THE
LAST PILOT

THE
LAST PILOT

Benjamin Johncock

PICADOR

New York

THE LAST PILOT. Copyright © 2015 by Benjamin Johncock. All rights reserved. Printed in the United States of America. For information, address Picador, 175 Fifth Avenue, New York, N.Y. 10010.

www.picadorusa.com
www.twitter.com/picadorusa • www.facebook.com/picadorusa
picadorbookroom.tumblr.com

Picador® is a U.S. registered trademark and is used by St. Martin's Press under license from Pan Books Limited.

For book club information, please visit www.facebook.com/ picadorbookclub or e-mail marketing@picadorusa.com.

Designed by Nicola Ferguson

The Library of Congress Cataloging-in-Publication Data is available upon request.

ISBN 978-1-250-06664-0 (hardcover)
ISBN 978-1-250-06665-7 (e-book)

Picador books may be purchased for educational, business, or promotional use. For information on bulk purchases, please contact the Macmillan Corporate and Premium Sales Department at 1-800-221-7945, extension 5442, or write to specialmarkets@ macmillan.com.

First Edition: July 2015

10 9 8 7 6 5 4 3 2 1

FOR JUDE

The field of consciousness is tiny. It accepts only one problem at a time.

ANTOINE DE SAINT-EXUPÉRY

THE
LAST PILOT

PROLOGUE

It was a stretch of wretched land bleached and beaten by the relentless salt winds that howled in off the Atlantic, forsaken by God to man for the testing of dangerous new endeavors. WELCOME TO CAPE CANAVERAL! the sign said. SPEED LIMIT: 17,400 MPH. Three miles south sat Cocoa Beach, the Cape's resort town, so low-rent that even the giant chiggers wanted to escape it. In daylight, Cocoa Beach was cobaltic blue, coconut palms and low-rise motels called The Starlite and Satellite and The Polaris, a replica rocket clasped above each name. The beach was like a strip of asphalt, long and wide and barren and hard. You could bend a spade on it. At sundown, mosquitoes the size of a clenched fist clustered at the water's edge. At night, it was infested with sand flies that stripped skin from muscle. The only visitors were young men racing cars and the occasional couple, lured out of their motel room by the slink of the murky sea and the promise of God knows what on the bare, hardback sand. Cocoa Beach was the kind of place where people ended up.

It was late, past nine, the diner was empty. George's had low lights, a high bar and a couple of Chesley Bonestell originals hanging on the wall. It wasn't a bad place. He came here because no one else did.

His heart hurt like hell. He pulled a half-pack of Lucky Strikes from his top pocket. He stuck one in his mouth and struck a match and lit it and waved the match until it went out. He looked at his hands, the thick hair on his fingers, his knuckles. He drank the rest of his beer.

Steely eyes gleamed down from a billboard across the street. Was it Shepard or Glenn? He didn't know, or much care; he just wanted the goddamn thing to stop staring at him. He stared at his food. He wasn't hungry.

A couple entered. The man held a gray hat between two fingers and the woman adjusted her dress as they waited to be seated. The waitress gathered plastic menus, ushered them to a table, presented the specials. The couple smiled at each other and he wondered if they were honeymooning. Smoke clung to the pine-paneled walls, lilting slowly toward the linoleum floor. The man approached his table.

Excuse me, he said, sir? Sorry to bother you an all but my wife—he glanced back—we was just wondrin, well, you're one of them, ain't you? What we been hearin about? The New Nine?

He stayed seated, pulled hard on the cigarette, his throat tightened.

I knew it! Honey, I was right.

The woman joined her husband. Her skin looked pale like a lake in late fall.

My wife, Betty, he said.

Pleasure to meet you, she said.

Now, which one are you? You're Borman, right?

Honey—

Lovell? No, wait, I know this.

You'll have to excuse my husband; we've heard so much about you all.

Harrison. Jim Harrison. I knew I knew it. Jim Harrison!

The man looked at the woman and the woman stared at the table.

Sure hope you don't mind us intrudin, the man said.

We've been staying down in Miami; at the Plaza, the woman said. It's been a wonderful three weeks, but the other night I said to Bill, Bill, let's get in the car, let's *explore* a little—

It's a Caddy, powder blue—a coupe.

—so we drove up the coast, the two of us.

I said, we should go visit the world's first *space-port*.

I didn't know what he meant.

But I never thought we'd meet one of you fellas.

A real astronaut, my goodness!

A thing like that!

Harrison put out his smoke and stood to leave.

It sure was good to meet you, Bill said, extending his hand. And thank you, for everything; really, thank you.

Harrison nodded and shook his hand. The couple returned to their table. In the restroom he pissed and thought and stood there for a long time.

At the door, the waitress rang up his check.

Everything all right for you, hon? she said.

He stared at the register. Hard cracks crossed the linoleum under his feet. His heart beat hard in his head.

Outside, the air was cool. It felt good on his bare arms. He stopped and stood on the near side of the sidewalk, against the mottled concrete wall of George's backyard. He held his head. He had to think. All he ever did was think. A man walked by and stared.

An hour passed. Inside the diner, lights were switched off in pairs, the couple left. Behind the wall, garbage sweltered and stunk. His breathing was heavy and his chest was wet. He felt dizzy. He had to move on, fill his mind.

The steely eyes followed him across the empty street. He could smell the sea; the salt and the sky. Wolfie's Cocktail Bar & Pantry was still open. Voices leaked out onto the sidewalk and echoed inside him. He walked on, past waiters licking spoons, clearing tables; past bars closing up. Air-conditioning units clung to gloomy walls, whining melancholic laments to men not yet home. The wind was hard with salt, the moon curled large and still. He reached Walt's Bar and stopped. He felt tense. Christ, he thought, I need to walk. I need to get to bed.

He got back to the motel at two. There were still people by the pool. Girls, mainly. A few men. They'd arrived soon after the first Mercury flights, the girls; eager young things, keen to become acquainted with the world's first astronauts. Cape cookies, Shepard called them. They'd been staying here since the beginning, the astronauts, enjoying the hospitality of Henri Landwirth, the Holiday Inn's manager. The rooms were stacked like cardboard boxes across two floors, encircling a bright blue swimming pool and a pink cocktail bar. Plastic chaise lounges, white like gulls, fanned the water. A racket of cicadas and crickets clattered loudly in the background.

Harrison entered the lobby. Standing by the pay phone at the foot of the stairs was a girl in a towel.

Hello, she said.

He didn't say anything. Smoke from a cigarette slunk around the brim of her straw hat. He could see small droplets of water on her bare shoulders.

Are you coming out to the pool with the rest of the fellas? she said.

I'm going to my room.

That's a much better idea.

That so.

It is.

What's your name?

Jane, she said.

She smiled, pulling the cigarette to her lips.

You drink whiskey? he said.

Got any ice?

He opened the freezer.

You're in luck.

He fixed two drinks. She sat in a chair, folding her legs over one of the arms. He stood.

Your room is kinda tidy, if you don't mind me saying so.

I don't.

Been here long?

A while.

Training?

He nodded.

Where you from?

You ask a lot of questions.

I'm a curious girl.

He held his drink at the back of his throat then swallowed it.

So we're going to the moon, she said.

Not yet.

How's that?

Takes time.

You fellas getting distracted? she said. It's been three years since

Glenn went up. Now that was something; felt like I had my own Lone Ranger watching over me.

Four days there, four days back, he said. Glenn was up for four hours.

Eight *days*? That even possible?

Record is thirty-four hours, nineteen minutes, forty-nine seconds. Gordo Cooper, Faith 7; the last of the Mercury flights. Hell of a mission. Took a nap on the pad during countdown. Ol Gordo, yeah; he's okay. Not the best, but he's all right.

Not the best? she said.

There's an old saying in flight test, who's the second best pilot you ever saw?

I like that, she said, lifting the glass to her lips. You going up? You bet.

She looked around the room, then said, why are you living in a motel?

He tipped the rest of the slug down his throat. How old are you? Nineteen.

Where you from?

Kansas.

You're not in Kansas anymore.

You've finished your drink.

She moved from the chair to the bed, tucking one leg beneath the other. He stared at the floor for a long time.

Tell me what you're thinking, she said.

He didn't say anything. He picked up the bottle, poured himself another.

You should go home, get some sleep, he said.

She emptied her glass slowly, eyes locked on his, ice accumulating along lips glossed with whiskey.

You sure about that? she said.

He stared at her and her legs unfurled and she walked toward him and placed a hand on his cheek. He shut his eyes.

Whatever it is, she said, it's okay.

She pulled the door tight behind her. He stood, eyes shut, bottle and glass hanging from his hands. He felt black, like he was falling, and he couldn't stop.

———

MOJAVE DESERT
MUROC, CALIFORNIA
OCTOBER 1947

———

The house was part of an old ranch stuck out in the desert scrubland near Muroc, in the high desert of the Mojave, fifty miles west of Victorville. It had a narrow veranda, dustbowl front yard and picket fence. It was called Oro Verde; Green Gold, after the alfalfa that once grew there. The ranch sat on the edge of Muroc Dry Lake, the largest slab of uninterrupted flatness on Earth. Forty-four square miles. Every December, it rained, the first and only of the year. Four inches would collect on the lake's dry surface in a slick pool. The wind pulled and dragged the water, licking the wet sand smooth. In spring, it evaporated and the orange sun fired the ground hard like clay, creating a vast natural runway. The sky was a dome, endless blue; vast and clear and bright. The high elevations of the Mojave were the perfect place to fly. In the thirties it had been home to some godforsaken detachment of the Air Corps, nicknamed the Foreign Legion by the locals: seventeen poor bastards who lived out on the desert hardpan in a dozen canvas tents, with no electricity or plumbing. The Air Corps used the dry lake for training, but the Muroc Field encampment was so remote and wretched that it had no commanding officer. When conscripts arrived to train for combat in the South Pacific, tar paper barracks were quickly constructed to accommodate them, and when men burned in the skies above Europe in the autumn of forty-two, the army installed a top secret flight test program to develop the turbo-powered jet. The flight test center turned permanent after the war, with a small detachment of test pilots, engineers, technicians and ground crew. The men were slowly eaten alive by the sun slung high in the day and, at night, they froze, the hard desert wind howling loud around them, stripping paint from the planes and the trucks.

Muroc Field's two Quonset hangars gleamed on the horizon as Harrison climbed the front steps of the house. He was slender, short, dressed in brown slacks and a shirt, open at the collar. It was Saturday; just eight. He'd been up at five, in the air at six. He pushed open the screen door and dropped his bag to the floor.

What are you doing home? Grace said, from behind the cellar door. Wasn't expecting you til later.

Thought I'd surprise you, he said, make sure you're not in bed with the mailman.

You seen the mailman?

I have.

You were right to come home.

I know.

Grace opened the door and stepped into the living room. She was tall, five-eleven, slight, with boney shoulders and fair hair, tied back. She wore a pair of crimson vaquero boots and a shirt tucked into dirty jeans.

What you doing back there? he said.

Fixing the door; damn thing's been driving me crazy, she said. How was it?

Fine.

That bad, huh.

She walked over, put her arms around his waist.

He yawned.

You tired? she said.

I'm beat.

Want to sleep?

Yeah, but I came home to see you.

You came home to make sure I wasn't in bed with the mailman, she said.

I came to make sure you weren't in bed with any man, he said.

You think I'm a floozy?

I think we got a lot of good-lookin municipal workers round here.

I hadn't noticed, she said, tipping back on the heels of her boots.

Yes you had.

You want to get into that?

Not really.

Let's get into something else, she said, tugging at his waist.

This is unexpected, he said.

Her lips touched his. They stood together in the sunlight.

You're not kissing me, she said.

Mmm?

You're not kissing me.

My mouth is dry; from the flight. Glass of water be good.

I'm sure it would. Help yourself, I'm going out.

She stepped away, her shirt creased from where it had pressed against him.

Where you goin? he said.

Rosamond.

Rosamond?

Post office has a package for us, she said, picking up her keys from the counter.

You're going to see the mailman? he said.

Your jealousy is oddly compelling.

You're oddly compelling.

You're tired, she said.

And thirsty.

Glass of water, she said, then take a nap.

I'm up again at eleven, he said. You know that's—

I know, she said. First powered flight.

Yeah. Be the fastest anyone's gone.

I know.

She stepped toward him.

Be careful, she said.

Always am, hon, he said.

He walked into the kitchen, found a glass and turned on the cold tap. Grace watched him drink slowly, then refill the glass.

I had a phone call, she said, leaning against the kitchen doorframe. They can see me on Monday.

Monday?

At ten.

He paused, looking at the water in the glass.

I didn't think it would be that quick, he said.

The lady said it's been quiet; she said—doesn't matter.

Want me to come?

No, maybe; I don't know.

I can speak to Boyd? The old man owes me some slack.

I'll be fine.

Ten?

She nodded.

Okay then.

Okay then.

The kitchen was small. It had a round table pushed into a nook at one end and a window that looked out over the open desert at the other. The planes took off over the roof, making the crockery rattle. But there were days when the blue of the sky was cut with a hard line of black smoke from the ground, the stiff air vibrating with the sirens of distant fire trucks. Those were bad days. There had been one a week since the end of August; seven in August itself. These grim streaks happened.

I'd better get going, she said, pushing herself off the doorframe with her shoulder.

Sure, he said, and paused. Rick Bong augered in yesterday.

I heard, she said. Janice told me. I'm going over to see Marjory on Wednesday. So's Jackie.

He was testing the P-80A, he said. Main fuel pump sheared on takeoff. Flamed out at fifty feet. No seat, so he pops the canopy, then his chute, but the airstream wraps him round the tail and they corkscrew in together.

He looked up at her.

He didn't turn on his auxiliary fuel pump before takeoff, he said. Jim—

How could anyone be so stupid not to turn on their auxiliary fuel pump before takeoff?

Sounds like it was just a mistake, Grace said.

There are no mistakes, Harrison said, just bad pilots.

She sighed. She stood beside him and pulled his head to her breast, holding it gently with both hands.

I'll see you later, she said.

Fancy coming over to Pancho's after? he said. Gonna be celebrating.

Maybe.

I'll be the fastest man alive, he said. Don't you forget that.

Doubt I'll be allowed to.

Well, it won't last long. Yeager'll go faster on Tuesday, assuming he don't drill a hole in the Sierras.

You should probably enjoy it while you can, she said.

You know, I think I will.

She kissed the top of his head.

Bye, she said.

Pick me up some Beemans, would you? he called after her. He rubbed his forehead and drank the rest of his water.

———

Pancho's place sat squat in six acres of bone-dry desert taut with Joshua trees. It had a wooden veranda, flyscreen door and looked like hell. She served scotch and beer and highballs and called it the Happy Bottom Riding Club. In summer, the temperature hit a hundred and ten and the bar would creak and groan. At night, it was close to freezing. The bar was part of a ranch that she'd bought from a farmer called Hannam ten years before, when the Depression sunk the price of alfalfa from thirty dollars a ton to ten.

It was still early, ten before nine, Pancho's was open. The desert was calm, the low sun nudging slowly west, burning the new day bright yellow and white. Stale carbon dioxide hung in the gloom of the bar like a bad mood. Harrison pushed open the screen door and stepped inside.

What do you want, you miserable pudknocker? Pancho said, looking up from her broom.

You know, he said.

You're early.

I'm up at eleven.

Gracie know you're here?

Practically her idea.

She's too good for a peckerwood like you.

Got any Luckies? I'm all out.

Get your ass over here you ol bastard.

She poured him a drink and he sat at the bar.

You know I love you, Pancho.

Well, don't I feel better.

I'm up again at one.

You're only up at one if you don't auger in at eleven.

Can't see that bein a problem.

You all never do, sweetie, she said, glancing at the wall where photographs of dead pilots hung. The frames began behind the bar, marring the far wall with grinning men standing beside cockpits and airplanes knocking contrails into the sky. Whenever someone augered in, she'd nail their picture up and say, dumb bastard.

Pancho had broad shoulders, dark hair and a face that looked like it was stuck in a nine-g pullout. Her real name was Florence Leontine Lowe. She grew up in a thirty-room mansion in San Marino, waited on by servants. Her grandfather, Thaddeus Sobieski Constantine Lowe, was an entrepreneur, engineer and balloonist; a hero of the Civil War. Papa Lowe doted on his granddaughter. When she was eight, he took her to the world's first aviation exhibition; a ten-day extravaganza in the hills above Long Beach. Florence watched Glenn Curtiss and Lincoln Beachey fly high and fast around the field in their biplanes for a three thousand dollar prize and was captivated. It wasn't the machines, it was the men. When she was old enough, she stopped riding horses and started flying airplanes. Her mother disapproved of her new lifestyle and, as soon as she turned eighteen, arranged for her to marry the Reverend C. Rankin Barnes. She lasted fourteen months as a minister's wife before disguising herself as a man and running away to South America as a crew member aboard a banana boat. She became a smuggler, running guns during the Mexican Revolution; later flying rumrunners into Ensenada and Tijuana. She spoke Spanish and Yaqui, slicked her black hair back with gardenia oil and lived like a peasant. She returned a year later with the nickname *Pancho* to news of her mother's death. She kept the name, inherited her mother's fortune and indulged her love of flying. She won races, broke Amelia Earhart's airspeed record and became one of Hollywood's first stunt pilots, throwing wild parties at her house in Laguna Beach. When the Depression ate its way into Southern California, it hit her hard. Broke, defaulting on loans, she sold up, headed out into the Mojave and bought Hannam's farm, just west of Muroc Dry Lake.

It won't give you no love, Hannam told her after the papers were signed. I used to get five, maybe six, cuttins a year; bale it, sell it on for a good price. Now, even with seventy or so acres planted up, man can't live on it, not now. It's all gone to hell.

Never did see myself as much of a rancher, she said.

That fall, she dragged out a private airstrip behind the hay barn with two English shire mares bought from the Washington State Fair then holed out a swimming pool. It wasn't long before she got to know the men from the base. They enjoyed her company; she knew airplanes and they got a kick out of her salty language and dirty jokes. In the evenings, the men grew restless, so they'd head over to Pancho's to take out her horses, have a drink, cool off in her pool. Pancho would curse and laugh and tell them stories and pour them drinks. Some nights she'd cook, a steak dinner; meat from her own cattle. She called up Bobby Holeston one morning and got him to turn the old cook's shack into a proper bar. She hired an enormous woman called Minnie to work the kitchen and Pancho had herself a business.

Harrison finished his drink and Pancho refilled the glass.

Help stabilize the system, she said.

He knocked it back and made to leave.

Hey, Harrison, she called after him.

He looked down at a half-smoked pack of cigarettes on the bar.

You're a peach, he said.

Get the hell out.

The screen door clattered shut, rattling the dead men hanging inside.

———

Pancho spent the morning running errands. Muroc was three miles north across flat dirt trails; a barren cluster of buildings founded on the Sante Fe railroad. The dull steel track stretched toward the horizon in both directions. Alongside the wooden station-house were three black sheds for the men who worked the rails. The main street was a dust strip. It had Charlie Anderson's store, Ma Green's café, and a Union Oil gas station, as well as a small post office and a one-man bank.

It was quiet. A slight wind caught a tangled cluster of loose telephone wires that grappled and rapped against each other. At the bank, Pancho settled three bills that she'd disputed the previous winter.

Anything else I can do for you, Pancho?

Nope, that's it, thanks Fredo. Good to see you.

How's things out in the boonies?

Can't complain.

Billy Horner still working for you?

Was when I left.

Be seeing you, Pancho.

You know it.

Don't be a stranger now.

We'll see.

Outside, the sun hurt her eyes. She pulled down on her old cowboy hat, lit a cigar and dropped the match into the dirt. Damn weenies. She had no problem paying bills, so long as they were fair. The smoke lingered in her mouth. There'd be more money soon. She crossed the street to Charlie Anderson's.

Well, Charlie, you ol bastard, how are you?

That Pasadena's First Lady?

Depends who you ask.

How's Rankin?

Wouldn't know.

Still in New York?

Last I heard.

When you gonna do it?

When I gonna do what?

You know.

She chewed on the cigar still burning between her teeth.

Now why would I go do a stupid thing like that? she said.

Case you meet a handsome fella.

Out here? I got prettier hogs.

Must be some swine. Maybe *he's* met someone?

He's pastor of the Pasadena Episcopal Church, Charlie. He meets women who want to marry him every day. First whiff of a divorce and the Church would haul his ass out of there. I won't do that to him. We write each other. Suits us fine.

What's he doing in Brooklyn again?

Who knows.

She pulled hard on her cigar. Two women, an aisle over, peered through the shelves.

Morning, ladies, Pancho said, blowing smoke through the gap. They disappeared. Pancho smiled. It was a small town; people talked. When folks heard about her swimming pool, they couldn't believe the extravagance. The first time she filled up her blue

Cadillac at Carl Bergman's Union Oil, he yapped on it for months. *It had no backseat,* Carl told the other ranchers. *It was full of dogs!*

Pancho got back to the ranch at eleven. Billy was serving two men at the bar.

Is it on? she said. Billy looked up.

Nope.

Quick.

The radio was wedged between the cash register and the rum. Close to the base, restricted exchanges could be picked up on the right frequency. Billy turned it on. The box popped and whistled.

Plenty fellas go up; you never listen, he said.

Shut up. Is it working?

Yeah.

This is different.

How you know?

This is not an airplane, Pancho said, least nothing a pudknocker like you'd understand one to be. It's a goddamn rocket with a tail; an orange bullet with razor wings and a needle-nose. They call it the X-1. And it's got one purpose: fly faster than sound.

That even possible? Fly faster than a man's own voice?

Maybe it is, maybe it isn't, Pancho said. That's what they been figuring out, and I promised a free steak dinner to any them weenies who does it first. Today's a big deal: first powered flight, pushing it up to point eight-two Mach. When Harrison hits that switch, the whole damn thing could go kaboom, or drop out the sky like a brick, or malfunction in a thousand other ways. There's no seat to punch out either; those razor wings would slice him in half. It's got to work, and he's got to land it, and he can't land it with any fuel left on board or the whole goddamn thing *will* go kaboom soon as it hits the lakebed. So, yeah, it's different, and everyone's got their jitters up.

Billy wiped the counter with an old cloth.

So how come you ain't down there? he said.

I seen plenty drop launches before, Pancho said, turning away to stack glasses.

At Muroc Field, a B-29 bomber took off from the south runway and climbed hard. Harrison sat on an upturned apple box behind the pilot with Jack Ridley, the flight engineer. The X-1 was strapped to the underside of the bomber. The B-29 reached altitude. Harrison climbed down the bomb bay ladder and into the X-1, the sound of the bomber's giant propellers roaring in his ears. In the tiny cockpit, he clipped on his lines and hoses; the oxygen system, radio-microphone and earphones, then pulled his leather flying helmet over his head. Stored behind him, at minus two hundred and ninety-six degrees was six hundred gallons of lox, liquid nitrogen and oxygen. Ridley climbed down after him, lowered the cockpit door in place, then returned to the bomber. Two chase planes, one flying high, one low, took off from the base to observe the X-1 in flight. Harrison's lips split, his breath condensing in the dark. In the gloom, he waited for the drop.

Pancho pulled a stool behind the bar and sat by the radio.

Listen, here we go.

Roger, take it easy son.

Ridley, Pancho said, to Billy. They heard Bob Cardenas, the B-29 pilot, announce twenty-six thousand feet, then begin his shallow dive.

Starting countdown . . .

Pancho leaned in.

Drop!

There was a sharp crack as the shackles released the X-1 like a bomb.

[. . .] looking at the sky.
Roger that, Jim.
Nose-up stall.
I see you, Jim—you're dropping like a brick.
Copy that.
[. . .]
Dive speed [. . .] too slow.
Walt, you got a visual from the ground?
Negative.
Twenty-five thousand feet.
Roger.
Twenty-four.
Say again, Jim? Didn't copy.
[. . .]
[. . .]
[. . .] Hey [. . .] fuel.
You're about three thousand pounds heavier than the
    glide flights.
Twenty-three.
Roger, Jim.
I feel it.
Copy that.
I'm gonna push the nose down [. . .] pick up speed.
Roger.

Leveling out.

[. . .]

You're at twenty-two, Jim.

Copy.

[. . .]

I'm level.

Good work, Jim.

I have a visual.

Copy that, Walt.

Lighting the first chamber.

Standing by.

Lighting one.

Roger.

Point four Mach.

Copy that.

Hey, Jim, you just passed me going upstairs like a bat
    [. . .]

Point five.

[. . .] shockwaves [. . .] from the exhaust.

You got eyeballs on that, Kit?

Confirm.

Lighting two.

Roger.

Point seven.

Hold steady.

Forty-five thousand feet. Lighting three [. . .] seven-
    five.

Jim [. . .]

Watch your nose.

Firing chamber four.

[. . .]

[. . .]
[. . .]

Pancho glanced at Billy. Billy shrugged his shoulders.

Point eight-three.
Copy that, Jim.
Say, Ridley, sure is dark up here.
Beautiful, Jim.
Jettison remaining lox, glide down.
Copy.
[. . .]
Jim?
Christ he's doing a roll!
Jim, that's not in the flight plan.
Zero-g [. . .]
Copy that, Jim.
Holy hell.
Engine cutout.
[. . .]
Ridley?
Fuel can't feed the engine [. . .] zero-g [. . .] down.
Level her out.
Leveling out.
Roger.
[. . .]
[. . .]
Walt?
[. . .]
Dick, what's his position?
Negative, can't see [. . .]
Walt?

Nothing.

I see him.

Confirm.

How's the fuel?

Terrific.

Them NACA boys sure gonna chew you out!

Copy that, Jack; couldn't resist. Lox spent, gliding
home.

Roger that, son.

Well, shit, Harrison! Pancho said. She looked up at Billy.

You want me in tonight?

You bet your sweet ass I do.

———

Harrison flew more powered flights that afternoon, easing the X-1
up to point nine-six Mach, encountering different problems each
time. Lakebed landings were also tough, with no markings and
too much open space. Depth perception was an issue; it was easy
to bend an airplane porpoising in, or flaring high and cracking off
the landing gear. On the last landing, Harrison let the airplane
settle in by itself, feeling for the changes in the ground effect as he
lowered down, greasing in at a hundred and ninety miles an hour.
With no brakes, it took three minutes to roll to a stop. The fire
truck drove out and he hitched a lift back to the hangar.

The men debriefed in Ridley's office, a small room on the second
floor of the main hangar. The windows were covered with dust, the
walls papered with enlarged photographs of instrument panels,
maps of the desert and hanging clipboards, fat with flight reports.

That low frequency rolling motion was most likely fuel sloshing,

Ridley said, looking at the clock on the wall. Nothing to worry about.

Well, that's sure good to hear, Harrison said. We done?

That's it, Ridley said. Let's go to Pancho's.

———

Grace took a left outside Rosamond, heading home, the package collected from the post office beside her. It was from her father. He sent occasional collections of miscellany; had done for years. There was usually a book, food (tinned or tightly wrapped in waxed paper), a small bottle of spirits, distilled himself, the odd trinket unearthed from the house that would inspire bursts of nostalgia. This haul included a pocket watch, Steinbeck's *Of Mice and Men*, an old photograph of her looking stern on a horse and a bundle of Beemans gum labeled FOR JIM, which saved her going back to the store; she'd forgotten to pick some up. Jim chewed it constantly. He said sucking on pure oxygen when he flew dried out his mouth, and that chewing helped equalize his ear pressure at altitude. Grace also suspected that the pepsin it contained proved handy in the cockpit.

It was almost noon. The hot sun hurt her face. A dust cloud churned up around the car as she drove; the monotony of the Mojave roads almost hypnotic. Her thoughts drifted from her father to her mother to her appointment on Monday. Her body stiffened. Her back began to ache. She leaned forward, against the wheel, stretching it out. She grimaced, then sighed. A sign on the roadside caught her eye. It was tied to a post marking a rough track that led up to Mac's ranch. She pulled up, let the engine idle, read the sign. She sat in silence for a minute. Then she drove up the track.

The ranch was quiet. Grace stood on the porch of the house, rapped on the door, took a step back. The air felt like sandpaper. She ran a finger across her forehead.

Hey, Mac, you home? she called out. She put her hands on her hips and looked down at the boards. Then she heard a grunt and iron pulling against wood.

Well, Grace! Mac said, standing in the doorway.

Hey, Mac, she said.

Come on in here, he said, standing back. How the hell are you?

Fine, she said. You?

Tired, he said.

The house smelled of hay. It was gloomy after the bright glare of the desert.

Can I get you something?

Something cold be good.

Have a seat.

It was a small room. A square wooden table sat at one end, the kitchen at the other. A black stovepipe ran up the wall from an iron stove. On the wall next to the pipe hung a framed family portrait, a large clock and an old .22. Grace sat down at the table. A small oil-filled lamp swayed above her head.

You broke in that grullo yet? she said.

Hell no, Mac said from the kitchen. That's one crazy goddamn horse. Should've never bought her. I'm gettin too old for this kinda thing.

The hell you are, Grace said as Mac walked back with two bottles pulled from the icebox. He set them down on the table and popped off the caps with an old knife. He had white hair and walked with a slight stoop. His face was brown and smooth, like every desert rancher. He handed Grace one of the bottles and sat down.

Ain't nothin better than a cold Coke on a hot day, he said.

Amen to that, Grace said, toasting him and taking a long swig.

Damn, she said, bringing the bottle down to the table. That's better. She belched.

Sorry, she said.

A skinned jackrabbit hung by a hook above the kitchen sink, pink flesh glistening in the low light. A pile of muddy potatoes sat piled on the side, waiting to be washed and peeled.

Nice of you to drop by, Mac said. I always told Rose this place was centrally located.

Middle of nowhere, Grace said, smiling and raising the bottle to her mouth.

I've said that one before, haven't I?

I think it's a common refrain.

Hell, I like it out here, Mac said. Rose, well, she weren't no rancher; she was too good for that.

To the wives, Grace said, holding up her drink again.

The wives.

They clanked bottles together.

So, Mac said. What can I do for you?

You still got those pups for sale? I saw the sign out front.

Only got the one left, he said. Half-thinkin on keepin him for myself.

Where'd you bury ol Sophie anyway?

Out back, under her favorite tree. Hell, I'm just a sentimental ol fool.

No you're not, Grace said. Least, no more than I would be.

Fourteen years, Mac said. Like havin another kid.

You see much of Johnny?

Not as much as I'd like. He's a cattle rancher down in Riverside County now. Got himself near-on thirty thousand acres in the Temecula Valley. Good grazin land. Leases most of it out. Smart kid. He got that from his mother.

So you gonna keep the pup?

Hell, probably not. He's a handful. You can have him if you want.

I'm just thinking about it at the moment, she said. Always saw myself with one, y'know? Growing up, a little girl . . . Guess that's just the way God made me.

She sighed, looked down at the table.

You ever had the feeling the future's become the past while you were busy being scared? she said.

Mac looked at her.

All the damn time, he said.

She looked away.

You wanna come see him? Mac said. He's out back.

Lemmie give you a call in a few days.

Sure, he said. No sweat.

She smiled.

Thanks, Mac.

How's that fine-lookin husband of yours?

Oh, fine, she said. His usual self.

Flyin today?

Just a few times.

Man's gotta work.

Think I saw more of him when he was flying over occupied France during the war, Grace said. Sure worried about him less. But I guess he knows what he's doing. At least in the air. It's down on the ground that's the problem.

Mac chuckled.

I heard they workin on some new type of airplane or somethin? he said.

They're trying to break the sound barrier, Grace said.

Why in the hell would anyone want to do that?

Jim says someone's gonna do it eventually. Better that it's us. Old allies aren't lookin so friendly anymore.

The Russians?

Grace shrugged. She drained her Coke, saw a deck of cards on a shelf near the table.

You wanna deal a hand? she said, nodding toward them.

Seems like you're in a good mood, he said, smiling and fetching the cards. Sure be a shame to spoil it.

Pipe down, old man, Grace said. You got anything proper to drink?

Shuffle, he said, handing her the deck. He walked through a side door and returned carrying a plain glass bottle, three-quarters full, and two glasses. He sat down.

Here, Grace said, passing Mac the cards. Now deal up, you ol cowboy.

———

It was just six and Pancho's was busy. A sloppy Cole Porter melody warbled, lost, into the desert night. There were already men on the veranda, surrounded by Virginia creepers, moonlight and girls, drinking scotch and laughing. Inside, the place looked like a cathouse, the piano smelled like a beer.

Pancho stood behind the bar, holding a framed six-by-four of Rick Bong in her hand.

Bing Bong, she said as she hammered it to the wall above the radio. You stupid bastard.

She turned and faced the crowd.

You know the problem with you sons-of-bitches? she shouted. You're all going crazy being horny and sober. We can fix one of them for you, but the other, hell, you're on your own.

There was laughter and cheering. Harrison dug out a cigarette and lit it; the match flared in his face. He walked through the crowd and sat down at a table in the far corner, where a man sat chewing gum.

Pancho wanted you to have this, Yeager said, pushing a glass toward him.

Scotch?

Rum.

Rum?

Best she's got, so she say.

Harrison tried it.

Ain't bad, he said.

Heard they dropped you in a nose-up stall, Yeager said.

You heard right, Harrison said. Thought they'd have to name an ass-shaped crater after me.

Yeager chuckled. He was short, with wiry hair and thin, blue eyes. He had a slow, West Virginian drawl and looked like he'd been left out in the desert for too long.

So how'd it go? he said.

Pretty much what we figured, Harrison said. Heavy trim pressure, Dutch rolls, massive shock wave buffeting, loss of elevator, pitch—

You lost pitch?

Point nine-four Mach, forty thousand feet. I pulled back on the control wheel and, nothing. Felt like the cables had snapped on me. I kept going, same altitude, same direction . . .

Christ.

I turned off the engine, jettisoned the fuel and landed, fast as I could.

Hell, Yeager said, no way I can get past point nine-four without a damn elevator.

You should've seen Ridley's face, Harrison said. He looked sick as a hog. We checked the data, turns out a shock wave caught the hinge-point on the tail.

What the old man say?

Shook his head, thought the program had reached the end of the line.

Ridley?

Thought on it for a minute, said maybe we could get by using just the horizontal stabilizer.

That's only meant for extra authority.

He did some calculations, thinks it could work.

What if the motor gets stuck trim-up or trim-down?

Then you got a problem.

Yeager grunted. What if the airflow overwhelms the motor and stops the tail from pivoting?

Then you got another problem, but nothing different than what I had today.

Could rip the damn tail off as it's pivoting too.

You got insurance, right?

Me and Ridley call this part the *ughknown*. He really thinks it'll work?

Tested the hell out of it today. Worked just fine. Point nine-six Mach. Felt a bit ragged, but it'll keep you in the air.

Anything else?

The windshield frosted over at one point.

It frosted? It usual' fogs. I just wipe it away.

That cabin's so damn cold. I took my gloves off, tried to scrape it, nearly lost my fingers.

How'd you land?

Kit was flying chase and talked me down blind. Said I must have been sweatin pretty hard to ice the shield like that.

Yeager chuckled again.

Listen, Yeager, Harrison said. That's the best damn airplane I ever flew, but it'll bite you hard in the ass when you least expect it.

One damn thing after another.

Yeah.

Get Russell to put a coating of Drene shampoo on the windshield tomorrow; that ought to sort it out. Best antifreeze there is.

Harrison nodded. You want another?

Hang on, here's Pancho, Yeager said.

Well, Pancho said. Look at this: my boys.

Rum was good, Harrison said.

I know. Yeager, you ol bastard, where's Glennis?

She's coming. Jus sorting out the babysitter.

How's Mickey and Don?

Doin good.

Those are fine boys you got there, Yeager, you hear me? Don't screw them up by doing something stupid like getting crunched.

She looked at Harrison.

When you gonna do the right thing like Yeager here? What have you got to show for your miserable existence on this rock?

Well, maybe when I reach the grand age of Yeager here I'll think about it.

I'll have a drink for that, kid, Yeager said.

They're on the house for you fellas tonight, Pancho said, so you can both shut up.

You're a peach, Yeager said.

A real peach, Harrison said.

And you two are a couple of miserable sons-of-bitches, but you're the fastest men in this room so I'll get Billy to bring you something over.

Thanks, Pancho.

She moved on.

Billy! Scotch for the two pudknockers in the corner. The good stuff.

Billy brought the drinks.

Shit, Harrison said.

What?

Doesn't matter.

Grace coming over?

Yeah.

You think Pancho's gonna keep goin on about kids?

He nodded.

Don't sweat it. Get outside, catch her as she comes in.

I'll see you, Chuck.

You bet.

Harrison started toward the door. A sharp sound cut through the noise and the singing. Pancho was standing on the bar, banging two empty beer bottles together.

Listen up, you sorry bunch of peckerheads. They say there's a demon living at Mach one. Well, maybe there is, maybe there ain't; all I know is Harrison and Yeager make you all look like goddamn mouse farts in the wind.

The bar roared.

Either that or the air force don't care if they get clobbered, a loud voice said.

Who said that? Pancho said. Gene May. Might have guessed nothing but horseshit could come out the mouth of a *civilian* pilot.

The screen door banged against the wall. Harrison looked up and saw his wife standing in the doorway. She stepped inside, leaned against the wall and folded her arms.

You young fellas, May said. What makes you think you can fly faster than sound *itself*?

These two men could fly right up your ass and tickle your eyeballs and you'd never know why you were farting shock waves, Pancho said. Get the hell out of my bar.

May took out a cigarette, lit it, looked around, shook his head.

You're gonna get clobbered and you're too stupid to see it comin.

He turned and left.

Harrison reached Grace and whispered, c'mon, let's get out of here.

Anyone else got something they want to get off their chest? Pancho said. Good. Where was I?

You were sayin Bridgeman flies like a mouse fart, someone shouted. There was laughter.

Grace smiled at her husband.

What? No. I just got here, she said.

I want you to forget everything you think you know about flying airplanes, Pancho said, not that you know that much, and raise your glasses, your bottles, your asses—I don't care what—to that ol demon. May he piss his pants when he sees you coming.

There was a cacophony of clattering glass.

Let's just hope, Pancho continued, that going supersonic don't turn them funny in the head, or—she winked at Harrison across the room—the balls.

What the hell was that? Grace said, turning to her husband.

Honey—

I saw that; that wink she gave you. What the hell, Jim?

She stared at him, eyes slick with tears.

Gracie—

She pushed the door open and left.

Christ, he said, and followed.

It was cold outside. The veranda was empty.

Goddamn it, Harrison called after her. Wait up.

Grace spun around.

I'm so mad I'm spittin nails right now, she said.

She doesn't know, sweetheart, she doesn't know.

That's our business, Jim, our *marriage*. She doesn't know what she's talking about.

I know.

Having kids, that's private; you and me—it's none of her goddamn business.

Let me speak to her.

No. I don't need you to speak to her, I'm plenty able to do that myself.

Where you going?

Where do you think I'm going?

Grace!

He ran after her. The back door to the kitchen was open. She ducked inside.

Grace, honey, stop, please.

In the kitchen, Minnie was turning six fat steaks on the grill. They smoked and crackled. She looked around.

Shit, sorry, Minnie, Harrison said.

Where's Pancho? Grace said.

Hello, Mrs. Harrison, Minnie said. What you all doin back here?

Sorry, Minnie, hi, is this the door to—

The door opened.

What the hell are you both doin back here? Pancho said. Party's out front.

It's none of your goddamn business! Grace said.

What ain't? Pancho said.

Jim and me; having kids.

Hon—Harrison said.

We can't.

Can't what?

Have kids, Grace said. We can't have children.

Pancho stared at her.

We're seeing the doc on Monday, Harrison said. Gettin some results. We don't know that for sure.

Well we sure as hell don't have any now, Grace said, and it sure don't look likely to change anytime soon.

Gracie, Pancho said, throwing her large arms around her slim frame. I had no idea. I'm so sorry. She held Grace tight, whispering something in her ear that Harrison couldn't hear. Grace was nodding her head. They parted.

Don't think I've ever seen you embrace anyone before, Pancho, Harrison said.

Shut your mouth, Pancho said.

Grace wiped her eyes with the undersides of her thumbs.

Right? Pancho said to her.

She nodded.

What? Harrison said.

None of your business, Pancho said. Between women. You'll tell me how you get on on Monday?

Grace nodded.

Here, Pancho said. Go home, take this.

She handed Grace a bottle of red wine.

You keep wine back here? Harrison said.

Keep that to yourself or I'll break your damn legs, Pancho said.

All right, all right, he said. I'll see you.

Yes you will.

Night, Minnie, Grace said.

Good night, Mrs. Harrison, Captain Harrison.

Good night Minnie, he said.

Get out of here, Pancho said.

Harrison slipped his hand into his wife's and they left.

She lay in bed, on her side, away from him; arm hooked beneath her pillow. The yellow light from the lamp felt warm. He pushed his face into the nape of her neck, hand resting on her belly.

Hey, he said.

She didn't reply. He kissed her back. He couldn't see her face.

Don't do that.

What?

Stroke my belly. I'm not a genie.

I know, he said.

She sighed. Wish I was, she said.

I know, he said.

I'm sorry, she said, and rolled over. Her eyes, narrow and full, flicked up to his.

It's okay, he said.

I just—

I know.

It'll be all right, he said.

She rubbed at a small scar on her forehead, like she always did. Monday—

Monday will take care of itself, he said.

Okay, she said.

Okay, he said, then, what's the matter?

I need to pee, she said.

He laughed. She slipped out of bed. He sat on the edge and stared into the empty room. The toilet flushed. He unbuttoned his shirt, pulled off his clothes, and got back into bed.

Not the eye mask, he said as she got back in.

It's too damn bright in here with a full moon, she said.

You a werewolf?

Werewolves change shape with a full moon, she said, not have a hard time sleeping.

You look like a giant fly.

Come here and kiss me, she said, lying down.

No way!

C'mon.

I don't want to kiss an insect.

She sought him out, buzzing through her teeth. He laughed. She climbed on top of him.

There you are, she said.

Get off, he said, laughing.

No.

Get off!

Never!

She stuck out her tongue and moved it toward him.

This is gettin weird, he said.

She took off the mask.

That's better, he said.

She bent down and kissed him and he turned her gently beneath him.

Oh, now you want some? she said.

I love you, he said.

I know, she said, giving a gentle gasp, and he kissed her.

She looked up at him, and he at her, and she touched his face, and he kissed her again, then said, but I'm on the flight line at five, so—he rolled onto his back—I gotta sleep.

You pig! she said.

Can I borrow your mask?

I can't believe I married you!

You are one lucky girl.

Go to sleep, she said.

Already halfway there, hon, he said.

She stretched out her arm and switched off the lamp. In the darkness, she said, Jim? Do you still love me?

He turned to look at her and stroked her face and said, I do.

———

They sat with six others on hard benches in silence. Stenciled in black on clouded glass spheres were three surnames, each hanging from a different door like droopy flower-heads. There was no clock.

The middle ball lit up and a loud buzzer sounded. A woman

stood, folded her magazine, placed it back on the table and walked through the door.

Then there were five, Harrison said. Who we following?

You didn't have to come, Grace said.

What's the matter?

I said I'd be fine. Margaret Anderson. And nothing's the matter. Keep your voice down.

You don't sound fine.

I'm just saying you don't need to be here; I know you want to get back.

When did I say that? Old man said take what I need.

Doesn't matter.

Right.

How much longer? she said.

Want me to ask? he said.

No, she said.

What's the time?

No clock.

You not got a wristwatch?

At the base.

What time we get here?

Ten before ten.

Must be gone eleven.

Uh-huh.

You want to get going? she said. I can get a ride back.

Nope, he said.

I know you don't like doctors.

I don't.

So go back. I'm fine.

I'm taking care of you.

I can take care of myself.

Knock it off, would you?

You're not the one they've poked and scraped.

I'm just trying to look after you.

I know.

Okay.

I'm sorry.

Let's just see what they say, he said. Find out what the hell's going on.

I don't want to know, Grace said, staring up at the door.

Two years, you don't want to know?

I want kids, Jim; I want to have kids.

I know you do, honey, so do I, but, you know, it isn't always possible for everyone.

A ball lit, the buzzer sounded. Another woman stood and disappeared through a door.

How much longer we gotta sit here for? Grace said.

Harrison got up and walked around the room. He peered at posters of dissected hearts and warnings about liver disease. Ten minutes later, Margaret Anderson rose and, twenty minutes after that, so did they.

Mrs. Harrison, please, take a seat.

The doctor gestured toward a chair in front of his cherrywood desk.

I don't believe we've met? he said, holding out a hand to Harrison. He shook it.

Jim Harrison.

Bob Roberts, pleasure.

Your name is Robert Roberts? Harrison said.

Yes it is, he said, removing his reading glasses from his front pocket and sitting down behind his desk. Care to take a stab at my middle name?

Harrison glanced at his wife.

I'm just kidding; it's David. Please, sit down.

Harrison sat down.

So, Doctor Roberts said, tucking the stems of his glasses behind his ears and flipping open a gray file. We have some results. I'm sorry to tell you that our suspicions were correct.

He removed his glasses.

You have Stein-Leventhal Syndrome, Grace, he said. Anovulation; that is, absent ovulation, excessive androgens and, from the X-rays—he pulled the glasses back to his face—ovarian cysts; a pretty thick covering, looking at these.

What can you do? Harrison said.

Not much, he said, lowering his glasses.

Can you fix it?

No.

Why not?

There's no cure; it was diagnosed only ten years ago.

So what have you been doing for the last ten years? Harrison said.

Jim, Grace said. Do you know what causes it?

We don't, Doctor Roberts said. We think it's an anatomic abnormality; a disorder, if you will. The ovaries produce excess androgens—male hormones—and develop thick cysts that cover the surface, preventing ovulation. And, as you are no doubt aware, with no egg, there can be no—

I get it, Harrison said. Honey?

I'm okay, Grace said.

It's not something we know much about, unfortunately, Doctor Roberts said.

Wonders of modern medicine, Harrison said.

It has its limits, it always has. Stein-Leventhal affects maybe four, five percent of women; maybe less. Out of those, some certainly go on to have children, but they *are* ovulating, if sporadically.

Is there anything we can do? Grace said. Anything at all?

Not much. Eat well, stay active. You know, I see women from time to time, struggling to conceive a child, and they sit in that chair and they tell me it's their right to have children; they want a baby and it's their right. I tell them it isn't a right; it's a privilege. Some women can't have children. That's a sad fact, and it isn't fair, but that's how it is. I'm telling you this, Grace, because I think you understand. Live your life. Don't waste it lamenting what you think is required to complete it. That disrespects the miracle of your own birth, and that of your husband's. Now, go, both of you, and get on with it. I'll see you again in six months for a checkup. You can make the appointment with Mrs. Webber on the way out.

Thank you, Doctor Roberts, Grace said.

You're very welcome. If you have any questions, anything at all, you can call me and we'll talk. That goes for you, too, Captain.

Outside, she leaned against the car and held her head. The car was hot from the sun.

Hey, he said.

She pulled herself into him.

I know, but just let me, let me—

It's okay.

She drove him back to the base. The car was an old Model A coupe that Harrison had been given. The engine idled. Outside the window, mountains rose in the distance.

You got any? she said.

He pulled a pack of cigarettes from his shirt pocket. She sighed.

You okay? he said.

She shrugged, tucked one behind her ear and put the other between her lips. She looked at the sky.

Here, he said, striking a match from the box on the dash.

Go on, she said. I got things to do.

He got out and she drove away.

Ridley was in his office, boots resting on his desk, reading and smoking. The sound of mechanics and technicians working in the hangar leaked up through the floor.

Mornin, Ridley said.

Everything okay? Harrison said.

Everything dandy.

Harrison sat down.

Jim.

Harrison turned to see Yeager in the doorway, young boy at his side.

Chuck, he said, and why if it isn't Don too!

Hi, Uncle Jim.

Don was three, dressed in blue, tatty cap on his head.

How's it goin, Don? Harrison said.

Good, Don said.

Here to see your daddy fly, ain't you? Ridley said.

Don nodded.

My Daddy never takes long, he said.

Ridley chuckled. All set? he said to Yeager.

Jus need to get changed.

The intercom on Ridley's desk buzzed, calling Yeager down.

Harrison stood.

You can watch me from here, Don, Yeager told his son. I'm goin that way. He pointed west, out the window.

You can stand on the radiator, Don, get a better view, Ridley said.

Let's get this over with, Yeager said. Jack? Be right back, Don.

Okay Daddy.

The two men left. Don tried to climb onto the radiator. It was too high. Harrison watched him look around; he watched him walk across to Ridley's desk, pick up an old flight helmet and carry it back to the radiator to use as a step. He stared at the boy, on the radiator, hands flat against the window, steam expanding and contracting from where his face pressed against the glass.

———

That night, at Pancho's, Harrison sat with Yeager, Ridley, Cardenas, Kit Murray and Bob Hoover and went over the flight plan for the morning. The men drank beer and felt good. When they were finished, Ridley stood up and said to Yeager, don't push her past point nine-eight-eight unless you're sure you can handle it. And we're on an unrestricted frequency, remember, so if the Machometer reads one or more, tell me the thing's playin up or something; I'll know what you mean.

Sure thing, Jack, Yeager said. Jim an me stayin for another; Glennis be here in a bit.

Don't you kids go stayin out too late, now, Hoover said, rising. Murray and Cardenas laughed as they stood.

After they'd left, Yeager said, jeez, I'm beat.

Yeah, Harrison said.

Old man took me aside yesterday an said, Chuck, lot of scientists, engineers still of the opinion that, at the speed of sound, *g-forces become infinite*.

What'd you say?

What we said. That the buffeting may decrease and things get easier as you approach Mach one.

What he say to that?

He opened the door to his office, where a bunch of fellas were waitin on him, and yelled, no rudder, no elevator, buffeting severe at one speed, mild the next, nose-up at point eight-seven, nose-down at point nine-zero: that airplane is liable to go in any direction, or all of them at once, but Yeager, Harrison and Ridley anticipate no difficulty, no difficulty at all, in attaining Mach one on Tuesday.

He sounds pissed.

Couldn't tell what he was; he was smilin half the time.

I noticed that about him. Says take it easy one minute; next he's champing at the bit.

Hell, Boyd's a pilot through an through. If it was up to him, we'd have done it a week ago.

The men sat for a moment in silence.

Harrison saw the door open; it was Glennis. Over here, he said. Yeager looked around.

His wife approached the table. Hi, hon, Yeager said.

Where's Pancho? she said.

Out back, in one of her rages, Harrison said. Some cop pulled her for having misaligned headlights.

Yeager chuckled.

Says she's gonna take him to court.

There's a woman you want on your side, Glennis said, sitting down.

Not sure bout that, Yeager said.

Pass me some of that, would you? she said to him.

He pushed his bottle to her. She took a swig and looked at Harrison.

What happened? What the doctor say about Gracie? she said.

He leaned back in his chair.

Jim?

There's a problem, Harrison said. It's rare.

Goddamn. How rare?

Four, maybe five percent.

Five percent?

Maybe less.

Can they do anything?

Nope.

Why the hell not?

Doctors don't know much about it. Only gave it a name a decade ago.

How's Gracie?

She's okay.

I'll bet she's not.

Look, we knew it'd be something like this, Glen.

Might not be a surprise, Glennis said, but that don't mean it hurts any less bad.

Just one them things, Harrison said.

I'm gonna come over tomorrow, see her, she said.

You're gonna have plenty enough on your plate tomorrow, he said.

Might need the company myself.

Thanks for the vote of confidence, hon, Yeager said.

If I didn't think you could do it, hotshot, I wouldn't be letting you fly, she said.

You're my good luck charm, Glen; I'm gonna paint your name on the nose.

You can't do that, she said.

Hell I can't, it's my ass on the line. Jim, let's get in early; I'll bring some paint.

Sounds good, Harrison said.

Glamorous Glennis, Yeager said.

Glennis cracked a smile. Pancho appeared behind the bar and called them all miserable pudknockers.

You havin a goddamn séance or are you gonna drink something? she said.

Scotch, Harrison said.

That's more like it.

Pancho brought four drinks and they sat around the table and toasted the *Glamorous Glennis*.

Best be gettin home, Harrison said.

Be good to that wife of yours, Glennis said.

He nodded. Five-thirty? he said to Yeager.

Bright and early.

Gonna be a hell of a day, Pancho said.

Say, hon, Yeager said to Glennis, what say we saddle up a coupla Pancho's best mares an have ourselves a little ride? Damn pretty night, tonight.

Sure, she said, assuming you can catch me.

Yeager watched her stand and leave. He smiled, then followed.

Harrison, Pancho said, come here, would you?

She led him over to the serving hatch and picked up a brown paper package.

Saw Gracie earlier, she said.

She told you?

Pancho nodded.

Couple steaks, she said, handing him the package. Give her a big kiss from me.

Thanks, Pancho.

Get out of here, would you? You're making this place look like a goddamn soup kitchen.

He got home at midnight. The bedroom was dark. Grace breathed into the silence, sleeping on her side. He sat on the edge of the bed, unbuttoned his shirt, unlaced his shoes. He pulled open the curtains. The desert was white. The milky light fell into the room. He felt heavy. He pulled a pack of Luckies from his shirt pocket, tapped it on his leg, put one in his mouth. He reached over to the box of matches on his bedside table. Grace stirred. The flame flared orange on her bare shoulder. He sat and smoked and thought of nothing.

First light was a diesel spill across the sky. The ground was gray. The hard silence of the desert sung. In the main hangar, men worked in old fatigues and brown coveralls. They worked in yellow light. When they got tired, they drank dark coffee from the pot at the back. When they got cold, they smoked cigarettes in the janitor's office. Black leads laid thick across the concrete floor. The X-1 sat quiet in the commotion. Harrison ate a sweet roll, drank hot coffee and watched the men work.

Anyone get that Drene? he said.

We got it, one of the mechanics called out.

Hey, Harrison, got a minute?

It was Yeager.

Sure.

They stepped out of the hangar to talk. It was cold.

Got me a little ol problem, Yeager said. Horse threw me at Pancho's last night. Sorta dinged my goddamn ribs.

What do you mean, sorta dinged?

Well, guess you might say I damn near like to broke a coupla sonsabitches.

You seen a doctor?

Hell, no. I made Glen call out the vet. Taped me up pretty tight. Told me to take it easy an get myself to a doctor. Old man ground me if he found out.

No doubt about that, Harrison said. How's it feelin?

Feels kinda okay now but last night damn near killed me.

Uh-huh.

If this was the first flight, Yeager said, I wouldn't even think about tryin it, but, hell, I know every move I gotta make.

Okay, Harrison said, if you think you can do it, but how in the hell are you gonna lock the cockpit door? That takes some liftin and shovin.

Hadn't thought of that, Yeager said.

Hang on a second, Harrison said. I got an idea.

He walked over to the janitor's office.

Hey, Sam, he said.

Captain Harrison. You look like a man who needs something.

You could say that. You got a broom?

Sure do.

Mind if I borrow it a second? We got a little situation here.

Be my guest, Sam said, nodding to where the broom leaned against the wall. Harrison picked it up and laid it on the table.

Here, he said to Sam. Hold this.

Sam held the end of the handle. Harrison found a saw and cut a foot off the end.

That ought to do it, he said.

Yes, sir, Sam said.

Thanks, Sam. Sorry about the broom.

What you got? Yeager said, as Harrison walked back.

Latest breakthrough in supersonic flight engineering, he said, handing Yeager the broom handle. That'll fit right into the door handle. You can use your left hand to raise it up and shove it locked.

Let's give it a try, Yeager said.

They walked back into the hangar, climbed up to the cockpit and tested the technique. No one saw.

Looks good, Harrison said. How you gonna get down the ladder though?

One rung at a time. Either that or Ridley can piggyback me.

You bring the paint?

Sure did.

Let's get on with it, case any brass show up.

The sun moved west a foot an hour. The sky was empty and long. Pancho stood outside, cigar burning between her teeth. The flight was scheduled for ten. Inside, Glennis sat up at the bar. Pancho took one last pull then put the cigar out on the rail and went back inside.

Get you anything, sweetie? she said.

No, Glennis said. Thanks, Pancho.

You okay?

Glennis looked up.

Never know how many places to set for supper, she said.

They sat and waited.

How's his side this morning? Pancho said.

Says it aches, but the vet fixed him up pretty good, least for today.

The radio was on. It was almost ten. Technicians were preparing the flight.

Gracie, Pancho said.

Glennis turned around.

Hey, Glennis said. I was coming to see you later.

She slid from the stool and the women embraced.

Thought I might as well be here, Grace said. Hi, Pancho.

You want a drink? Pancho said.

I'll have a beer.

Grace, honey, I'm so sorry, Glennis said, sitting back down. Jim told me last night.

It's fine, Grace said, really.

Let me come over later.

Sure, that'd be nice.

Pancho put a bottle down in front of her.

I just want this over with, Glennis said.

Almost ten, Pancho said. Sure you don't want nothin?

Beer'd be good I guess, she said.

On me. Both of them, Pancho said, reaching beneath the bar and passing her a bottle.

Glennis stared at the bottle of suds, turning it clockwise with her fingertips.

There's this thing, she said, happens time to time. Sure wish it didn't. Don't know how I see it, but I do; I always do. I'm on the airplane with him. He's strapped in, door locked, waiting for the drop. And I see, over his shoulder, the pressure fall on the fuel gauge. Needle drops fast, to zero. Only he doesn't see it, so I tell him, Chuck, your fuel pressure's dropped, you need to call for an abort, but he can't hear me, so I shout at him to check his dials—which, course, he does anyway—and I feel so relieved. He turns everything off and calls for an abort over the loop. Tower hears him, Jim and Kit flying chase hear him, boys in the NACA truck hear him—I hear him—but the B-29 pilot up there—and I never know who it is—doesn't hear him. He's accidentally got his finger punched down on the microphone transmission key. I *know* because, my God, I can *see* it; I'm there in the B-29 cockpit too. So I start shouting, *Don't drop him!* but he can't hear me and he starts the countdown, ten through one, which everyone on the loop hears, including Chuck, who starts yelling, *Don't drop me! Don't drop me!* and Jim and Kit and the others are yelling *Don't drop him!* and I start screaming *Don't drop him!* until I'm hoarse and crying and the countdown finishes and he reaches over to the handle and releases the plane, and . . . that's when I wake up screaming.

Christ, Pancho said.

What you tell Chuck? Grace said.

That I had a bad dream.

You tell him about it?

I can't. It don't feel right. Like I'd be damaging his confidence. And if I do that, it might affect the flight. Just thinking it feels wrong; like letting the thought in is enough to . . . I tell him, one of the kids had a fall, or got hit by a car; something like that.

She drank her bottle down.

That's why I didn't want my name on that damn airplane, she said, wiping her lips. Ain't nothing glamorous about it.

Grace nodded. On the radio, Ridley said, let's go.

They listened as the B-29, with the X-1 mated beneath it, rolled down the runway, took off and began to climb.

It's a beautiful day, Grace said.

Yes it is, Glennis said.

The women sat and drank and the sun beat down on the bar.

Harrison's voice; Pancho looked at Grace. He was taking off in a Shooting Star, flying chase with Kit Murray. Pancho poured herself a scotch. From the mothership, they heard four minutes called, then two minutes, then Ridley's voice again, to Yeager, waiting in the plane below.

You all set, Chuck?

Hell, yeah, I'm tired of waitin; let's drop this crate.

Countdown numbers tumbled from the radio. Pancho turned up the volume. The X-1 was dropped. They stared into their drinks and listened. Yeager lit the four rocket chambers and climbed, steep, up. His voice on the radio was faint, that West Virginian drawl.

Had a mild buffet [. . .] jus the usual instability.

The X-1 reached point nine-six Mach.

Say Ridley, make a note here [. . .] elevator effectiveness regained.

The Mach needle moved to point nine-eight, fluctuated, then went off the scale. Pancho heard a sudden, hard crack; sharp and loud enough to ripple the beer in the bottles and rattle the frames on the wall.

Say Ridley, make another note, will ya? There's something wrong with this ol Machometer . . . it's gone kinda screwy on me.

If it is, Chuck, we'll fix it. Personally, I think you're seeing things.

Well, guess I am, Jack, an I'm about to punch a hole in the sky.

They heard Yeager chuckle to himself. Glennis smiled. Pancho slammed her hands down on the bar.

Yeager! she said. That miserable sonofabitch! *Just the usual instability?* Man doesn't have a nerve in his goddamn body!

Glennis laughed, Grace squeezed her hand and Pancho made martinis to celebrate.

The desert cooled, night fell. Yeager claimed his free steak dinner at Pancho's.

Got you a present, Harrison said, handing him a brown paper package tied with string.

Thanks, he said, pulling at the string. Inside was a raw carrot, a pair of glasses and an old length of rope.

All cowboys use rope, Harrison said. You can use that to tie yourself to the horse.

Tricky seein things in the dark, Ridley said. Jackrabbit holes, corral gates . . .

Why, thanks a whole lot, Yeager said. One thing about you guys, you're real sincere.

He stuck the carrot in his mouth, put on the glasses and swung the rope around his head.

The men laughed. Pancho came over.

How's the Lone Ranger? she said.

All right, all right, Glennis said. Time to give the fastest man in the world some peace.

There was cheering.

Don't feel right, Pancho said, not celebrating properly.

Orders are orders, Ridley said.

This is the most historic flight since the goddamn Wright Brothers and the air force wants to keep a lid on it.

Just the way they figured it, Harrison said.

Well it's a crock of shit, Pancho said.

Matters that we busted that ol sound barrier; doesn't matter who knows.

You can't keep a thing like that secret, she said. Word'll get out and every hot pilot in the country will know this is the place to aim for. This here's the new frontier. Everything's gonna change. So tell Boyd I'll keep his little secret—hell, I'm keeping enough of his dirty ones anyways—but tonight, we're celebratin.

Pancho threw out anyone not involved with the X-1 program and declared the bar gratis. She always had her booze flown up from Mexico, telling everyone it tasted better tax-free. Grace handed out cold cuartito bottles of Pacífico from a crate on the floor. Harrison and Ridley grabbed Yeager and wrestled him onto the bar. He stood and swayed and they toasted him three times.

It was nearly two. Yeager and Ridley were head-to-head across a table in a shot contest, slowly downing then inverting their glasses in turn. Pancho refereed, calling odds, collecting money. More glasses were empty than full. Harrison cheered and wondered where his wife was. He knocked back his scotch, put down his glass and searched her out.

He found her outside, sat on the steps of the veranda, drinking a warm beer.

There you are, Harrison said.

She looked up at him. Today is a good day, she said.

It is, he said.

It hurts, she said.

I know, he said.

Here. She tapped at her chest.

He sat down. She took a drink of her beer.

Plenty more good days comin, he said.

She offered him the bottle, he took a swig.

Why don't you give Mac a call, see if he's still got that pup? he said.

She looked at him. She nodded. She looked down at the dirt.

When I was a girl, she said, Daddy would take me out riding. Growing up on a ranch, horses were just how we lived; but it was different when he took me out. We'd be gone for the whole morning sometimes; other times longer. We'd ride out together, same horse; a beautiful brown mare he called Lightning—not for her speed, though she was no slouch; she'd been born in a storm. He'd give me the reins from time to time and sometimes we'd stop and fish or catch a jackrabbit to take home with us, but mostly we'd just ride, for the sake of riding. Can't ride a horse without thinking about him. Warm breeze in your face, dirt kicking up behind. It felt good, just to ride.

He offered back the bottle; she shook her head. They sat together in silence, smoke curling away in the wind.

———

MOJAVE DESERT
MUROC, CALIFORNIA
JANUARY 1959

—————

The blanched beans steamed thin trails that coiled up from a pan in the sink. She watched them twist slowly, the desert flat and wild and wide out the window behind. For a moment, the steam seemed to rise up from the sagebrush itself; a column of smoke. She looked down at the floor, and gripped the edge of the sink.

Shit, she said. Shit shit shit.

Grace shut her eyes and stood still, heart lilting in her chest. She left the beans in the sink and walked out of the kitchen.

Milo! she said. Milo!

The dog ran to her from the sofa.

Good boy, she said. Let's take a walk.

She dried her hands on the back of her jeans and pulled on her boots.

It was eleven and the mountains shimmered in the distance. The sun scolded the sky steel blue; orange gleams snagged the underside of gaunt clouds high in the thin air. She walked across the hardpan, away from the house. Milo ran ahead, darting between the black Joshua trees. She whistled and he returned to her side, nuzzling her legs. She pushed her fingers into his hair.

All right, she said. The dog ran off again. She glanced up at the horizon toward the base. The sky was clear. They walked for an hour.

When they got back, she went to bed and slept. She did not dream. When she woke, she was not alone.

Jim? Is that you?

You're awake.

When did you get in?

She sat up on her elbows, pulling the eiderdown to her chest.

You look so peaceful, he said, stroking her head.

How was the flight?

It was okay.

She turned on the bedside light.

Jesus, Jim—what happened to your eyes?

Same old; I'm fine.

Don't give me that crap.

She got up on her knees, put hands either side of his face, looked into him.

It looks like someone's gone at your eyeballs with a knife! she said. She sat back on her legs. You've been pulling heavy g's. What happened?

Just a tight spot, hon, nothing to worry about.

Are you okay?

Got a little beat up. Guess my eyes got themselves a little blood-shot. I'll live. I'm stiff right through though, so I'm gonna take a hot bath.

Grace sat on the edge of the bed in the half-light. Harrison removed his shirt and walked out to the bathroom.

Bud Anderson shot a bunch of ducks this morning, he said, said we could have one if we want. Hon?

Sure, she said.

Great; I'll bring it home tonight. Maybe make a stew or something?

Grace didn't answer. In the bedroom, she rubbed her face, her neck, and pulled on her pants.

Any chance you could fix me up a cheese sandwich or something quick? I got to be back at base for a debrief at three.

Planning on eating it in the bath? she said.

Can I?

She appeared at the bathroom door. He was in the tub, soaking. The old pipes banged behind the wall.

My mother always said there was no place for food in the bathroom, she said.

Your mother said a lot of stuff.

You should have heard what she said about you.

We used to talk a lot about fishing, he said. Woman loved to fish.

Grace looked down at her husband, half-submerged, skin brown and smooth and wrinkled from the beating it took from the desert sun day after day. His ears were pink from the hot water. All she could think was how vulnerable he seemed; this mass of flesh and hair she loved so deeply, floating naked in the bath. There was a small cut on his face, above his left eye, near the hairline. He moved in the bath, exposing his shoulder. It was yellow.

Your shoulder, she said.

Dinged it pretty bad, he said. Hurts like hell.

She knelt beside the tub and ran her fingers across the bruising. She kissed it.

Head's pretty sore too, he said.

She pushed her lips to his forehead.

And here, he said, pointing at his lips.

She leaned in and kissed him.

I'll make your sandwich, she said, but you're eating it downstairs.

Later that afternoon, when Harrison had gone back to work, she put Milo in the car and drove to Rosamond, twenty miles west of the base, and pulled up outside the First Baptist Church. It was a small building with alabaster walls and a domed bell tower. A single Joshua tree stood outside next to the veranda, its crooked arms reaching skyward like a penitent sinner. The engine idled. She drummed her hands on the wheel.

C'mon, she said, and turned off the engine.

She tied Milo to the corner of the veranda.

I'll be back in a minute, she said.

Inside was gloomy and cool. A lone figure sat hunched at a wooden table in the northeast corner, sunlight falling on a smooth head of Brylcreem from a small window cut high in the wall above him. He looked up when he heard the door close, hair gleaming white in the gloom.

Grace, he said as she approached him, this is a pleasant surprise. He rose and walked over to greet her.

Good afternoon, Reverend Irving, she said. I hope you don't mind me—

Not at all, not at all, he said, please, come in.

I was just passing by and I thought I'd stop in, see how Virginia Allen was doing.

You're very kind, he said. She's bearing up. Her fever peaked over

Christmas; the doctor says that's the worst of it. She needs to rest now, rest and eat. We miss her on a Sunday.

You'll tell her I stopped by? She's such a sweet old lady.

Of course, she'll be delighted. Thank you.

I'd better get going, she said. Milo's outside.

It's good of you to stop in. Milo's your son?

My dog, she said. Milo's my dog. Tied up, out front.

Ah, he said, well. It's good to see you, Grace. God bless. You're always welcome.

She thanked him and left, the cold air slugging her like a gang of thugs as she stepped outside; Milo, whimpering, pressed his body against the dirt.

———

The next day was a Thursday. It was a quarter before ten and she was alone in the house. Milo's paws clicked on the hard linoleum of the kitchen floor as she pulled laundry into a basket to hang outside.

What's the matter, boy? she said. You been poking about all morning.

The dog paced the room. Grace glanced up at the clock. She carried on with the laundry, folding and smoothing the sheets, ignoring the forty-five-minute chasm between when Jim said he'd be home and what the clock now read. Three words were trying to get her attention, like a small child. *Something has happened.* She folded and smoothed. She could recall the entire conversation. She was used to conversations at five in the morning. He dressed for work, she lay in bed. He would be home by nine.

Fold and smooth. The house was silent and still; slowly, the chasm grew. She listened. She listened for a car turning off the main highway. She listened for the wail of a siren. She listened for the telephone. No one had called. The other wives; there would be calls. A collective assimilation of information and, one by one, elimination of their husbands' names: a grim game of chance. *Something has happened.* The silent telephone was good. Unless it was very bad. She knew the procedures; they all did. In the event of Something Having Happened, a strict protocol was swiftly adhered to. No information pertaining to the freshly deceased would be released until the man's wife—widow—was informed, in person, by an appropriate party; a superior officer, a comrade or, often, the base's chaplin. The chosen messenger would advance slowly upon the departed's front door, headwear stowed beneath the left arm, face set in a way that spoke the news, the words that followed a horrible formality. The man would close the front door behind him. He would assist the crumpled woman to a place of comfort. He would leave. Grace stared at the telephone. The sky was silent.

There was a hard knock on the door.

She felt nothing; just a distant confusion: in her nightmares, it was always a doorbell. It occurred to her, for the first time, that they had no doorbell. She wanted to shout, but had no voice. Instead, she watched a phantom arm, her arm, reach out from her unfamiliar body and push open the door.

Mornin, Mrs. Harrison! Oh, you look terrible. Are you okay?

Dougie, she said.

What's happened?

She stared at him. He was wearing a light blue shirt with short sleeves. Under his arm he carried a package.

I'm fine, she heard herself saying.

You sure? You don't look right, if you don't mind me sayin.

I must have stood up too quick, got a little dizzy.

Well, so long as you're sure . . . Got a package for you—Jim, actually. Damn heavy, glad you're in. Didn't much fancy lugging it back.

He lowered the box gently to the ground.

Where do you want it?

There's fine.

She felt sick. She held the doorframe.

Hey Milo, Dougie said.

The dog ran outside.

Well, guess I'll be seein you, Mrs. Harrison. Don't be movin that yourself.

He smiled. She thanked him and shut the door. In the kitchen, she made up a little hot milk, with a measure of bourbon and a spoon of sugar, and sat down at the kitchen table to drink it. Then she cried. Four sharp sobs. She stopped herself, wiping her eyes with the palm of her right hand. Her husband was still missing. Milo stalked the yard in circles. She stood at the window and watched him. She glanced at the telephone again, then walked over and dialed the base. The duty officer answered.

This is Grace Harrison, she said. I want to speak to Captain Harrison please.

That's not something—

Please, she said, surprising herself. I want to speak to my husband.

I—

It's very important.

Her voice was beginning to break apart.

Let me see what I can do, he said. The voice rung off.

Hello? she said.

Yeah? a third voice said.

Jack? Grace said.

Who's this? Jack said.

Jack, it's me, it's Grace.

Gracie? Are you okay?

I know I'm not supposed to call the base—and I never have, not once, in ten, twelve years—but, Jack, have you seen Jim? He told me he'd—is he—

Why, he's right here, Grace—hang on.

Jim?

Gracie?

Jim.

Hon, what's the matter?

Nothing, nothing's the matter. I'm sorry; I shouldn't have called.

Hey, it's okay, he said, slow down and tell me what's goin on.

It's me, I'm sorry, nothing's going on, it's just . . . you said you'd be home at nine, and I know you were taking up a Starfighter this morning and after . . . what happened to Kinch . . . I hate that damn plane.

Honey, honey, it's okay. Jack needed my help on this profile. Said I'd be home closer to eleven, remember?

I—no?

When I was looking for my watch.

I must have dozed off . . . goddamn it.

It's okay.

It's not.

Honey—

I've made myself half mad with worry this morning. What's wrong with me? I'm so embarrassed.

Gracie, hon, don't even fret on it. Air force pays my wage, trains me to wear the Blue Suit, but they don't do a damn thing to train the wife of a Blue Suiter. You're doing just fine. Look, I'm just about done here. I'll head back now.

No, no, it's okay, stay; Jack needs you. I'm going to get out, take Milo for a walk or something. I need to clear my head.

Well, okay, as long as you're all right?

I am now.

Okay then.

I'll see you later.

You bet.

Okay.

He rang off. It was nine fifty-five. Grace put Milo in the car and drove to Rosamond.

The hardware store was the only place they could get dog food. Charlie Anderson used to sell it, but Charlie was dead, tuberculosis, and his store, hundred and sixty acre homestead, and the town of Muroc itself, had been bought up by the air force and dismantled to make room for the expanding base, renamed Edwards, after Glen Edwards, who augered in testing a prototype jet-powered heavy bomber called the Flying Wing that had the look and aerodynamics of a banana.

After she'd bought the dog food and hauled it out to the car, she leaned against the door and lit a smoke and the metal against her back felt hotter than the burning cigarette tip flaring orange sending smoke twisting away in a sinewy line that her eyes followed; the thin column turning and rising. Her hand trembled and a brittle ashen hulk broke off and fell to the ground. She stared at the charred lump at her feet. *Burned Beyond Recognition.* That's what they called it when a human body was exposed to the intense heat of combusting aviation fuel. Her heart hammered hard inside her. She dropped what was left of the cigarette, pulled Milo from the car and started up Main Street.

———

Grace, I wasn't expecting to see you again so soon.

Reverend Irving was at the lectern. He collected his papers, picked up a small Bible and stepped down from the platform.

How are you feeling today? he said. You look tired.

She sat down on the front pew. Irving joined her.

Grace? he said. Has something happened?

She stared down at the smooth floor.

Hasn't happened in years, she said.

Can you tell me about it?

You know my husband, Jim, she said, sitting up. He's a test pilot at the base. He came home once, few years ago, with bright red eyes. You've never seen anything like it; I thought his eyeballs had burst or something. He'd been pulling heavy negative g's. They call it *red out*; the blood vessels in the eyes rupture. He looked terrible. Skin was so gray. He just sat in the kitchen, drinking a glass of milk. I asked him what had happened and he said, nothing much, bit of a corner; managed to luck out of it. *A corner. Lucked out of it.* I couldn't blame him, or Jack—his engineer—for wanting to beat Scott Crossfield's Mach two record, especially with the Wright Brothers' big anniversary thing coming up a few days later and the celebration the navy had planned for Scotty, but the Bell guys, the engineers who built the plane, told them—told them straight— the X1-A could be pretty . . . *unforgiving* at speeds above Mach two; that it might, uh, *go divergent*. Which is a pretty little way of saying the airplane might suddenly lose all aerodynamics and fall out of the sky like a brick. Air's pretty thin at seventy-five thousand feet. Sky's purple, stars are flickering. You slide around like a car on ice. Every airplane has a performance envelope, its critical limits. Jim says flight test is all about *pushing the outside of the envelope.* That's what they all talk about. That's all they talk about. Well, in this case, the envelope didn't want to stretch at all. At seventy-five thousand feet, above Mach two, the envelope was full of holes. Those Bell guys were right. The airplane just . . . *uncorked*. Started pitching and yaw- ing *and* rolling, all at the same time. There isn't anything you can do to maneuver out of a hypersonic tumble. In fact, almost anything you *do* try is going to make things a whole heap worse. They call it inertia coupling, but that don't do a real good job of explaining what actually happens. You fall out of the sky, rolling and spinning and tumbling, end over end. Jim was thrown around so violently that he busted the canopy with his helmet and was knocked unconscious. He fell ten miles in seventy seconds before coming round at thirty thousand feet in an inverted spin. You wouldn't wish an inverted spin at that altitude on anyone, but an inverted spin is something he knows how to get out of. So he wrestles the airplane into a normal spin then pops out of it, twenty-five thousand feet from the farm. You know what the sonofabitch says on the way down? That they won't have to run a structural integrity test on the airplane now. It was a joke. He was making a joke. He put her down on the lakebed and everyone said, how the hell are you still here? He was home for lunch. I didn't find out about the new record until I ran into Jack the next day. Mach two point four. Fastest man alive. They gave him the Harmon International Trophy. That was nineteen fifty-three. I had nightmares about it for a year. And then he shows up again, yesterday lunch, with bloodred eyes.

She started to cry, then stopped herself.

You know, she said, we went to this party, the year before, I think, old friend of mine; she'd moved east, New York, after the war. She was a journalist, worked at *Time* and a bunch of other places, then managed to get a job copywriting for one of those big advertising agencies on Madison Avenue. She spent the whole evening telling me how ruthless it was, how *cutthroat* and *dog-eat-dog*. I asked her how many of those men would still go into a meeting if there was a one-in-four chance of them not making it out alive. We lost sixty-two men over a thirty-six-week stretch once. That's nearly two a week. I had to buy another black dress; I couldn't get the one I had clean and dried in time. So I had two, on rotation. You want to know why I'm here? I remembered something. Back in fifty-three, Joe Walker, good friend of Jim's, test pilot for the NACA—the NASA now—came over when he heard what happened to Jim in the X1-A. Tells Jim inertia coupling hit him hard a couple of times too. Jim asks how he got out of it. Joe pulls that big Huck Finn grin of his across his face and says, the *JC Maneuver*. In the *JC Maneuver*, he says, you take your hands off the controls and *put the mother in the lap of a su-per-na-tu-ral power*.

She gave a little laugh.

Sorry, Reverend, she said. I remembered that yesterday.

She looked down again at the hard stone floor.

Kinda thing I could use right about now, don't you think? she said.

I'm glad you came back, Irving said. And I'm glad you've shared this with me. Where did you grow up?

Midwest. On a ranch. My father didn't hold much with church. Figured that, with his mother outliving his wife, there wasn't much of anyone watching over him.

I've met Jim before, he said, few times, over at Pancho Barnes's place. He still the fastest man alive?

She smiled.

Mel Apt beat him to Mach three in fifty-six, she said, but . . . Mel bought it with that one. It had a seat, and Mel tried to eject, but . . .

I'm sorry.

Jim always says there's no point trying to punch out of a rocket plane; it's like committing suicide to keep yourself from getting killed.

The Lord will give you strength, Grace. He will hold you up. Would you like me to pray for you?

She nodded. Irving said a prayer. Then he said, you should come along on Sunday.

I can't, I'm sorry, Reverend. He can't know I'm here, no one can.

You feel that prayer would undermine his confidence in the air?

It's more than that—these . . . *things*, they're not talked—

I understand.

Thank you, she said.

Psalm one thirty-nine says, *Whither shall I go from thy spirit? Or whither shall I flee from thy presence? If I ascend up into heaven, thou art there: if I make my bed in hell, behold, thou art there. If I take the wings of the morning, and dwell in the uttermost parts of the sea; Even there shall thy hand lead me, and thy right hand shall hold me.* It's funny, in a way; I'm already directing my prayers into the atmosphere, after the Sputnik.

Jim said it was nothing to worry about, it was so small.

Don't let size deceive you. Look at the H-bomb. This country has always been protected by the vast oceans that surround it. Imagine if that could be breached, at any time, in minutes, by a Sputnik carrying an atomic bomb? What if it could shower us with radiation like a crop-duster as it passes overhead? This time last year, Rickover told the Senate he didn't think the American people understood that we were at war. They need to hear shells! What we'll be hearing before the year is out will be louder than shells, I assure you.

You really think so?

Only last week the Soviets launched another Sputnik—Mechta, whatever that means—that flew to the *moon*, then into orbit around the sun. The sun! How are they doing this? How are they doing these things before us? McCormack's right, you know, we're facing national extinction if we don't catch up, and catch up soon. We simply *must* capture the high ground of space. Our survival— the free world, the church—depends on it.

He paused.

The Communists aren't supposed to be good at technology. He sighed. I'm basing my next sermon on it.

On how the Communists are supposed to be technologically backward?

On us getting soft, he said. We're standing still. The American man is drinking beer on his sofa in front of his new television set, while the Soviets are toiling, sweating and bleeding, becoming masters of the universe. Maybe Average Joe should concern himself less with the depth of the pile in his new broadloom rug, or the height of the tail fin on his new car. Maybe then we'd prevail. May I read you something?

She nodded. He opened his Bible and began to read from a newspaper cutting pressed between the pages of Leviticus.

Control of space means control of the world. From space, the Reds would have the power to control the Earth's weather, to cause drought and flood, to change the tides and raise the levels of the sea, to direct the Gulf Stream and change temperate climates to frigid.

It's a battle, Grace, he said. It's a battle for the heavens. It's good versus evil and we're on the front line. You know, I might use that. These things are so difficult to write.

He made a note.

I pray for this country, Grace. I pray for the president, I pray for Vice President Nixon, and I pray for Premier Khrushchev. And I will pray for you and Jim.

I should go, she said. Thank you, Reverend.

God bless you, Grace.

In the car, driving home, she thought back to the fall of fifty-seven, sitting outside Pancho's with a warm beer; Jim and a few of the others passing round the binoculars, trying to see the Sputnik as it passed overhead.

Ike said anything? Pancho said.

Why the hell should he? Harrison said.

You can certainly hear the damn thing, Ridley said.

Cardenas had pulled his car over. KCAW was broadcasting the satellite's transmission live. You sure we're gonna be able to see it? he said.

Damn right, Pancho said. I can't get that goddamn bleeping out of my head. You think it's a code, or something?

Hang on, Harrison said. Listen.

—launched earlier tonight. The official Soviet news agency TASS says that the man-made satellite is circling the Earth once every hour and thirty-five minutes. The rocket that carried the artificial moon into space left the Earth at five miles a second. It has a diameter of twenty-two inches and weight a hundred and eighty-four pounds. Nothing has been revealed about the material of which it is constructed, nor where in the Soviet Union it was launched from.

What's the big deal? Harrison said.

Beats me, Ridley said.

Both us and the Russians have been talking about launching an Earth satellite since fifty-five, for chrissake; part of the International Geophysical Year. Why the surprise? The Naval Research Lab's launching ours on a Vanguard in December. That right, Jack?

That's right.

Whole lot of fuss over nothing, Cardenas said.

Well I sure as hell don't like the idea of some secret Commie machine buzzin me fifteen goddamn times a day, Pancho said.

I don't like it either, Grace said.

Wait til the X-15 rolls out, end of June, Ridley said. It's been designed to fly at two hundred and eighty thousand feet—that's fifty miles up—beyond where the atmosphere ends and space begins.

Scotty's already in training to fly it. Jim here, a few other fellas—an maybe a coupla boys from the NACA—will follow. Forget satellites, they'll be the first *men* in space.

Grace stared at her husband. He shrugged his shoulders.

You fellas got your sights set on space? Pancho said.

We been goin higher an faster the last ten years, Ridley said. Next logical step for the X-series.

Sounds like a whole heap of pie in the sky, Pancho said.

North American's already working on the follow-up, Harrison said. Two pilots will fly it into orbit, take a few little turns around the Earth, land on that glorious ol lakebed out there.

Hold on, Cardenas said, binoculars pressed against his eyes. I think I see it.

They watched the white grain glide across the silent dark sky as the country slumbered below.

Feels strange, Grace said. Creepy. Like we've invaded the heavens or something.

Harrison looked at her and frowned.

What I mean is, she said, no one's been up there—*out* there—before, ever; now here we are.

We're not, the Reds are, Cardenas said.

Makes you wonder what else they got up their sleeves, don't it? Pancho said.

You don't feel it? Grace said to Jim.

Feel what?

Like something's shifted.

No one's going to remember this in a year's time, Harrison said.

Hey, Ridley said. I can see it without the bins.

On the radio, the announcer said, *listen now for the sound that forevermore separates the old from the new.*

That next morning, Grace went to Rosamond and bought as

many newspapers as she could carry. When she got home, she spread them out on the kitchen table in front of Jim.

SOVIETS FIRE EARTH SATELLITE INTO SPACE

RUSSIAN MOON CIRCLING THE EARTH

SPACE AGE IS HERE!

COMMUNISTS WIN RACE INTO OUTER SPACE

TRACK RED MOON BY RADIO

He put down his coffee.

What the hell? he said and started to read.

You think the press is going to give a damn about the X-15? she said.

The Sputnik in its flight across the world may be a courier of such dire portent to national security that considerations of partisan politics have no place in the discussion of how this happened and what to do about it, he read.

He looked up at Grace, who was reading the *Washington Post*.

Says here that Johnson has opened a subcommittee of the Senate Armed Services to look at American defense and space programs *in light of the Sputnik crisis*, she said.

What crisis?

Listen to this, she said. *The Roman Empire controlled the world because it could build roads. Later, when men moved to sea, the British Empire was dominant because it had ships. Now the Communists have established a foothold in outer space.*

That Johnson? he said.

Yup.

Johnson is an asshole.

I'm just telling you what they're saying, she said. The Soviets are masters of the universe, according to Bill Kreagor at the *New York Times*. Christ, Soapy Williams has written a poem about it.

Why's he written a poem?

Oh little Sputnik flying high
With made-in-Moscow beep,
You tell the world it's a Commie sky
And Uncle Sam's asleep.

How the hell are we asleep? he said. We flew a rocket faster than Mach one *ten years* ago! The rocket program at Edwards is the most advanced in the world! Ike's the only one talking sense.

He sounds old-fashioned.

He sounds measured.

He's out of touch.

Because he's not hysterical?

Because he doesn't get that everyone's terrified! Terrified that the Soviets can and probably will drop atom bombs on any American city they want, whenever they want, with no warning.

You really worried? he said.

I'm concerned; sure I am. When the *New York Times* says we're in a *race for survival* and the Senate majority leader says the Reds will soon be dropping bombs on us from space like kids dropping rocks onto cars from freeway overpasses then, yeah, I get a little jittery.

This country's gone nuts, he said.

Grace stopped reminiscing; she was nearly home. Milo's tongue lolled from his mouth, head stuck out the open window. Armageddon felt far away. She had enough to worry about. When she got in, Harrison was upstairs, packing a bag.

Honey? he said.

Hey, she said, walking into the bedroom.

Where you been? he said.

Out, she said. Shopping.

Shopping?

Milo needed food. What's going on?

I've got to go away for a few days.

Away?

I'm real sorry, hon.

What? Why?

Sealed orders. Top secret. I've got to report to Washington, D.C. for a classified briefing first thing tomorrow.

———

He stepped out of the taxi onto the corner of H Street and East Executive Avenue. The Washington air was so cold he thought the day might snap in two. He turned up his collar; drew himself together. He felt uncomfortable. The strict geometry of his suit made him feel like a patsy. It was the only one he owned. He pulled at the knot of his tie. He was standing in front of an unremarkable townhouse in downtown D.C. He checked his orders again. *Dolley Madison House.* He was in the right place. It didn't make any sense. Why was the briefing here and not at the Pentagon? He'd been ordered to dress as a civilian too. The whole deal was odd.

The receptionist told him to wait in the auditorium, where he found thirty or so men, milling around, also wearing unfamiliar suits. They were, he could tell, all air force and navy pilots; the odd Marine flyer. He recognized Jim Lovell and Pete Conrad from the navy's Test Pilot School at Pax River, their prime test center. Wally Schirra too. Harrison looked around for anyone else from Edwards. There was Howard Lane. And there was Deke Slayton. Deke was a prime pilot in Fighter Ops; a good guy, doing solid line-testing work.

Deke, Harrison said, approaching him.

Jim!

The men shook hands.

Fancy running into you here, Harrison said.

Fancy that, Deke said.

Any idea what this is all about?

Beats the hell outta me. Plenty Blue Suiters though.

Plenty navy too.

Uh-huh.

What's his name? Harrison said.

Who?

Over there.

John Glenn. Flew the first supersonic coast-to-coast. Set a speed record.

That's the one, Harrison said. Marine, isn't he?

Yeah.

Jim Lovell approached them, smiling, and shook hands with Harrison.

Jim, Harrison said, this here is Deke Slayton. Jim finished top of his class at Pax River.

Pleasure, Deke said, shaking Lovell's hand.

Edwards?

Deke nodded.

Harrison turned to Lovell. They still call you Shaky? he said.

Only Conrad.

Shaky? Deke said. Bad name for a pilot.

That's pretty much what he had in mind when he came up with it, Lovell said. And here he is now.

Jim! Conrad said to Harrison. Good to see you.

Hey, Pete, Lovell said.

Shaky! Say, that was weird this morning, weren't it?

Lovell laughed.

It sure was, he said.

What happened? Harrison said.

We ran into each other at dawn, Lovell said, in the parking lot, sneaking off base to come here.

We had strict orders not to tell anyone—including each other, Conrad said.

And we followed our orders to the letter, Lovell said.

My money's on this being about space, Conrad said.

Smart money's on a new type of rocket plane, Lovell said.

Here? Deke said.

Maybe, Lovell said.

X-15B is already being designed by North American, Harrison said. Then the X-20 will follow it.

That the one they're calling the Dyna-Soar? Deke said.

Dynamic Soarer, yeah, Harrison said.

They're space-planes, sure, Deke said, but they're a way off.

Too far off, Conrad said. My guess is, they're in a funk after the Vanguard fuckup.

That was bad, Deke said. Real bad.

Why the hell did they televise it? Harrison said. It made us look stupid.

Stupidest thing I ever seen, Conrad said. Two months after the Sputnik, Khrushchev laughing at us already; here's our chance and the thing doesn't make it six inches off the goddamn pad! Just does this little fart then collapses and—

Boom, Harrison said.

Boom, Conrad said. What a joke.

What was it they called it? Deke said. *Kaputnik?*

Something like that, Harrison said.

So I'm sticking with space, Conrad said.

The men fell silent and scanned the room.

No Yeager? Lovell said.

No college degree, Harrison said.

Damn shame, Deke said. I thought they wanted the best?

Well, they've only called in test pilots under thirty-nine, under five-eleven with at least fifteen hundred hours of jet experience—and a college degree, Lovell said. Which must rule out a bunch of fellas.

Crossfield? Walker? Conrad said.

Too old? Deke said.

Civilians, Harrison said.

Right.

A man shut the door at the back.

Here we go, Harrison said.

The men took their seats and stared at the podium. A short man walked onto the stage. He looked as comfortable on it as the men felt in their suits.

Gentlemen, good morning, he said. My name is Doctor Robert Gilruth; you may call me Doctor Gilruth. We've asked you here to-day to discuss Project Mercury.

He had their attention.

As you are probably aware, Gilruth continued, in October, the president expanded the role of the National Advisory Committee on Aeronautics to include vehicles able to extend beyond the confines of the atmosphere. The highest priority of this new National Aeronautics and Space Administration is to put an American into Earth orbit within three years. The program, headed by myself, is called Project Mercury. We're looking for the best pilots for these missions. The hazards will be considerable. As such, the first men in space will be chosen on a volunteer basis. Should any man decide not to volunteer, it will not be entered onto his record, nor will it be held against him in any way. The NASA will be a civilian agency, so every man would keep the same military status and rank.

Deke turned to Harrison.

Civilian? he said. That don't sound good.

Gilruth, gently perspiring under the hot lights, explained that the space vehicle was to be a funnel-shaped capsule, just six feet across and nine high. The volunteer would be strapped to a form-fitted couch, sealed inside, and placed atop a ballistic missile capable of three hundred and fifty thousand pounds of thrust. A man on the ground would light the missile and fire it into space.

That is the stupidest thing I ever heard, Harrison said to Deke.

Any questions? Gilruth said.

The men murmured a mixture of amusement and incredulity. A few raised their hands.

The missions will be controlled automatically from the ground, Gilruth said, in response to the first question. The pilot will have no control over the capsule during the flight.

No landing, he said. The capsule will splash-down in the ocean.

No prototype of the capsule has been built yet, he said. We're putting together some first-rate blueprints.

Well, I see your point, he said. A *reputation for blowing up* is perhaps a little strong . . . but, yes, there have been a few incidents with the Atlas in the past and it's being worked on.

Harrison sat back in his seat. No flying? It wasn't even a ship or a craft, it was a goddamn tin can. They sealed you in, shot you into the sky like a cannonball and prized you out in some remote and turbulent part of the Atlantic. Assuming you survived the ride, of course. The only prerequisite skill seemed to be the ability to take it. Sure, if the thing malfunctioned up there, the pilot could take over, push a button, fire the retro-rockets to pop it out of orbit and splash-down prematurely, but that was about it. No, a real pilot would take her up, fly the thing himself, grease it in like a man and make it to Pancho's in time for beercall. That's how it was done. Harrison looked up to Gilruth on the stage. The man was good; Harrison gave him that.

The first men in space, Gilruth said, will be known as *astro-nauts*, meaning *star voyagers*.

* * *

That night, the men were put up in hotels around town. Harrison was in the Marriott on Fortieth Street with Lovell, Conrad and a few others from Pax River. They dumped their bags as soon as they arrived and met in Schirra's room, pulling chairs into a circle like it was a séance. They wanted to chew over this Project Mercury business together, in private; Schirra even locked the door.

There were six of them, sat in a circle, filling their glasses from a bottle of scotch being passed around. Lovell, Conrad and Schirra, he knew pretty well. There was another navy guy, Al Shepard, an experienced test pilot who'd previously been an instructor at Pax River. Harrison knew him by reputation. The other man was from Edwards, Gordon "Gordo" Cooper, but wasn't involved in either the X-series or Fighter Ops, so Harrison didn't know him. Deke, along with Howard Lane and a few others from Edwards, were staying in another hotel across town.

So, gentlemen, Lovell said. What do you think?

The men looked around at each other.

It ain't the X-15, that's for sure, Conrad said.

It's hazardous duty, *that's* for sure, Schirra said. I'm not worried about putting my ass on the line, I'm worried about putting my career on the line.

The men around Harrison nodded in agreement. The quickest way to screw up your career was to get caught up in some crackpot program that floundered on, leaving you two, three years behind in flight test and promotion. Schirra was higher up the ladder than most of his navy brethren, and had the most to lose.

It's the most harebrained thing I've ever heard, Harrison said.

Suppose it works out how they say? Lovell said.

We're not all in line to fly the X-15, Gordo said. No offense, Jim.

None taken.

First man in space, Shepard said. I could live with that.

They haven't even built the damn thing yet, Conrad said.

Even if they do, Harrison said, you're not gonna be able to *fly* it at all. You'll be a guinea pig; a lab rabbit, with sensors taped all over and a thermometer up your ass. Anybody goes up is gonna be nothing more than Spam in a can.

I'd feel a hell of a lot better if it wasn't the Atlas, Lovell said.

I heard its walls are so thin they collapse if they're not pressurized, Shepard said.

Lighter it is, faster it goes, Conrad said.

And the higher it blows, Lovell said.

Schirra, who'd gone silent, said, we used to call this kinda thing *innovative duty*. He stopped smiling. Any one of us would be nuts, he said, to get tied up in this. And you, Jim, he said, looking at Harrison, you'd be nuts to walk away from something like the X-15 for some lunatic Rube Goldberg thing like *Project Mercury*.

Damn straight, Conrad said.

Well, Harrison said, been real good seein you fellas, but I expect I'll be headin home.

He took the elevator back to his room. What a crock, he thought. Still, there was something about it he couldn't shift. He felt something, but didn't know why. He thought about Lindbergh, the *Spirit of St. Louis*; wind and wood and wings; the gray sea below, cold Atlantic air burning his face. It was almost eleven. He opened the door to his room. A note had been slipped under it. He sat on the edge of the bed, picked up the telephone, and dialed home.

Honey? he said. I just got a message to call you. Is everything okay?

Jim, she said.

What is it? he said. What's the matter?

I'm pregnant, she said.

———

He was home by dawn. He slung his bag down and embraced his sleepy wife standing in the kitchen.

Thought you'd decided to stay? she said.

Couldn't keep away, he said, arms around her middle. How come you're up?

Been sick again, she said.

Again?

That's why I went to see Doctor Roberts in the first place.

When were you sick?

Uh, I don't know; yesterday, couple of times the day before; last week.

You didn't tell me?

Why would I tell you?

You were sick!

Yeah.

And I'm your husband.

And?

And you should tell me this stuff.

She put on a pot of coffee, glanced out the window, got out the milk.

You gotta tell me this stuff, hon, he said, leaning against the counter. I need to know.

Jim, there's a whole entire *crater* full of stuff I don't tell you about, she said.

What? But why wouldn't you tell me if you were sick?

You were at the base the first time it happened. Few weeks ago. I felt better after. And that was it. Sometimes, believe it or not, I don't want you distracted, especially if you're flying some important program.

She poured the coffee into two chipped mugs and set them down on the round table. The morning sun fell across it like a drunk.

So I deal with it myself, she said, sitting down. Like all that trouble last year with Hank Roosey.

What trouble with Hank Roosey? he said, joining her at the table.

I can't believe we're having this conversation.

What trouble with Hank Roosey?

It doesn't matter, she said.

What he do?

I took care of it.

I want to know.

It doesn't matter.

Matters to me.

No it doesn't, she said. You just can't stand not knowing. You have to control everything, because if you're in control, everything will be okay, right? But let me tell you something. That's not how life works. And you know what? When this little thing—she pointed at her belly—comes out, there's gonna be a whole heap of chaos in your life that you'll have zero control over. So get used to it.

Okay, he said, picking up his mug.

Okay?

Okay.

Okay then, she said. I'm sorry, I'm a little cranky right now.

I'd better get used to that too, right? he said.

A laugh escaped her. She looked at him over her mug.

It had something to do with a hog, she said.

I knew it! That miserable sonofabitch—

Jim, forget it, it was eleven months ago. I took care of it. The point is I knew you'd get worked up like this so I didn't tell you. Just like three weeks ago when I woke after you left for work and was sick in the sink. I thought I'd eaten something bad. Or the week after that when I was hurling most of the afternoon. I just assumed it was some bug. So when it didn't seem to be going, I called up Doctor Roberts and made an appointment. I would have told you about it but you were in Washington for the briefing. I *did* tell you when Doctor Roberts called me with the test results; at least, I tried to, I had to leave a message.

What tests did he do?

Blood test; had to pee in a cup—let me tell you, *that* wasn't easy.

I'll bet.

Then he asked me a bunch of questions.

Like what?

General stuff—how much I smoked, what I weighed, family history—that kind of thing.

Harrison sat back in his chair.

He mention anything about you expectin? he said.

Not til he called, she said. I think he suspected at the time but didn't want to give me any false hope.

What—*how*—did this happen? Harrison said.

You want me to draw you a diagram?

Is he sure?

Yeah, Jim, it's real; this is happening.

But—

I know, I think I was in shock too when he called and told me. I had to sit down. I didn't think that happened to people. I just sat on the floor and cried. He was very understanding. He talked me through the whole thing.

So how . . . ?

You're gonna love this: he doesn't know.

He doesn't know?

He said some women, a small fraction, once diagnosed, *can* go on to have children, but it's dependent on them ovulating, even if very infrequently.

And that's not something you've done?

I mean, I can't remember last time I had a period. It's been years.

You tell him that?

Sure, he knows that, she said. But he says sometimes these things just happen, and we should be happy when they do. Said that there's plenty in the world to worry about, so why add to it?

Harrison didn't say anything.

Look, she said, I know it's a shock. You get used to one thing then everything gets turned on its head, but this—this is amazing—

It's a goddamn miracle, is what it is, he said, cracking a grin. My beautiful wife! he said, banging his hands on the table. We need to celebrate!

Well amen to that!

Wait—everything's okay with the baby, right? I mean, does the condition—is it dangerous?

Everything's fine, Grace said. No reason why there should be any problems. No reason at all.

Doc Roberts say that?

He did.

And you're seeing him again?

Next Tuesday.

Next Tuesday.

Wanna come?

No thank you, he said.

There you go, she said.

He drunk his coffee and stared at her.

So, May, huh? he said.

Yup.

Guess I'd better figure out a nursery.

* * *

Pancho proclaimed it a genuine miracle by Jesus Christ himself and cleared a prime space on the wall above the bar for the first baby photo. She said it was about time they had some goddamn life in the place instead of a bunch of pudknockers who couldn't fly for hog-shit. The men hollered at the swollen moon and the coyotes howled at the men. At midnight Pancho threw the others out and fetched a bottle of Glenfiddich that she said Howard Hughes had given her on *Hell's Angels* and Glennis raised a toast and Pancho insisted they call the baby Florence if it came out a girl and Grace laughed and said we'll see and they talked and drank til dawn.

Ridley lit a cigarette, sighed, sat down at his desk. Harrison was listening to the radio. It was early April. The sky was cyanide blue.

You still listening? Ridley said across the room.

Uh-huh.

Why in God's name are they holdin a press conference *before* anyone's gone up?

Beats the hell outta me.

Who's that?

That, my friend, is Walter Bonney, Harrison said. The NASA's director of public relations. Listen in, it's quite a show.

What's goin on?

Well, they got all seven of the Project Mercury pilot-volunteers sat up there onstage and Bonney's got the press askin them questions.

Bet they love that, Ridley said.

Nobody's asked them about their flyin experience yet though; not a damn word on it.

What they talkin about then?

You want a coffee? Harrison said.

Yeah.

Harrison walked over to the pot. The question just asked, he said, pouring them each a cup, was if their wives or children had anything to say about them volunteerin for the program.

You're not serious, Ridley said, sitting forward in his chair.

Sure am, Harrison said.

What the hell they say to that?

Not much.

Figures.

Until they got to Glenn.

The coast-to-coast guy?

Yeah, Harrison said. Glenn comes out with a whole goddamn *speech* about how he couldn't go on with something like this without the backing he gets at home. Starts talkin about his wife's attitude to his flyin career—the whole thing; I swear, I nearly choked up he was so goddamn sincere.

Since when does the *attitude of his wife*—

Beats me. Here—

He handed Ridley a mug.

Thanks.

Then he was off again talkin about church and Sunday school and God and family—

Who shoved an apple pie up his ass? Ridley said.

Not the Marines I'm guessin, Harrison said. You see him on that show?

Hmm, yeah; think so.

Name That Tune.

With the kid singer?

Yeah.

Charming sonofabitch.

Yeah.

Harrison sat down with his coffee and turned up the volume on the radio.

Why are they having a press conference again? Ridley said.

To introduce the world to America's first astro-nauts, Harrison said. He sipped his coffee. You hear what I been hearin?

Sending a monkey up first? Jesus, I laughed my ass hard off when Walker told me.

Funniest damn thing I ever heard, Harrison said. A monkey's gonna make the first flight!

Oh, boy, Ridley said, beginning to laugh.

A guy called from some newspaper yesterday, Harrison said. Told me he wanted to ask the X-15 pilots how we felt about not being part of Project Mercury.

What'd you say?

I told him Project Mercury didn't really require a pilot, there wasn't any real flyin involved. Plus I didn't want to sweep monkey shit off the seat before I sat down.

Oh, boy, Ridley said.

Well, he asked.

He sure did.

Harrison cocked his ear toward the radio.

Who's this Carpenter fella? Ridley said.

Navy guy, Harrison said. Never even been in a fighter squadron. He's only got two hundred hours; been flyin multi-engine propeller planes! Not that Bonney's mentioned it, of course.

And these are supposed to be America's finest pilots? Ridley said. Wasn't Cooper in *engineering*?

Heh, yeah. He was in Wally's room for the meeting that night. I think he sees it as a shortcut up the pyramid.

There ain't no shortcuts, Ridley said. You either got it or you don't.

Shepard's done good work though, Harrison said. Nothing like the X-series, and he's never been in combat, but he's a good guy. I like him. Grissom? Never heard of him. Was at Wright-Patterson, I think, doing all-weather testing. Wally wouldn't stop goin on about what this thing might do to a man's career—but there he is— Jolly Wally—not feeling quite so jolly in front of all them reporters. They got one good pilot, I guess.

Deke?

Yeah.

Surprised he volunteered.

Me too. Lot of people round here liked what he'd been doing.

Harrison shrugged and turned the volume down.

How's Gracie doing? Ridley said.

Struggling in this heat.

I'll bet. When's it comin again?

Early May.

You got the nursery all finished?

Just about. Air force should be payin me to fix up their property. There isn't a whole heap of room, but how much space does a baby need?

You're askin the wrong fella. Hal pleased?

All I could do to stop him movin in.

Ah, he just wants to look after his own little girl.

We don't have the space. He's just been by himself for too long.

When'd June die? Ridley said.

Twenty years last fall, Harrison said.

Hell of a thing, Ridley said.

Yeah, Harrison said. My old man died when I was five.

I didn't know that, Ridley said.

He worked the railroads; West Virginia mainly—Deepwater, Indian Creek, Greenbrier and Eastern, Kanawha Central. Died of a heart attack, right there on the tracks. He was a big man; strong, shoulders that sloped off him like hills. Only really got one memory of him. I must have been three, maybe four. We were living on this small homestead in Wheeling, up in the Northern Panhandle. His old man had been a coal miner. Tough work. Had to lease his tools from the company, pay them rent, and his wages were only good in company-owned stores; some strange currency they paid. Anyway, I remember this one time a wolf or a hound or something was lyin badly hurt out back of our place. Must have escaped a trap in the woods somehow. His back leg was all mangled up and he'd lost a lot of blood. He was all done howling, poor thing. We spotted him just before sundown. Dad told me to stay inside. Ma must have known what was going on because she told me to go to my room and not come out til she said so. But I crept out of my window and onto the roof. Laid flat on my belly. The animal was right there below. It was a hot night. I saw Dad appear from one of our outbuildings carrying a shovel. He pushed it into the earth alongside the wolf and bent down. He stroked the animal's head for a minute, whispering in his ear. Couldn't hear what. Then he stood up and brought the blade of the shovel down hard on his neck.

Jesus, Ridley said.

I guess he must have buried it after, Harrison said. I don't remember. He marked it with a stone; a big blue thing. It stayed there for a couple of years; vanished sometime after that.

You ever get back out that way? Ridley said.

Harrison shook his head. Ma was a strong woman. Raised me herself; just the two of us. Never too proud to ask for help if she needed it. That was a good quality. We had a friend, Annie, who lived close by. She was a remarkable woman. She helped Ma out a lot. You want another coffee?

Nah, I'd better be on my way.

Sure thing, Jack. I'll see you.

Tell Gracie I said hi, Ridley said.

I will.

Ridley left. Harrison sat back in his chair and turned the volume up again. On the radio, a reporter said, *could I ask for a show of hands of how many are confident that they will come back from outer space?*

Jesus, Harrison thought, lighting another cigarette. What the hell kind of question was that? What a bunch of dopes. Harrison switched the radio off and went down to the hangar.

———

It was late, gone midnight, bone-cold. Grace pulled herself from the car, walked slow to the house, holding her back, fighting the wind.

Real howler, Harrison said as he got out. Wait up, would you?

If she said anything, he didn't hear. He went to help.

Get off, I'm fine, she said, pushing him away.

You don't look fine, he said.

Unlock the goddamn door, she said. I'm freezing.

Harrison did as she said and shut the door and the desert behind them. He switched on the light.

I'll make you a hot milk, he said.

I don't want a hot milk, she said. I just want to sit down; my back is killing me.

You got to stop doin so much, he said.

Sure, she said, that's the problem; nothing to do with the other human I'm lumping around inside me.

I'm just sayin you need to take it easy, he said.

I don't *want* to take it easy, she said. I want this damn baby out of me.

Well, you're not due for another week or so, so—

Thank you for letting me know, she said, because I had no idea.

Her hair was up; she pulled it down.

Well, you look good, he said.

I look like a goddamn mess, she said.

Hey, I'm just tryin to help, okay?

Well quit it, would you?

Jeez, he said.

And stop complaining, she said. You're not the one carrying a baby around inside you.

Her palms cupped around her swollen belly.

Where's my milk? she said.

You didn't want any! he said.

Yes I did, she said. I always have milk before bed.

You're turning in? he said.

Yes! That's why I want my milk!

I—he said, and stopped. I'll get you some.

She sighed, sat down, sank back into the sofa.

Nice evening, huh? she called out to the kitchen.

Yeah, he said. Lotta fun.

She sure can cook, Grace said.

Sure can, Harrison said. Joe's a lucky son of a gun.

How long they been in that place? she said.

Don't know, he said.

I like it.

What?

Joe and Gracie's house—I like it, she said. The kitchen.

Uh-huh, he said.

She rolled her eyes but he didn't see.

I'm tired, she said.

I know, he said, walking into the living room with her milk.

Here you go, he said.

Thank you, she said. Hey, you okay?

She stroked his face. He nodded.

You sure?

Yeah.

She kissed him.

I love you, she said.

Love you too, hon, he said.

C'mon, she said. Let's turn in; I'll drink this in bed.

Jim. *Jim.*

Uh, he said. What?

It was dark; he was asleep.

Jim wake up.

What? What is it? What's the matter?

My water's just broke, she said.

Huh? he said.

Wake up, she said.

He switched on the lamp.

Jesus, he said. What time is it?

Ten to four, she said.

He rubbed his face.

We got to move fast, she said.

How come? he said. You said labor was long. If we go in now, they'll only send us home.

Yeah, she said.

That's what you told me, right?

Yeah, she said, but I've been in labor pretty much since we came to bed.

What? Why didn't you tell me? he said. He was sitting up now.

Didn't see the point, she said. They told me I had to relax; said that was the best thing I could do. Figured you being asleep would probably help.

Thanks.

Looks like I was right.

Jesus, Grace, he said. Are you okay?

Uh, they're getting pretty painful now, she said. Faster.

What the hell is this? he said, jerking his hand up from the bed.

I told you, she said, my water's broke.

He pulled a face that Grace said was unhelpful and he wiped his hand on the sheet and said, what do we do?

Get dressed, she said. I got a bag all packed. We need to get to Lancaster.

He helped her into the car. It didn't start.

Too damn cold, Harrison said.

What?

The engine.

He turned the ignition again. The engine chugged then wailed.

Damn it, he said.

What the hell, Jim? she said.

It's four in the morning, he said. Usually warms up twenty degrees or so before anyone drives it.

Jesus, she said.

Don't worry, hon, he said, we got the motorcycle out back.

She looked at him.

The Triumph? she said. Are you fucking kidding me?

What?

It's a wreck!

I fixed it up pretty good, he said.

Her hands clung tight to the dashboard.

Jim, she said, it's pitch-black, freezing cold and I'm having a baby, and if you think I'm getting on the back of a *goddamn motor-cycle* you're out of your—

She yelled out and gripped the dash.

Hon? Hon? What's the matter? he said.

I'm having a baby what do you *think* is the matter.

I'm gettin the bike, he said, and got out.

Jim!

He ran down to the barn, threw the tarp off the Triumph, got it running.

All right, he said. He opened the throttle, warmed the engine and drove back to the car. Grace got out.

Hold tight to me, he said. Use the footrests; you'll be fine.

Jim, she said, I can't . . . I . . .

Yes you can, he said. I got you.

I'm scared, Jim.

Nothin be scared about, hon, he said. We'll be there in no time. Think of it like a horse. Nothin to it.

She held his back and slowly pulled herself on.

That's it, he said.

She gripped his waist, baby cocooned between them.

Meant to say, he shouted over his shoulder as they accelerated, light's bust. Wasn't expecting to ever take it out at night.

Her face was pushed hard into his back. She didn't reply.

Don't worry, he said. I know these roads pretty good.

Grace groaned and hung on.

They reached the Antelope Valley Hospital in Lancaster thirty-five minutes later. He helped her down from the motorcycle. She began to wander off.

Grace! he said. Where you goin?

She kept on walking. He caught up with her.

We got to go that way, he said.

She mumbled something.

What? he said.

Leave me alone, she said.

Jeez, he said. Let's get inside.

He led her through two heavy glass doors. The lobby was dark. There was no one around.

Stay here, he said. I need to figure out where we go.

He found a directory on the wall by the elevators. He went back for Grace but she'd gone.

Jesus, he said, looking around. He found her wandering down a dark hallway toward Cardiology.

Where you goin? he said. We need the fifth floor.

She was mumbling again, head low, gripping the wall.

C'mon, he said.

Look, he said. Service elevator. He pulled her gently toward the doors and they rode up to the fifth floor.

Rows of identical black chairs ran back to back across the room. He sat still, clock thunking on the wall. The waiting room was empty.

He waited.

At six-thirty, a man came in, nodded at Harrison, sat down. He was younger, unshaven, large hands thick with black hair and a small tattoo on each wrist. He looked over at Harrison, sighed, said, first? and Harrison said, yeah. The man hunched forward and stared at the floor and sat there for a long time. Then he rubbed his face, looked up at Harrison and said, you'll get the hang of it soon enough.

Harrison nodded.

Got three, he said. Handful.

Harrison didn't say anything.

Made sure I had this for the second.

He brought a small hip-flask from his shirt pocket. He unscrewed the top, took a slug, passed it to Harrison.

Thanks, Harrison said. He took a mouthful, handed it back. The man drank again, offered more, but Harrison waved it away. The man smiled.

The door opened and a nurse stepped in.

Mr. McKay? she said.

The man stood, tucking the flask into the back of his jeans.

Everything's fine, the nurse said. You've got a handsome son.

Well how bout that? the man said, smiling.

Congratulations, Harrison said.

Can I see em?

The nurse nodded.

Good luck buddy, the man said. He left with the nurse and Harrison was alone again.

Captain. I'd ask that you mind your language. Please step back outside of this office and try, if at all possible, to put a lid on it. You dislike waiting. You dislike not knowing. You dislike not being in charge. I've seen this before, many times. Although this, I have to say, is the first time I've ever heard someone offer to help. Your wife is in the advanced stage of a very routine labor. The last thing anybody—including your wife—either wants or needs is a *husband* thinking he should run the show. I'm sorry but you're going to have to get used to this, Captain. Now go back to the waiting room, sit down, and *wait*.

* * *

An hour later, another nurse came in to fetch him. He followed her through a series of swinging double doors into a bright ward of shrouded beds. The nurse led him to a bed at the far end and pulled back the curtain. Grace looked up and smiled.

The nurse pulled the curtain closed as she left.

Hey, he said to Grace.

Hey. Shh. Come see.

She held a white woolen blanket in her arms, so small; a red face, a knitted blue hat. Harrison went over, kissed his wife and bent down, breaking into a lopsided grin. He touched the baby's cheek.

It's a girl, Grace said. She smiled.

How you feelin? he said. You okay?

Hair matted either side of her face, blotched red and white but gleaming; her lips fuller than usual.

I'm fine, she said.

You look awful, he said.

Gee, thanks, she said. You look worse, actually. You been drinking?

No, uh, no, not really, he said. Doesn't matter. I can't believe we have a little baby girl.

The baby lay silent and still, eyes shut, warm, with a belly full of milk.

Looks pretty straightforward, he said.

You should have been here half an hour ago, she said.

They wouldn't let me, he said.

I heard.

Grace looked at her daughter.

When can we get out of here? Harrison said.

I'll find out, Grace said.

Can I hold her? he said.

Sure you can, daddy-o, she said.

Grace carefully lifted the bundle toward his outstretched arms. He held her gently, his left hand bigger than her head. She coughed. It felt good to know there were doctors nearby. He held her close.

She smells good, he said.

That'll change, she said.

He walked around the room with her, feeling her knees press against his rib cage.

You know, Grace said, Florence isn't such a bad name.

Florence, he said. Florence Mayton . . .

Mayton? she said.

My mother, he said.

Really?

Yeah.

No, I mean, do we have to?

I'd like to, he said.

Florence Mayton Harrison . . . she said. Yeah, okay then.

Yeah? he said. That's what you want?

Sure. You?

He thought for a second then said, yeah.

Okay then, she said. Here, let me see her.

He brought her over.

Florence . . . Grace said, as Harrison held her up. Florence . . .

You're gonna be a daddy's girl, aren't you? he said, bringing her closer to his face. We're gonna go huntin, fishin—

Probably catch more than you do, Grace said.

Well someone's feelin perkier, he said.

He pulled over a chair with his foot and sat down, Florence resting across his chest.

I could still use a sleep, Grace said.

You must be beat, he said.

You betcha, she said, already sliding away. Harrison smiled and put his head back, feeling the warmth of his daughter through the blanket, and something in his heart kicked.

He took a few days from work. Ridley brought them home in his truck; the four of them crammed in the front, the old Triumph laid flat in the back.

My own bed, Grace said when she saw it.

Don't get too comfortable, Harrison said.

They took Florence to her nursery. It was still unfinished; half-painted, pale green, boxes stacked waist-high on one side, waiting to be stored.

She won't notice, Grace said. Or care.

I'll finish it, he said.

The first days passed fast. He learned how to sterilize a bottle, make up formula, wear Grace's pink gown to keep warm in the kitchen during early feeds. Florence cried hard when hungry and it cut into him; not the volume, or the sound, but the need. And it came with no warning, on no schedule, and took priority over all else. He didn't like it. What did you expect? Grace said.

They had visitors. Grace Walker brought a stew, Pancho arrived with whiskey.

We called her Florence, Grace said.

Pancho pretended not to hear and complained about a bill she'd got from the vet.

* * *

He took Florence to the base, held her tight against him, this little thing, showing her to everyone.

He sat with her in Ridley's office, pointing out airplanes in the hangar below.

Sure hope she can fly better than you, Walker said.

Damn sight smarter than you, Ridley said, not looking up from his report.

That night, Harrison put her to sleep in her crib, tucking the blanket in tight, stroked her head. She looked up at him. He folded the top of the blanket down, retucking it on either side. He frowned.

What are you doing? Grace said, walking into the dark room.

What if she wriggles in the night? he said. Pulls the blanket over her head?

She won't.

But what if she does?

The blanket is woven loose, Grace said. Look.

He looked.

Is it too tight? he said.

It's fine, she said.

Harrison sighed.

I can't get the damn temperature in here right, he said.

She'll tell you if she's cold, Grace said. Quit worrying.

Later, on the sofa, Grace said, I never much thought of being a mother til I met you.

That so, he said, next to her, feet up on the coffee table.

Guess being an only child, it never really crossed my mind.

Too busy with the horses?

She gave a little laugh. Yeah, she said. Guess.

She sought out his hand and held it.

Then, after the war, she said, I don't know; it was just there, in me, somehow.

Uh-huh.

You notice that funny noise she makes? she said, looking at him.

Yeah, he said. Like a quack, or something? Kinda cute; and a bit strange?

I think it's cute, Grace said. She's such a tiny thing, isn't she, Jim?

Yeah, he said. He looked at her and smiled.

Our girl, she said. Say, you'd better turn in; you're due on base at five.

Got Ridley to reschedule it, Harrison said.

Really? Grace said. He spoke to the old man?

Figure they can cut me some slack, Harrison said. Program's ahead anyway.

She kissed his cheek.

What's that for? he said.

Thank you, she said.

I need a drink, he said.

I'll get you a beer, she said, standing, stretching, walking to the kitchen.

We can hear her down here, right? Harrison called out.

They'll hear her in Rosamond, Grace said from the kitchen.

He grunted, reached for the newspaper, put it back down again.

I'm gonna get some air, he said.

What? she said.

Outside, the control tower glowed red spilling a dim light over the desert salt pan. He lit a cigarette, smoked it, went back inside. Grace had gone to bed. He sat in the kitchen and drank his beer.

———

MOJAVE DESERT
MUROC, CALIFORNIA
FEBRUARY 1961

The sun lulled brittlebush to early flower, full corollas turning the desert floor yellow. Harrison slid up his sunglasses, grinned, pushed open the door.

Daddy! Florence said.

Hey there, Duck, he said, stooping to pick her up. You had a good day?

Daddy's home!

Grace leaned against the kitchen doorframe, wiping her hands on a towel.

Why yes he is, she said.

Harrison kissed his daughter on the cheek, then repeatedly under her chin. Florence threw her head back and giggled.

Least someone's pleased to see me, he said.

Just surprised, is all, Grace said, walking toward him. Wasn't expecting you til after five.

She kissed him.

Got off early, he said, putting Florence down.

Lucky you, Grace said, then sighed. Sorry, she's been a handful. You okay?

Yeah, he said. Same old.

Daddy come with me, Florence said, cause you have to come with me.

Grace frowned and Harrison followed Florence to the kitchen.

Cookies! he said. Why, Duck, they're my favorite!

Florence ran to her mother.

Daddy's favorite! she said.

Isn't he a lucky man, Grace said.

Florence turned to her father, who was eating a cookie, scowled, and said, you are lucky.

Harrison narrowed his eyes and finished the cookie; does somebody want a horse-bite? he said.

Florence squealed and ran to the sofa. Harrison ran after her, hands held open like claws. She buried her head in the cushions. Harrison grabbed the back of her thighs.

Horse-bite! he said.

Florence screamed and wriggled away. He growled and crawled after her on his hands and knees.

Mommy! Florence said.

Don't hide behind me, Grace said. When your daddy's in one of these moods, there's not much anyone can do.

Florence ran back into the kitchen.

What's got your goat? Harrison said to Grace, sitting up.

Nothing, she said, sorry; I'm just tired. Listen, instead of horsing around, I could use some help with dinner?

Sure, he said, standing up. Duck, he said, you're safe now!

No, Daddy, she said. Cause you don't do that.

C'mon, he said. Go play til supper.

Florence wandered off. Harrison turned back to Grace, who was staring into the steam rising from a pan of boiling water.

Hon? he said. You okay?

What? she said. Yeah, I'm fine.

She turned back to the vegetables on the countertop.

What can I do? he said.

You could set the table, she said.

Sure.

He began to set the table.

How about me takin Duck on her first fishin trip soon.

Jim, you can't take her into the mountains; she's way too young.

Kern River, he said. Nothin crazy. Cast a few lines, stick our feet in the water, have a little fun—that kinda thing. Might even catch us a trout or two.

She dropped the chopped vegetables into the pan of water and turned to look at him.

And how you gonna get there? she said.

Take out one of Pancho's horses, he said. The gentlest one she got. Saddle her up, strap Duck to me; off we go.

And what happens when Florence loses interest and you can't keep an eye on her because you're fishing?

Well, I could take a good length of rope; tie one end around a tree, the other around her waist; pack a few toys for her.

Jim—

That's not such a bad idea, he said. Relax. Look, we'll be gone half a day, tops, and most of that'll be ridin.

Grace looked out the window.

Well, okay, she said.

Hey, Duck, he yelled. Where'd she go?

Florence? Grace said, stepping into the living room.

Maybe I left the door open? Harrison said.

Jim, Grace said, the fence—

Her heart lurched.

You haven't fixed it yet!

Shit, Harrison said, and ran outside. Grace followed. He looked around the yard.

She's not here, he said.

Jesus, Jim—if she gets lost in the desert—

Call Ridley, get him in the air! he said, and jumped over the fence. Florence!

Grace ran back inside and dialed the base.

C'mon, she said, c'mon.

As the call connected, Harrison burst into the living room with their daughter under his arm.

Look what I found running around the Joshua trees, he said.

Florence, she said, thank God. Jack? Sorry, Jack, we had a missing girl for a while there, but it's all okay now. Yeah, we're fine—she looked up at Harrison—I will. Thanks, Jack; bye.

She replaced the receiver, took Florence from her husband's hands, and raised hell.

We could have *lost* you, Florence.

Sorry, Mommy, Florence said.

Grace sighed, and put her down.

That's okay, sweetheart, she said, just . . . don't do it again.

Florence stepped back to her father and wrapped her arms around his legs. He put his hand on her head. There was a terrific rumble from outside. Harrison cocked his head.

Quick, he said to Florence.

They ran into the yard.

Look! he said.

The airplane was barely fifty feet off the deck, climbing toward them from the runway. It grew larger and louder; he had to shout to make himself heard over the roar of the rocket plane.

It's an XF-92, he said.

Florence covered her ears.

Delta-wing prototype!

She said something, but he didn't hear.

Controls are hydraulically operated, he said. Very sensitive. Sneeze on the stick and you'll corkscrew in.

They watched the plane pass overhead. The thunder fell to a low grumble.

That was Pete Everest, he said.

Florence, hands still covering her ears, stared at him reproachfully and said nothing. Over her shoulder, in the doorway, Grace smiled.

LONG BEACH,
CALIFORNIA
APRIL 1961

Most days, the three of them stayed by the pool. They ate salty fries and drank cold Coca-Cola through colorful straws. In the early evening, they'd walk along the beach, the heat bearable by the water, the sun a fat orange closing in on the sea. Their room was a double with a sofa made up for Florence, who would kick off her blankets in the night and wake early, cold from the air-conditioning.

It was late morning, ten before twelve, hot outside. Sunlight slid down the balcony door and lolled in a silver pool beneath the glass, starving the room of color.

Honey? Harrison said. Hon? Where's my slacks?

Why are you yelling? Grace said. I'm in the bathroom, not Texas.

The gray ones? With the pockets? What time we meeting her?

Twelve-thirty, Grace said.

Goddamnit!

Jim!

Dadammit, Florence said.

See what I mean, Jim?

Jeez Louise, he said. Sorry already.

Who is Louise? Florence said.

We need to go, Harrison said.

The toilet flushed, Grace washed her hands and stepped out of the bathroom.

The diner is just around the corner, she said. Florence, get off the bed. Your slacks are hanging up in the bathroom. Florence! How many times do I have to tell you not to bounce on the bed?

But I'm bouncing, Mommy.

Off!

She slid off the mattress on her tummy. Harrison went into the bathroom, picked up his slacks, and came out.

Listen, Duckie, he said. Could you do Daddy a special favor? I need my watch from the table—he bent down—can you see it? Think you could get it for me?

Florence nodded and ran around the bed to fetch it.

We're gonna be late, he said to Grace.

Then put on your slacks and find your shoes. And redo that tie. And stop worrying.

Here's your watch, Daddy!

Well, hey, thanks Duck! he said. He kissed the top of her head and slid the heavy piece over his wrist, fixing it underneath.

Daddy gave me a kiss! Florence said.

Yes he did, Grace said. Now, come on, Duck, we need to find your shoes too. Jim, pass me your tie.

Harrison dressed and Grace handed back his tie, neatly knotted. He pulled it over his head and combed his hair in front of the mirror.

Right, he said. Let's go.

Turn the light out, Grace said. I got the key.

I need to pee Mommy, Florence said.

Goddamnit, Harrison said.

Jim! How many times? Sweetie, do you really need to go? Can you hold it?

Florence shook her head.

Jim, go downstairs, Grace said. We'll meet you in the lobby.

The diner was busy, full of families on vacation like them. Red plastic tables curled around the kitchen in a half circle; tall windows looked over a bright blue pool, its surface gilded with broken sunlight.

Maybe we should have chosen someplace else? Grace said, looking around.

It's fine, Harrison said.

Yeah?

She'll love it.

Sure is noisy, Grace said.

She don't hear too good, Harrison said.

That's why I'm worried.

It'll be fine, he said.

Florence was holding her mother's hand. I'm tired, she said.

Do we just sit down? Grace said.

Guess so, Harrison said. Look, over there.

They walked over to an empty table, nested in a horseshoe-shaped booth, and slid in.

Who is coming? Florence said, sitting between them.

An old friend of Daddy's, Grace said.

Her name is Annie, Harrison said. She's very old.

Old? Florence said, scrunching up her nose.

She's eighty-one years old, he said.

She's very old, Florence said.

Yes she is, Grace said, but it's rude to say so.

Your mother's right, he said.

I'm very old, Florence said, resting her head on the table.

Jim, that's her, isn't it? Grace said.

Harrison looked up toward the door, smiled, and said, yes it is.

He slid out from behind the table to greet her.

Annie walked slowly, with a stick. She was short, hair sewn up in a tight bun, her dress a deep indigo. When she saw Harrison, she smiled, dark skin folding softly like a newspaper.

Jimmy, she said. They embraced. Several people at nearby tables stared. Harrison ignored them and brought her back on his arm.

Gracie, Florence; this is Aunt Annie, he said.

You're very old, Florence said.

Florence! Grace said. I am so sorry, Annie.

Annie laughed.

Don't be, she said. She's a precious one.

Annie smiled at Florence and said, and who might you be?

Florence hid her face in her mother's arm. Annie chuckled.

I'm only teasin you, Annie said. Your daddy told me all about you!

It's so great to finally meet you, Grace said.

It sure is good to meet you too, Annie said. And little Jimmy here! My goodness! Ain't he turned out handsome?

That's a matter of opinion, Grace said.

Haven't seen your daddy since he was nine years old, Annie said.

Why are you a funny color? Florence said.

Jesus, Harrison said.

That's *enough*, Florence, Grace said.

That's all right, Annie said, let her be; nothin more beautiful or true than what comes from the mouth of a child.

Annie dipped her head toward Florence and said, I do look different to you, don't I; but you look different to me!

She chuckled and continued.

God made us all different colors and shapes! Be pretty borin if we was all lookin the same now, wouldn't it?

Florence nodded.

Aunt Annie was a good friend of my mother—my mommy—Duck, Harrison said.

Your grandma was a very beautiful woman, Florence, Annie said. You have her nose.

Her nose?!

Yes. And I miss her a *lot*, Annie said.

Where is she? Florence said.

Harrison glanced up at his wife.

Why, she's in heaven, sweetie, Annie said.

Heaven? Florence said. With Billy Horner's dog?

Uh, yeah, sweetheart, Harrison said.

Who told you that, Duck? Grace said.

Aunt Pancho did, Mommy. Is Aunt Pancho going to heaven?

Grace and Jim exchanged another look.

Let's get Aunt Annie a drink, shall we? Grace said.

Aunt Annie wants a drink, Daddy, Florence said. Cause she's thirsty.

Why, thank you, Florence, Annie said. I *am* thirsty. Annie chuckled. Ain't she a precocious little thing!

Tell me about it, Grace said.

Well, Duck, Harrison said, guess I'd better call someone over.

He looked over his shoulder toward the kitchen. Women wearing white dresses with red frills milled about, carrying drinks, taking orders.

Be right there, hon, one of them said as she passed, carrying two plates of hot food.

Harrison turned back to the table.

Everyone hungry? he said.

Everyone was.

The food, when it came, was good.

You know, Florence, Annie said, leaning in towards her, I brought your daddy into this world!

You were a midwife? Grace said.

Never lost a baby.

What's a midwife? Florence said.

Grace shot her husband a look. I can't believe you never told me!

Harrison shrugged.

He was a tough one, Annie said.

Well he sure as hell didn't get any easier, Grace said.

Hey! Harrison said.

Annie laughed and Florence looked at her and laughed too.

You too, huh, Duck, Harrison said.

I stayed on after little Jimmy was born, Annie said, helped out with the house; just a couple of weeks, til his mama was back on her feet. I'd just lost Emery; my own place was feelin mighty empty. After that, Mayton an me; well, Florence, we became the best of friends.

Can we be friends? Florence said.

Friends? Annie said. Why, Florence, we're family!

Florence turned to her father and smiled.

What made you move west, Annie? Grace said.

My bones, Annie said.

Your *bones*?! Florence said.

My old bones ache, Florence, Annie said. Gets worse, colder it gets and the older I get. West Virginia is bitter in winter, so I came out here to keep warm. And all my life I've wanted to see the Pacific blue.

And? Grace said.

It's a beautiful thing, Annie said.

My bones are sore, Florence said.

No they're not, Grace said.

I have to pee, Florence said.

Grace sighed and said, come on then, trouble; we'll take a trip to the ladies' room.

They slipped out from behind the table and Florence skipped ahead of her mother. Annie folded her napkin, smoothed the crease.

What a fine little girl you have, Jimmy, she said. Two fine girls! You done well for yourself.

We'd love to have you stay sometime, he said. It's real peaceful out there. And hot. You'd like it.

I would like that, Jimmy, she said, but I don't travel too good no more. Comin out here, to California, movin all this way, damn near killed me.

Your cousin's family, they helped move you?

Bill and Marcie, yeah, she said, they sure did. You know they met at Annabel's funeral?

That Bill's first wife?

Yeah, she said. Marcie and Annabel were old school friends from Pennsylvania.

Guess these things happen, he said. Must have been tough.

Life is long, Annie said.

Sure don't feel that way at the moment, he said. One minute, I'm sittin in a hot waiting room in Lancaster near-on all night, next Florence is tellin me not to forget my lunch as I head out the door.

Annie smiled.

That's kids for you, she said. Life happens; sure as hell ain't gonna hang around for you to catch up. Makes it hard to keep your bearings.

Harrison looked at the table. Then he looked out the window. Then he looked at Annie.

Sometimes I wonder if I should quit the flight test business; do something less likely to bust my ass every day, he said.

I remember you building them little model airplanes, runnin round your backyard, as a little boy. Drove your mother half-mad to keep findin propellers or part of a wing all over the house. She told everyone she met you could fly before you could drive.

He turned an empty bottle of beer in his hands.

Sure miss her, he said.

Think about her almost every day, Annie said. But then, I don't have kids to worry about.

I haven't been back there for so long, he said.

Your mother ain't where they laid her, Jimmy.

He nodded, took a swig from the empty bottle.

Wish I'd written you more, he said.

Jim, you were a young man and young men need to be out in the world doin things; not tellin an old woman what they *want* to be doin. You wrote me plenty. I enjoyed every letter.

He nodded.

Daddy!

Florence ran over and sat on his lap.

Hey, Duck! he said.

Can I have an ice cream, Daddy?

Please, Grace said, behind her.

Please?

Don't see why not, he said.

We gonna have ice cream! Florence said to Annie. I like strawberry. Daddy, can I have strawberry?

Sure you can, Duck, he said, nodding to a passing waitress.

Four ice creams, please, he said. All strawberry.

Sure thing, the waitress said.

Annie folded her napkin again, smoothing the crease.

When I was a little girl, she said to Florence, we couldn't

afford ice cream; we didn't have it. I was sixteen before I ever tasted it. Oh, it was a hot day. My daddy was takin me to see his aunt on a great, long silver bus but none of the windows would open. Took nine hours, forty minutes. Nine hours forty minutes with the sun shinin hard on the windows. We stopped halfway, stretched our legs, while the driver bought tobacco. There was this little hut sellin cigarettes, newspapers, candy; that kinda thing—and ice cream. Well, I begged my daddy. And I got lucky. He'd sweated up a storm in that ol bus too. He bought us one each and we sat out on an old telegraph pole we found lyin by the road and we ate them fast as we could. Best thing I ever tasted, before or since. Now, whenever I have ice cream, I'm sittin on that pole in the heat with my dear daddy and that's a magical thing.

Harrison took care of the check and they parted, promising to stop by Annie's place before heading home at the end of the week. Back at the hotel, Florence slept, Grace read on the balcony and Harrison sat on the bed, reading the paper and smoking.

She's such an incredible woman, Grace said, stepping inside and pushing up her sunglasses.

Huh? Harrison said.

Annie. Amazing woman. Matches?

He tossed her the box.

Woman practically raised me when dad died, he said.

Wish I'd met her sooner, Grace said.

Harrison looked up.

I'm just glad she's moved out here, he said. She looked old.

She is old.

Older. You know. I guess you read a letter, you hear a voice.

She's not going anywhere yet, Grace said.

Yeah.

Grace sat on the edge of the bed alongside him.

You okay? she said.

Sure, he said.

You want a drink?

He frowned.

Come and sit outside with me, she said. It's a lovely day.

The room was gloomy. He looked across to the open balcony doors, the blue beyond the light.

Listen, he said. We're on vacation. What do you say we eat out tonight? Just us?

What about Duck?

We'll get a sitter.

In a hotel?

Sure, he said. You know why we're stayin here and not someplace else, right?

You know the owner.

Right, he said. Sammy. We go way back.

And?

And Sammy's got a fifteen-year-old girl savin for a record player.

You want the hotel manager's daughter to babysit for us?

Betty'll be up around seven, he said.

She smiled. You've already arranged it.

It's done.

Can we afford it?

The sitter? he said.

The meal—we already ate out once today, Jim.

She pulled the sunglasses from her head and placed her hands on her lap.

I've been keepin a little back, he said.

She smiled.

Well, aren't you full of surprises, she said, and kissed him. Thank you. I'll have to get Florence in bed and asleep before this girl comes though, otherwise she'll never go down.

Whatever you think's best, hon, he said.

She looked over to where Florence was sleeping.

I'd better get her up now, then, she said.

I got us a reservation at the Manderville, he said.

Well then, she said, turning back to him. It's a date.

They went out, dressed smart, had a good time and got back at eleven, a little drunk. Betty had spent the evening reading on the balcony.

Felt like I was on vacation myself, she said as he paid her. She tucked the folded bills into the front pocket of her jeans.

You kids fancy another night, she said, just tell my dad.

Harrison opened the door, thanked her again and wished her good night.

Sweet kid, Grace said. I'm beat.

Me too, he said. Feel like I've eaten half a cow.

Come to bed, she said, so he did.

The next morning, at breakfast, Florence asked if they could go to the beach.

Grace looked at Harrison.

Honey, Grace said, I think it's going to be too hot for the beach today.

I want to go to the beach, Florence said.

It's very hot already, Grace said, and it's only just eight.

But I want to go, Florence said.

I know you do, sweetheart; maybe we can go tomorrow.

I don't want to go tomorrow.

We'll do something else fun today, and go to the beach tomorrow, Grace said.

I want to go to the beach today, Florence said.

Florence, Grace said. We are not going to the beach today, okay? It's too hot.

How about a picnic instead? Harrison said.

A pic-nic? Florence said.

In a park, he said. We'll find one. Get some food, find a nice spot in the shade, maybe there'll be swings?

Jim, Grace said.

I want to go to the swings Mommy! Florence said.

Well, okay, Duckie, Grace said. We'll see if we can find a park with swings. But if there aren't any swings, we'll just have a picnic, okay?

Okay Mommy, she said.

It'll be perfect, Harrison said.

We going on a pic-nic Daddy!

Yes we are, Duck, he said. And we're gonna have to find ourselves a blanket. You can't have a picnic without a picnic blanket.

The park had trees and the trees had shade. There were swings, and a merry-go-round too. The park was neat, quiet, with a large fountain at the center. They found a spot on a slope beneath a gnarled sycamore. Grace unpacked the sandwiches; pickle and cheese, apples, a pie; a can of soda each. When they finished eating, Harrison took Florence to the swings and then to the fountain. He left her scooping the water with her hands, and returned to their spot where Grace was reading.

Is she okay? she said.

She's fine.

He sat down, took in his surroundings and watched his daughter run about, lost in her own world.

At three, the air cooled as a slight southeasterly roamed ashore as though drunk and looking for a good time.

Let's head back, Grace said, sit by the pool, cool off. Duck could sure use some quiet time. I don't think she'll nap today.

Harrison nodded in agreement and called out to Florence who came running up the slope and tripped and fell on her face. She screamed.

Duck! Harrison said, running toward her. He bent down, pushed the hair out of her face and examined the bump already wide and red on her forehead. She cried hard. He scooped her up and carried her back to her mother.

Mommy! she said when Harrison lowered her into Grace's arms.

She's fine, Harrison mouthed to her.

Ooh, Duckie; you had a little fall, she said. Should I kiss it better?

Florence nodded miserably.

Oh, you've got a little nosebleed too, Grace said. Here, hold this tissue on your nose, put your head back—that's it—hold it like that for a minute. It's okay. Shh. It's all right. There. Look, it's stopped already. That wasn't so bad, was it?

No, she said, quietly.

Now let's clear up your face and wipe your nose, Grace said. She exhaled and looked up at Harrison, who laughed a little. They packed up the picnic, said good-bye to the park and headed back to the hotel.

Grace drew a bath for Florence at bedtime. Her skin smelled of chlorine and her hair was full of sun lotion. Harrison sat on the balcony, smoking, with a cold beer.

Jim? Grace said from the bathroom. Jim, can you come here a minute?

He frowned, put down the bottle and went inside.

What is it? he said, stepping into the bathroom, closing the door behind him.

Take a look at Florence's eyes, would you? she said.

Florence was standing up in the bath, covered in bubbles, head tilted back.

What's the matter? he said, moving closer to look. You okay, Duck?

I feel sick, she said.

He looked at her eyes.

You see? Grace said.

Yeah, he said. Don't look right, do they?

Concussion?

I don't know.

Sweetheart, he said, do you feel sick?

She nodded.

He looked at Grace.

What do you think? she said.

Let's get her to bed, he said. See how she is in the morning.

Okay, Grace said. It's all right, honey, she said to Florence, you can sit down now.

Florence sat down and stared at the taps. Harrison watched her.

Maybe we'll try and see a local doctor tomorrow, he said. Reception will know someplace we can go.

I think that would make me feel better, Grace said.

Right, he said. Okay. Time for bed, Duckie. You'll feel better in the morning. Sleep well now. He kissed her on the head and went back out to the balcony and sat down and drank his beer and thought about his daughter and stayed there for a long time.

* * *

The next morning Florence climbed into their bed at five and vomited. They got the telephone number of a local doctor from the hotel's receptionist.

Eleven-thirty, thank you, Grace said, and hung up the telephone.

Okay, she said, sitting on the edge of the bed. We've got you an appointment at the doctor's. He's going to take a look at you. Make you feel better.

Florence looked downcast. She hadn't been sick again but felt dizzy. Her face was hot. Grace tried cooling her down with a cold wash cloth.

Just after eleven, the family made their way downstairs, out of the hotel, to the doctor's. It was a ten-minute walk. Harrison carried her.

I don't like doctors, Florence said into his shoulder as they arrived.

You and me both, Duck, he said.

The doctor examined her.

Well, she's not concussed, he said, sitting down at his desk. I can't see anything wrong with her. You'll probably find Florence feels better in a day or two. She might have picked up a bug. You say you've been spending time at the pool?

Grace nodded.

If she's not better by the time you get home, he said, take her to see your regular physician.

The white fan on his desk oscillated, pushing hot air into their faces.

Enjoy the rest of your vacation, he said as they left.

Outside, Grace sat on the wall of the parking lot and said, now what?

Well, Harrison said, we can either have another day here, maybe stay around the hotel, or we can pack up now and get back. What do you think?

Grace looked at her daughter on the wall next to her, feet dangling down, still.

How you feeling, sweetie? Grace said.

I feel sick, Mommy, Florence said.

Grace looked up at Harrison and said, she's not right.

Harrison bent down and looked at her eyes again.

What are you doing, Daddy? she said.

Just looking at your eyes, Duck, he said.

It was hard to look *at* them, rather than into them, but after a minute he stood and said, we should probably get back.

At the hotel, Florence slept on their bed as they packed around her.

We should call Annie, Grace said, tell her we're leaving. Soon as we get back, we'll take her to see the pediatrician in Lancaster.

Yeah, he said. We should call ahead, fix an appointment.

I'll do it, she said.

Thanks, he said. I'll go settle up downstairs.

It was a three-hour drive home. Florence slept, her head on Grace's lap in the back. They got back late afternoon. Harrison carried his daughter upstairs and Grace started dinner.

The Antelope Valley Hospital in Lancaster was a dirty white shoebox. Doctor Rivers, Florence's pediatrician, was thin and tall with a single black eyebrow that reminded Florence of a giant hairy caterpillar.

Look up at me and don't move, he said.

She stared at the caterpillar as he peered into her eyes with a small flashlight.

Thirty minutes later, he referred them to an ophthalmologist on the third floor. They sat on hard seats in the waiting room for an hour. Florence snuggled into the crook of her mother's arm. Harrison got up and walked around and looked at the art on the walls.

The ophthalmologist, Peter Sturm, was Minnesota-born and recently hired; facts he presented as they entered. He sat and looked into Florence's eyes; her head on a chin rest, a metal frame surrounding her head.

Okay, so, seems we do have a problem here, he said, pushing his chair backward and whizzing over to his desk. He collected a file, kicked out a foot and shot back again.

What kind of problem? Harrison said.

To be honest with you, Sturm said, I'm not sure. Yet.

Why can no one give us a straight answer? Grace said.

Honey, Harrison said.

It's okay, Sturm said. I said yet. I'd like to see Florence again in a few days, if I may? Perhaps Monday?

You'll know then? Grace said.

Let's see how she does over the weekend, Sturm said.

What can you see? Harrison said. Is there a problem with her eyes?

Sturm scratched the black hair on his arms.

Yes, he said. Florence's eyes; they're slightly misaligned. Although the problem might be something else entirely and this merely a side effect. The misalignment is nothing to be too worried about, but I see from her notes that she had a small fall recently— is that correct?

Yes, Grace said, we were on vacation, at Long Beach. She tripped and fell in the park on Wednesday.

Sturm unbuttoned his sleeves and rolled them down.

Any dizziness? he said.

A little, Grace said. And she had a slight nosebleed. We told all this to Doctor Rivers.

I understand. Is this where she bumped her head?

He pointed to the bruise on Florence's forehead as he did up his cuffs.

Yes, Grace said.

Florence, head still sat on the black plastic chin rest, was silent.

Okay, Sturm said, pushing back again. Let's give it the weekend, and I'll see her again Monday.

He signed a form and passed it to Harrison.

If anything changes, bring her straight in.

Thank you, Grace said.

Thank you, Florence said.

You're welcome, Sturm said. See you Monday.

The weekend was busy. Harrison went to work, caught up with Ridley. Grace drove to Rosamond with Florence to fetch groceries. In the afternoon, they did chores. On Sunday, to distract Florence, they took her to Patty Keller's birthday party. Her father, Emmett, was an engineer at the base; Dorothy, her mother, a nurse. Colorful streamers hung from trees in the Kellers' backyard. The smell of cooked meat floated around the men and women holding bottles watching their children run and scream. The wind was flat and low.

Jeez, Harrison said. Emmett's got half a damn cattle on there.

He found a tin bucket beneath a dressed-up table and pulled a beer from the cold water.

You want one? he said to Grace, who shook her head. He sighed and pulled the cap from the neck with a nearby opener.

Jim, Emmett said, walking over, bottle in hand.

Emmett, he said. Helluva party.

At least I got to choose the food, Emmett said.

Smells good.

Ten minutes. You hungry?

Sure.

Grace here?

Over there.

Come on, he said. I want to say hi.

They stayed for a few hours, the children wilting in the stifling heat. Everybody knew everybody; the Mojave was big but small like that. The air cooled and the wind picked up. Harrison sat in a chaise lounge and looked at his watch. He was about to get up and find Grace when she came over and said, have you seen Duck?

She's inside, I think, he said. With that tall kid—Ray?—and Don.

As Grace walked back toward the house, Dorothy rushed out, carrying Florence.

Grace, she said.

What happened? Grace said, running to her. Is she okay?

Dorothy set Florence down.

I've been watching her for the last half hour or so, Dorothy said. I was clearing up in the kitchen. Florence tripped—none of the boys were near her—so I went over and picked her up. Her eyes looked odd somehow. I couldn't put my finger on why, so I didn't think anything more of it. But then she tripped again, a few minutes later, and I saw her eyes, and they were crossed. I sat her up, gave her some water; she said she felt fine. Her eyes straightened out after a minute or so but I think they're getting worse now.

Grace bent down.

Florence, honey, are you okay? she said.

I feel funny, Florence said.

Funny? Funny, how?

I feel funny.

Okay, sweetheart, she said, brushing Florence's hair away from her face. Grace straightened up and told Dorothy what had happened on vacation.

Look, Dorothy said, I'm not a pediatric nurse, but if I were you, I would get her to the hospital as soon as you can, so they can run some tests. Forget about the Antelope. Take her straight to the Daniel Freeman, southwest of downtown LA; in Inglewood. Ask for Burt Lapitus—he's their senior neurosurgeon.

Neurosurgeon—Dorothy?

Get her checked out properly.

Right now? Grace said.

First thing tomorrow. And call me after. Let me know how it goes.

Okay, thanks, I will; first thing tomorrow. Burt Lapitus.

Come inside, Dorothy said. I'll write it down.

A few minutes later, Harrison appeared in the kitchen. Grace looked at him.

What? he said.

I'll tell you in the car, Grace said.

They put Florence straight to bed when they got home.

Mommy, Florence said.

Sleep tight, Grace said, pulling the blanket up to her chin.

She kissed her and stood and turned out the light.

Downstairs, Harrison opened a bottle of beer from the fridge.

I'm going to sit down, he said, when she appeared at the kitchen door.

Grace nodded and he passed. She looked at the time. It was nearly six. She thought about Irving; his gleaming hair, that measured tone. She glanced at the telephone. There was a pack of Lucky Strikes on the table. She picked them up, found some matches and went out to the backyard.

———

In the morning Grace drove to Los Angeles with Florence sat in the back, eyes still awkwardly askew. They stopped at Little Sam's Roadside Eatery, just outside Littlerock, for breakfast. They ate waffles, Grace drank coffee and Florence was allowed a strawberry milk shake.

Four bucks for some milk and ice cream, Grace said as they left.

Why we driving, Mommy? Florence said, as they pulled away in the car.

Because we're going to LA.

Why we going to *elay*?

To see a doctor to make you better.

Why we seeing a doctor?

Doctors make us feel better.

Why?

Because that's what they're trained to do.

Why they trained?

Because they want to.

Why they want to?

Because it feels good to help people.

Why?

It just does, okay?

We going to *elay*, Florence said, sitting back.

Yeah, Grace said, we are.

The Daniel Freeman Memorial Hospital was on North Prairie Avenue, near the Inglewood Park Cemetery. Florence was struggling to speak clearly. At the front desk, Grace spoke to the receptionist.

Hi. I called this morning—early—we've got an appointment with Doctor Lapitus at nine-thirty?

Your name? the lady said.

Grace Harrison. The appointment is for my daughter, Florence.

First floor, left out the elevator, waiting room B.

Thank you, Grace said, heading in the direction the receptionist was pointing. Florence squeezed her hand tight. In the elevator, her eyes started to roll.

Jesus, Grace said.

They got off at the first floor and waited to be called.

Harrison was in the hangar talking to one of the ground crew when the call came through. Ridley, expecting it, yelled down to him. Harrison cut short his conversation and ran up to the office.

Yeah? he said, picking up the receiver from where Ridley had left it on his desk.

It's me, Grace said.

You okay?

Yeah.

How's Duck?

She got worse, Jim; on the way over.

Worse? How?

She started slurring when she spoke, and when we got here, her eyes, they started to roll—not much at first, but when they called us in, I had to carry her.

Christ, he said.

Oh, Jim; you should have seen her. I mean, she's fine in herself, it's not like she needs the emergency room or anything, it's just . . .

It's okay, hon, he said. What's happening? You see Lapitus?

Yeah, he's a nice guy. Gets kids, y'know? He wants to run a bunch of tests.

Sure, whatever they need to do.

There's so many . . .

It'll be okay, hon; these men, they know what they're doing. These tests; they need to find out what's going on.

One of them's called a *Pneumo-cepo-gram*? Something like that?

Okay.

It's so they can look at her brain, Jim.

Don't worry, listen; everything's going to be okay, he said. They need to cover everything. Probably doing it because she banged her head, is all.

Grace sighed.

I'm right here, he said.

It sounds pretty bad, the test, she said. They've got to do a spinal tap; inject air into her spine.

She's a tough kid, he said. She'll be fine. And you'll be right there with her, right?

Grace nodded, inaudible, but he knew.

Think we're gonna be here all day, she said.

Yeah, he said.

Ridley reappeared in the office.

Hon, I gotta go, Harrison said.

Sure, she said. I'll speak to you later. What time you home?

Seven, most likely.

Okay.

Okay. Call me here if you find out any more. And tell Duck I love her.

I will.

Okay then.

Okay. Bye.

Bye.

It was close to four and he had a day's work behind him. His body was tired. He stood at the sink in the men's room and ran a little water and it collected in a small pool and he dipped his hands into it and brought it to his face. He looked in the mirror. He had been clean-shaven that morning. There was one more flight scheduled. He and Walker had been pushing the X-15 higher and faster each time they went up. Walker had just set a new speed record of Mach three point three one. If everything went well, Harrison's flight profile was aiming for an altitude of a hundred and thirty-six thousand five hundred feet, or twenty-six miles up, which would be a new altitude record. He looked at his watch. He pissed, changed into his flight suit, left the locker room. He saw Ridley heading down the stairs toward him. Their eyes met and he knew then that something was very badly wrong.

Phone call, Ridley said.

Harrison was alone in the office. He looked at the telephone on Ridley's desk. The receiver lay on its side like an injured animal. He walked over and picked it up.

Jim, is that you? Grace said.

Yeah, it's me, he said. What's the matter?

Oh, God, Jim. She's got a tumor; a tumor in her brain stem.

Harrison sat down in Ridley's chair.

Jim?

What did the doctor—what did Lapitus—say?

I—

It's okay, he said. Hon? It's okay. Tell me what Lapitus said.

He—they—said, they came in with a nurse, the nurse said why don't I take Florence to the rec room to play for a few minutes so you can have a chat with the doctors and I said, okay, and they left, and Lapitus said, we've got the results back. And I knew, I knew right then . . .

It's okay, Harrison said, swapping the receiver to his other ear. What did he say?

He said the X-rays showed Florence has a *glioma of the pons*, and I said, what's that? And the other doctor—I can't remember his name—said the pons was the stem of the brain and a glioma was a malignant tumor.

Malignant? What is that? Harrison said.

It means it's cancerous, she said. They want to start treatment on her straightaway, X-ray treatment, to shrink the tumor.

Where is she now? he said.

They've got her a bed; she's sleeping, she said.

Is she okay? I mean, right now?

She's tired. I told her that the doctors have figured out why she feels sick, and they're going to start giving her some special medicine in the morning.

Grace began to cry.

I feel like I'm lying to her, Jim; I can't bear it.

You told her enough, hon. I'll come straight out.

No sense in you racing to get here tonight—Duck'll sleep til morning and I'm about to collapse. Go home, get some rest.

Okay, he said. I'll be there first thing.

Okay.

Hon?

Yeah?

It's gonna be fine; just wait and see. Might be in for a tough time, but she's a tough kid. She gets that from you.

I'll see you in the morning?

You bet.

Jim? I love you.

I love you too, hon.

He put down the receiver and stood up.

Ridley appeared at the door.

All set? Harrison said.

You all right? Ridley said.

She fueled?

Waiting on the main runway.

Okay.

Why don't we call it a day; head over to Pancho's?

You got the profile?

Sure do, Jim.

Then let's hit the sky and light this candle.

The sky bled red and the sullen yellow sun sunk fat and weak. Black Joshua trees cut the sharp horizon. Harrison hung around after the flight. His coffee steamed in the cool air. The base was quiet. The ground crew was finishing up. Ridley stepped out of the hangar and said, well buddy, looks like that's a new world altitude record. A hundred and thirty-six thousand five hundred feet. Nobody's flown higher. That's one magnificent beast.

A real Black Beauty, Harrison said.

Pancho's? Ridley said.

Gonna head home, Harrison said.

Sure.

Harrison drank his coffee. The men stood in silence.

You need a hand with anything, let me know, Ridley said. Grace, she, well, filled me in on your little, uh, situation.

Sure appreciate that, Jack, Harrison said. Just got off the phone with the old man; got a week off. Heading down there first thing. I got to pack some bags.

Well, how you gonna get them there?

I was gonna see if I could borrow Reggie Withers's truck.

Reggie Withers'll be under a bottle of piss-poor rye by now, Ridley said. Take my car. I got it here.

How you gonna get around?

I'll use your bike. We'll swap.

Harrison nodded. Okay.

Key's upstairs; hold on.

Harrison pulled a cigarette from the pack in his shirt pocket and struck a match and lit it and stood and watched the sky and the earth. The world was beautiful. Ridley returned with his keys. They swapped. Harrison said, could you stop by, look after Milo til I'm back and Ridley said, sure.

Thanks.

Give Florence a big hug from her Uncle Jackie.

Harrison nodded.

I'll see you, Jack, he said.

He packed three bags without thinking and collected a few of Florence's toys together and pushed them into a suitcase and went into the bathroom and vomited. Downstairs, he gave Milo some water, ate a slice of leftover pie from the refrigerator and locked up. He sat up in bed, smoking, reading a little of the paperback on his bedside table, then turned out the light and went to sleep.

———

Daddy!

Well hey there, Duck, he said, setting the bags down at the foot of her bed. How you feelin?

Better, she said.

Well, I'm glad to hear that, he said.

Florence sat up. Small machines sat on blue metal trolleys beside her. The room was bright. A small window overlooked the parking lot, five floors below.

Hey, you've got a great view here, Duck, he said, peering out the window. Think I can see the sea.

Mommy's gonna take me to the beach soon and we're gonna go cause we have to play in the sand, cause we're going to the beach.

That right? Harrison said. Hi, hon, he said to Grace. He leaned over to where she sat and kissed her.

Hey, Grace said. You get here okay?

No problems, he said. Jack lent me his car.

That's good of him, she said.

Yeah, he said. And Uncle Jackie gives you a big hug, Duck.

Yeee! Florence said.

I'm tired, Grace said.

I bet, he said.

Thanks for bringing out all our stuff.

Anything I've forgotten, just buy here.

Can I have another kiss, Daddy?

Sure you can, sweetheart, he said, and kissed her cheek.

Daddy! she said. You're all prickly!

No time to shave? Grace said.

Packed my razor, Harrison said.

Honey, Grace said, turning to Florence. Do you want to tell Daddy your news?

Florence looked at her for a second.

You do it, she said.

What is it? Harrison said.

Well, Duck has to stay in bed for a while, cause she's having some trouble standing and walking—isn't that right, sweetheart?

Florence nodded.

Well, okay then, Harrison said. That looks like a pretty comfy bed. Seems like a good place to be.

You get in with me, Daddy?

Oh, well, I don't think there's enough room for me, he said. And I'm very heavy.

Daddy's very heavy, Florence said to Grace, who smiled.

Grace, want some coffee? Harrison said.

I'm okay.

Can I have a coffee, Daddy?

No you can't, Grace said.

Aw, Florence said.

All right, Harrison said. Be back in a minute.

Earlier, at seven, Lapitus had stopped by to say good morning. Treatment was scheduled to start at eleven. A nurse called Clara came by at ten and said she'd found a motel with a double room right around the corner, if they wanted it. Harrison, who had just returned with his coffee, said they did and thanked her.

She's such a sweet girl, Clara said. She hasn't complained, at all.

Lapitus came in a little later. He introduced himself to Harrison, and explained the treatment plan to them.

We'll be using radiation therapy, Lapitus said, as you know surgery isn't an option. We'll keep her here for a week, then we'll see her as an outpatient for an additional six.

And that will get rid of the tumor? Grace said.

It's hard to say at this stage, Lapitus said. You will see a big improvement in her symptoms during the treatment, though.

She'll be able to walk? Grace said.

Most likely. I understand Clara found you a motel?

Yes, Grace said, just around the corner, thank you.

Our pleasure, Lapitus said. Now, Captain Harrison—

You can call me Jim.

Jim. Let's take a walk.

Harrison looked at his wife who nodded and he left the room with Lapitus.

The smell of the hospital gave him comfort. Lapitus led him down murmuring hallways with vanishing points that seemed to move, across wide atriums and through crowded lobbies. Harrison quizzed Lapitus about Florence's condition, the treatment, the tumor as they walked.

Brain tumors in children are rare, Lapitus said. There's only about fifteen hundred diagnosed a year, but what Florence has accounts for just one in ten of those. They are, as any pediatric oncologist will tell you after a few drinks, dreaded.

They moved through a busy elevator lobby.

Jim, Lapitus said, I haven't told Grace this yet; I wanted to wait until you were here. I'm afraid the prognosis for Florence is not good.

The elevator doors opened.

The radiation is likely to improve her symptoms dramatically during and after her treatment but, unfortunately, we tend to find that, six, seven, eight months down the line, the problems usually recur—and progress rapidly when they do.

Bodies spilled into the lobby.

Most children die within a year of diagnosis, Lapitus said. It's extremely unlikely she'll survive past Christmas.

The men walked through the crowd and emerged in an empty hallway. Harrison stopped him, turned to him.

What else you got? Besides the radiation. Don't hold out on me.

Lapitus considered him for a moment, looked at the floor, then said, it's a measure of last resort.

Harrison held his eye. Sounds like that's where we're gonna be, he said.

Cobalt, Lapitus said.

Tell me about it, Harrison said.

It's new, Lapitus said.

How new?

Few years. With X-ray treatment, the X-rays struggle to penetrate tumors that have developed deep inside the body. The cobalt machine uses a gamma-ray beam that's produced when radioactive cobalt sixty breaks down. It goes deeper. Much deeper. But there's a cost. The cobalt doesn't discriminate. It's very good at what it does—very, very good—it kills cancer cells, yes; but it also destroys healthy ones too. For a child so young, it could be worse than the cancer itself.

A janitor pushed past with a mop and bucket. Harrison watched him lope along the hallway; his slow gait, the steel bucket, the wooden mop.

Appreciate you tellin me, doc, Harrison said.

It's not something I'd recommend until we've absolutely reached the end of the line, and even then, it would warrant extremely careful consideration. To be honest, it probably isn't even worth mentioning to Grace yet.

Harrison nodded. The janitor disappeared, lost in the long lines of intersecting hallways. Lapitus started to walk again. Harrison followed, in silence. After a few minutes, he said, where we headed? Lapitus took a sharp left, pushed through a set of heavy double doors and said, where we started. They stopped in front of a single door and Harrison looked at it.

I find it better to talk about things on the move, Lapitus said. You're both welcome to see her as much as you like this week. Come and go as you please.

Thank you, Harrison said.

Lapitus put his hand on the door handle and looked at him. Harrison nodded. Lapitus opened the door.

Florence was asleep. They stood around her bed.

So, Lapitus said, we'll start her on two thousand three hundred roentgens—that's the maximum, the highest amount.

Is it painful? Grace said. I mean, will it—hurt her?

No, not at all, Lapitus said. She'll just have to keep still.

Okay, Grace said.

Each session will last between fifteen and thirty minutes, Lapitus said. They'll get shorter as we progress. And most of that time will be us making sure we aim correctly. We have to be precise, to avoid delivering radiation to the surrounding healthy brain tissue.

Grace looked at Harrison.

I'd wake her soon, so we can start, Lapitus said.

Do you have any water? Grace said.

I'll get Clara to bring you some, Lapitus said.

Thank you.

You're very welcome. I'll leave you alone for a bit now.

Lapitus smiled and left. They watched their child sleep.

———

In the motel that night they pushed their clothes into shallow drawers in silence. Grace went into the bathroom. Harrison sat on the edge of the bed, took out his cigarettes, lit one. He tossed the pack onto the bed and sat forward and rubbed his face. He stood and walked to the window. He walked back to the bed and sat down and stared at the wall for a long time. The motel was quiet. He wondered about the time. Then he heard a noise from the bathroom, halfway between a laugh and a shout. At the door, he said, hon? She didn't reply. He pushed at the door. Grace sat on the toilet seat, half undressed, fingers clutching her face, crying. He pulled her head to his body and held her.

In bed, Grace said, what are you not telling me? He lay on his back, heart held taut behind his ribs. Nothing, he said.

Did Lapitus say something to you? she said.

He could make out her face, pale in the gloom. He thought about the hundreds of variables that made it beautiful to him, as though it was a cipher, the sharp edge of a key. She switched on her bedside lamp.

Jim? she said.

Yeah, he said. Lapitus talked to me.

When?

Out in the hall. Took me for a walk.

Tell me what he said, she said.

She did real good today, he said.

Jim, please.

He sat up and looked at her.

Lapitus told me the radiation will make her better, but after a while, maybe a few months, she'll likely get worse again, and quickly.

You mean we'll have to do this over again? she said.

He shook his head.

What do you mean? Why not?

Not an option.

Why not?

Just isn't.

There's other things they can do, right? Other treatments?

There aren't many options.

But there are options, right? Jim?

There's one.

Just one?

He nodded.

Well what is it? she said.

Cobalt, he said.

What's that?

It's new, a real breakthrough, apparently.

Okay, that sounds good; that sounds promising.

Yeah.

What's the matter? Can't we use it?

He paused.

No, he said, we can use it.

What's the problem then? she said.

He sighed.

Seems cobalt's pretty effective at killin cancer cells; only trouble is, it kills the healthy ones too.

The healthy cells?

Yeah.

It could damage her? she said.

He nodded.

Badly?

He nodded again, then shut his eyes, and opened them again.

Lapitus isn't sure her body could take it, he said.

Oh God, Jim.

Don't, he said.

Don't what?

Just—

He got out of bed.

What are you doing? she said, sitting up.

He went into the bathroom and locked the door. At the sink, he ran the tap cold, scooped his hands beneath the surface and put his face into the water. He pushed his fingers into his hair and turned and sat on the toilet. His elbows dug holes in his knees and he shut his eyes. He could hear her sobbing in the bedroom. He felt sick. He went out and held her. After a while, she said, she handled it all so well.

Yes, he said, she did.

Our girl.

Our girl.

She's tough, Jim; she's got so much spirit, so much fight in her.

It doesn't matter, hon, he said, gently.

She's not like other kids; of *course* it matters.

It doesn't matter.

Stop saying that, would you? She's a fighter, she can *beat* this.

No, he said. She can't.

Grace stood up, her eyes silver in the low light.

Stop it! she said. Jesus Christ! Just shut up, would you? Just *shut up*!

Grace—

What the *fuck* is wrong with you? She will *beat this*.

No, honey, she won't, he said. He looked at the floor. She'll be dead by Christmas.

They slept fitfully. A glittering darkness pervaded their dreams. Harrison stood outside a house. Men were working on it. He recognized it as the house he'd lived in as a boy. He felt excitement. One of the men said, you want to look inside? He nodded. The door opened. Inside, in vivid detail, he saw things from the first years of his life. A clock. A vase. A chair. A painting. He didn't realize, until then, that he'd remembered them. And he felt a terrible ache inside him. And he cried with nostalgia, and he cried with joy, and he woke, and there were no tears on his face, and his eyes were dry. Grace murmured next to him. He breathed hard into the silence. He held on to his sleep, and disappeared again.

———

At the end of the week the nurses brought Florence a cake and hung red balloons above her bed and everyone sang Happy Birthday and Florence blew out two tall candles and they all clapped.

Happy birthday, sweetheart, Grace said.

Thanks for doing this, Harrison said to Clara.

My pleasure, Clara said. She's so sweet.

The other nurses smiled and Lapitus came in and said, what'd I miss?

My birthday! Florence said. I got two candles.

So you did, he said. And this is for you.

He handed her a wrapped package. Happy birthday, he said.

Mommy I got a present! she said.

Yes you did, Grace said. What do you say?

Thank you, Florence said.

To Doctor Lapitus.

Thank you, Florence said to Lapitus.

You're very welcome, Lapitus said.

Are you going to open it? Grace said.

Inside was a cotton head scarf, patterned with yellow, pink and red flowers.

Thank you, Grace said to Lapitus.

He smiled and said, now, you'll have to excuse me, I have rounds to do.

Thanks, doc, Harrison said.

Lapitus left. Grace helped her daughter with the head scarf. The X-rays had left Florence with a large bald spot beneath her crown.

Just what you need, Duck, Grace said.

Anyone want a drink? Harrison said.

You going down to the lounge? Grace said.

Yeah.

I could use a coffee.

Sure thing.

Ladies? he said to the nurses.

Thanks, but we'd better get on, Clara said.

The nurses wished Florence a happy birthday again and left.

Be back in a minute, Harrison said, and followed them out.

The lounge was on the first floor. He took the stairs. He could see the concrete floor of the basement, six stories below. He held on to the handrail and walked down. The lounge was full of people. They stood around a television set that had been wheeled in, black power cable curling through an open door nearby. Harrison frowned, walked over, stood at the back of the crowd next to an old man in a robe.

What's goin on? Harrison said. The man turned and looked at him. Then he looked at his feet and walked away. Harrison frowned, turned to his left, where a surgeon in blue scrubs stood holding a coffee.

More riots? Harrison said.

The surgeon shook his head and said, no—Shepard.

Harrison shifted his feet and managed to see the screen.

This is incredible, the surgeon said. This is insane. I actually feel a little sick. He laughed.

How come?

I guess the excitement. Maybe the danger? I don't know; we're about to put the first American in space, stick it to the Reds, show them they can't just take over the world. I wish I was down there, at Cape Canaveral, see it for myself. You see the rocket tests on TV?

Harrison lied, said he hadn't.

Oh, boy, the surgeon said. Last month, the one on the pad right now, the Redstone, was supposed to put a dummy into orbit. Forty seconds after launch, it went crazy. They had to blow it up by remote control. Next one, three days later; thirty-three seconds. And last summer? When it exploded midflight? Worst was when they flew all those VIPS down. When the countdown reached zero, nothing happened. The Redstone just gave out a little groan. Didn't move. Then the escape tower popped off the top and floated down under this little white parachute and plopped into the Banana River. Boy oh boy, what a joke. I bet they wet their pants in Moscow over that. Remember *Kaputnik*? And that was only a satellite! I mean, you must have seen them?

Harrison shook his head.

That is one brave sonofabitch, the surgeon said.

The television showed a live feed from the pad: the Redstone rocket, the tiny Mercury capsule perched on top; behind it, an infinite blue, the odd seagull.

He's sitting right on top of that thing, the surgeon said. Risking his life. For us. What the hell do you think goes through the mind of a man at a time like this?

It wasn't *blowing up*, Harrison thought. It was *fucking up*.

Who the hell knows, he said.

In the chaos of the last week, he'd forgotten about the planned launch of Freedom 7, the first manned flight of NASA's Mercury/Redstone program. He'd watched the ape, Ham, go up in January, flip his switches, splash down in the Pacific. A great crowd had gathered at Edwards to watch it on the small black-and-white television in Bob White's office. The men were in good spirits, watching little Ham do his job. They cheered when his chutes opened and clapped at his splashdown. Little Ham; a monkey; the historic first flight. Project Mercury was a circus stunt, no two ways about it.

On the television, Cronkite was broadcasting at the Cape from the back of a station wagon. The countdown had been stopped several times already.

Four hours, Cronkite said, *four hours since Shepard was inserted into the capsule. We have another hold at T minus six—that's six minutes before the completion of the launch sequence; we have a hold.*

Harrison watched with the surgeon as more people gathered around the television. They could hear, as Cronkite could, the clipped words of the engineers in the blockhouse; the radio static an electromagnetic conduit for their collective anxiety. No one wanted to be responsible for killing America's first astronaut. The countdown began again. The Redstone, tall and slender and filled with liquid oxygen, rumbled and squealed on the pad.

Jesus, the surgeon said.

T minus two minutes and forty seconds; that's another hold, Cronkite said.

More chatter on the loop. Now the Redstone's fuel pressure was running high.

They could be about to call an abort, Cronkite said. *The pressure valve in the booster might need to be reset manually. That would delay the mission for at least another two days.*

On the loop, the engineers chattered and fussed. Shepard lost patience. His voice cut in; the voice of the pilot.

All right, I'm cooler than you are. Why don't you fix your little problem and light this candle*!*

Harrison smiled, the surgeon leaned in and the audience began to vibrate as the engineers each declared their systems GO and the candle was lit and the rumbling Redstone howled like a beaten animal until it cleared the tower and fired Alan B. Shepard Jr.—naval aviator, test pilot, husband, father of three—off the face of the Earth. Harrison looked at the surgeon; there were tears in his eyes. In the lounge, the audience cheered and the surgeon clapped and Harrison took out a cigarette and lit it and shook out the match.

Fifteen minutes later, it was over. Freedom 7 dropped into the cold Atlantic like a stone. Shortly after, Shepard was heaved aboard the aircraft carrier *Lake Champlain*. The audience applauded. Harrison chuckled, cigarette dangling from his lips, and clapped. Shepard stood on the deck and waved. The surgeon turned his head and said, where do we get such men?

Back in the room, Harrison sat, drinking his coffee.

I can't believe I missed it! Grace said.

There wasn't much to see, Harrison said.

Maybe not for you—

Or him.

But for the rest of us.

Honestly, you didn't miss much.

Is he in space now? Florence said, from her bed.

No, honey, Harrison said. It was just a suborbital ballistic lob—a little ride, Duck—he's home now.

Is he in space?

No, sweetheart. He isn't.

I want to go to space.

You, my little Flo-Flo, Grace said, need to rest.

I don't want to rest, Florence said.

It's been a long week, Duck, Harrison said.

Can we go home? Florence said.

Yes, he said. In the morning.

Okay, she said.

Grace smiled and stroked her forehead until she fell asleep. That night, in the motel, Grace said, I'm scared, Jim, and Harrison said, everything will be okay.

———

They left Los Angeles early. It was Saturday.

Grace carried Florence up the stairs when they got home.

At around two, Pancho stopped by.

Aunt Pancho! Florence said when Harrison brought her down.

Hey, kiddo, good to see you, Pancho said. I heard you done real good at the hospital.

I was at the hospital, said Florence. There was a doctor and Daddy bought me an ice cream.

I'll bet he did, Pancho said. I'm gonna cook you up some sausages. You still like sausages, don't you?

I like sausages, she said.

Good, cause I invited a few people over.

Grace decided not to stress. An hour later, the garden was full and Pancho stood in a cloud of hot smoke and put raw meat on the grill and piled it onto a plate when it was cooked. Joe Walker, who couldn't make the party, buzzed the house in a F-104, flying so low and so fast that it shook the glass in the windows and caused a plate to fall off the sideboard and smash on the kitchen floor. Harrison carried his daughter around on one arm and held a bottle of beer in his spare hand. Florence still wasn't able to walk. She wore the head scarf that Lapitus had given her. Grace stood outside and looked at the salad she'd made and considered making more.

Hello, Grace, a voice behind her said. She turned around.

Reverend Irving, she said. You—I wasn't expecting you.

He smiled. I'm sorry, he said, I should have called ahead. Pancho told me what was going on when I visited the base last week. I've been praying for you all.

He was dressed in black and holding a bottle of beer.

No, no it's fine, Grace said. I'm sorry, I was just—

Surprised to find me in your garden?

She smiled and nodded.

Have you had any salad? she said.

I have. It was good, he said.

Good.

It looks like she's doing well, he said, looking over to where Florence was playing in the grass.

Who knows, she said.

And how are you? he said.

She looked at the sky curling overhead, a weak blue. It's good to be home.

I'm sure, he said.

We've got another six weeks to go, she said. As an outpatient.

In Los Angeles?

She nodded. I'll take her back during the week, stay down there, bring her home on weekends.

You have somewhere to stay?

A friend of Jim's moved to Long Beach not too long ago. Said we could stay. Jim's got to work.

How have things been?

She looked down at the salad bowl she was carrying.

I didn't mean to—

No, it's okay, she said, looking up. Better, thank you. Much better. Having Florence really turned things around. I don't know why, but there you go.

Well, nothing never happens when we pray, he said.

I like that, she said.

He smiled.

Me too, he said.

Thank you, Reverend, she said. Really.

It was my pleasure, he said.

I'm going to—she held up the bowl.

Of course, of course!

She smiled and walked back to the house. The wind picked up. Irving finished his beer. He spotted Mel Apt's wife, Faye, and her two children, and went over to speak to them.

Grace stood in the empty kitchen. The house was cool and quiet. She could hear Jim, outside, talking to someone about the X-15. She walked into the living room and sat down on the edge of the sofa, her arms around the salad bowl, and cried. She looked at the wall. Then she looked into the empty bowl. Then she stood and returned to the kitchen, fixed more salad and went back outside.

Harrison poured himself a black coffee and sat down. His body ached from the flight. He'd flown the X-15 just shy of Mach five. He wanted out of his pressure suit, but first he wanted a coffee. Ridley stepped in from the hangar.

Good flight, he said.

Sounded like someone was banging on the side of it with a goddamn hammer, Harrison said.

That's the slots expanding, Ridley said.

Felt like I was flyin an oilcan.

One of the pleasures of flying at hypersonic speeds. Metal expands. Not much else we can do about it.

I need to get this goddamn suit off.

Ridley sat down on the bench next to him. Can you believe Jack Kennedy? he said.

Hell, after that stunt he tried in April, think the man must have been dropped as a child, Harrison said.

You hear the budget?

No.

One point seven *billion*. And that's just the first year.

Jesus.

They're gonna need a lot more than that to get to the moon. And they'll get it.

He really serious about this nineteen-seventy deadline?

Yup.

That's nine years.

Yup.

And all they've done so far is lob Shepard through the sky like a stone. Suborbital. Hell, I just done pretty much exactly that. Hundred and sixty-seven thousand feet. There's no air, no aerodynamic controls—that's why we got the damn hydrogen peroxide thrusters!—I hit five g's on the way up; Shepard did six. He was weightless for five minutes; I was off the seat for two.

I know, Ridley said.

Landed it myself, too—I didn't need the whole goddamn navy to fish me out of the ocean. Christ. One point seven billion?

Seems catching up is all that matters.

The man's obsessed, Harrison said.

The world's judging him—judging this country—on how we do in space.

Talk about takin a longer stride.

You thinking about it?

Hell, no. Got everything I need right here.

Attaboy, Ridley said.

Two hundred a week and the Blue Suit, Harrison said. Everything a man could ask for.

Amen, Ridley said. He looked at the lockers. How's Florence?

Doing good, Harrison said.

Yeah?

No sickness at all.

That's great.

Yeah. And they're giving her the maximum dose of X-rays too, Harrison said. Twenty-three hundred roentgens.

I'll be damned, Ridley said. She's a tough little cookie. Gets that from her mother, mind you.

She started crawling again pretty soon after they started. And she learned to walk again last weekend.

That's good news, Jim.

Yeah.

Her eyes still crooked?

Nope. Straightened right out. The doctors are doing a great job down there. And she gets to come home on weekends.

You been cookin?

Nah. Pancho's.

I gotta get out of this suit, Harrison said, standing.

Ridley pulled out a pack of Pall Malls and said, I'll see you at the debrief.

———

The swimming pool in Lancaster was long and thin and blue and Grace moved almost silently through the water, hands cutting the surface with precision, legs beating hard behind her. They used to come here every week before Florence got sick. Now that her treatment had finished and they were back at home, Grace brought her almost every day. In August even the high elevations of the Mojave were almost unbearably hot. It had been a hundred by ten every morning that week. As she swam, her mind rested. Milo was at home, indoors, out of the heat; Florence was by the kids' pool with Jenny and her daughter, Megan. After the Yeagers had moved, when Chuck stepped away from flight test work to command a squadron of F-100s up at George, Grace had found herself without a confidante. Glennis had always been there, stuck out in the boonies too, but now she was fifty miles away, raising three kids on her own while Chuck worked long hours. Grace fantasized about their life: out of the test business, squadron commander, air force still making him shake hands with Important People, make speeches, stand on podiums. For a moment she thought about the risks of standing on a podium. They weren't great: you could fall off, fall over, clam up, get hit, get booed. The only thing that was potentially life-threatening was getting hit.

Florence didn't know Jenny and Megan that well; the next length would be her last. Jenny lived north of Lancaster; her husband, like most of the people around who weren't ranchers (and increasingly there were less of them), worked at the base, as an engineer. Megan was three. It was good to have company again. Milo wasn't much of a talker. When Grace reached the end of the pool, she pushed the water from her face and removed her cap. She pulled herself out and walked, dripping, over to the kids' pool. Jenny was perched on the little steps that led into the water with the children alongside her.

How was your swim? Jenny said.

Good, Grace said, sitting down with them. Everything okay?

No problems, Jenny said.

Florence wants to tell me something, Megan said, but she doesn't make sense.

Oh, thank you, Megan, Grace said. Florence, sweetheart, you okay?
Florence nodded.

Darn it, Jenny said. Look at the time. I need to get going. We've got the dentist this afternoon.

Lucky you, Grace said. What's that, Duck? Speak up, I can't hear you. Don't pull that face; come on, we need to get going too.

Florence shrieked and put her hands over her ears.

Florence! Be quiet! What do you think you're doing? Grace said, then, to Jenny, Jesus, what's gotten into her?

Been there, Jenny said.

Out, Grace said to Florence, or I'm going to pick you up and carry you out.

Florence stood up and started to walk out, then fell over.

Will you *stop* messing around, Grace said, yanking her up from beneath her arms. Florence stood and began to walk back to the changing rooms, but veered left on the way, heading toward the main pool.

Florence! Grace said, going after her.

No! Florence said, kicking her legs as Grace picked her up from behind and carried her to the changing room.

What's gotten into you today? Grace said as she rubbed her dry with a towel.

Florence said something, but Grace couldn't make it out.

What? Grace said.

Florence spoke again; a tumble of vowels and consonants. Grace froze.

Oh, God, she said.

———

Jim? Jim it's me.

Honey? What's the matter? You all right?

It's Duck—she, she—

What?

She can't talk.

What?

Her words, Jim; *she can't talk.*

I'll be home in an hour, he said. Have you called Lapitus? Call him.

———

It was a different room, but it looked the same.

Okay, Lapitus said.

Florence was asleep. She looked serene; her almond skin perfect in the retreating light. Grace stroked her forehead. She was so small.

I'll be back in an hour, Lapitus said. Take some time; have a talk.

Harrison took a seat next to his wife. They sat in silence. After a while, he said, what do you think?

She lay her head on the bed next to her daughter and started to weep.

Hey, he said, sliding his arm across her shoulders. Hey.

They stayed like that for a long time. Outside, it was dark. Grace was thirsty. He poured her a glass of water. There was only one glass so he waited until she'd finished then poured himself one.

Lapitus said it was the measure of last resort, Grace said.

I know, Harrison said.

She looked at her shoes, then the ceiling.

Is that where we are? she said.

He nodded. She held her head in her hands. He drew her near. Over her shoulder, their daughter slept on.

She's always been strong, Grace said.

He nodded. She pulled away and ran her fingers beneath her eyes.

I'll tell Lapitus, he said.

Can you stay? she said. The program—

I can stay, he said.

Her smile was weak. They held each other tight. Harrison slipped out of the room and returned with Lapitus.

We'll do everything we can, Lapitus said. We'll start tomorrow.

Within two days they knew it wasn't going to work. Florence was too young, her body too weak. We have to stop, Lapitus told them. She can't take it. They sat in Lapitus's office in silence. Harrison looked at the clock on his wall. It marked something, but he didn't know what. He reached for the pack in his shirt pocket. There was only one cigarette left. He tapped at the pack, fumbled the cigarette and dropped it on the floor. He reached down and picked it up and said excuse me and left the room and walked to the men's room and stood panting at the sink.

Later, they met with Lapitus and his staff and agreed that the best place for Florence was at home. There were forms that needed signatures. A schedule was drawn up. The nurse booked monthly check-ins September through December and said they could book in more dates in the New Year. Grace picked up on the nurse's assumption. She clamped her teeth together and tried not to cry.

They drove Florence back to the Mojave late afternoon when the temperature had dropped. She slept, sprawled on the blue leather seat in the back. When they got home, Harrison reached down and scooped her up and carried her to bed. She murmured but didn't wake. After they'd carried everything in from the car they stood in the kitchen and Grace made them hot milk on the stove that they drank standing up. It was nine-thirty. The house was still.

Every day Florence had a visitor. Pancho usually arrived at breakfast. She brought meat, milk, sometimes tinned fruit, beans. Reverend Irving would stop by and have tea with Grace in the kitchen while Florence played on the floor. By mid-October she couldn't walk but she could crawl and she laughed as if it were some great discovery. Jenny and Megan came over once to play, but it was awkward, and Grace didn't ask them back. Every Tuesday, though, she'd dress Florence in a pretty dress and drive over to Grace Walker's place near Lancaster. Florence would play in the garden, the novelty of new toys keeping her attention while the women sat and talked.

Joe can't see it, Grace Walker said of her husband on one of these occasions. She held her one-month-old daughter, Elizabeth, on her lap.

The forehead, the smile, Grace said, looking over at them.

I know.

Look at that!

A wide grin had transformed Elizabeth's face.

Her mother laughed.

She's so sweet, Grace said.

It's probably wind.

Treasure it, Grace said.

Can't help but, she said, stroking Elizabeth's cheek with her finger.

Grace looked at where Florence was playing in the grass. Elizabeth grunted and started to cry.

I'm going to put her down, her mother said, standing. Do you want to try Florence on some ice cream in a minute?

Sounds good.

Hang on.

She took Elizabeth upstairs to sleep.

Mommy, Florence said. Will you come play with me? I'm making a farm.

Sure, Duck, Grace said.

In the shade, the grass was cool. Grace felt a heavy sadness fall on her. It was so sudden and so powerful she gasped. It was as though her bare feet were touching the floor of existence. She felt black. She stood, took a breath. A voice from the house said, she went down like a dream; shall we try that ice cream now? Grace nodded and called out, sure, and tried not to cry.

It was two weeks before Christmas. The sky was a slab of concrete. The lakebed cracks ran deep and the desert animals were restless for the winter rains. Clouds bore down. The ground grew closer to the sky.

In the locker room, Harrison removed his pressure suit. He paused, rubbed his face, and sat down. Ridley entered, holding a bunch of paper.

I'm headin home, Harrison said.

Hell you are, Ridley said. It's only four, and I got the data. Don't you want to see it?

I gotta go.

Sixty-five miles, Ridley said. That's space. Kármán line's at sixty-two; air force *and* the FAI say so.

I know where the damn Kármán line is, Harrison said.

He pulled on his clothes and began to button his shirt.

Hell of a day, Ridley said.

Yeah, Harrison said. He stared at the watch in his hand, then at the floor. She's been coughin a lot, he said. Up most of the night.

Ridley looked at him.

Sure sorry to hear that, he said.

Gracie had to call a nurse out earlier, Harrison said.

You spoken to her?

The nurse?

Gracie.

Not yet.

Ridley didn't say anything.

Not since the nurse came out, anyway, Harrison said. It's happened before, them sending someone. They got some real good staff up there at the Antelope.

Don't doubt that. When you due next in LA?

Not til after the holidays now.

Make sure you tell that little girl what her daddy did today.

Harrison grunted. Think it'll rain?

Can't even remember what it looks like.

Yeah.

Give her a big hug from me.

I will.

See you tomorrow.

See you, Jackie.

Harrison clambered into the Model A just as it started. Heavy drops thumped on the roof.

Shit, he said.

The car had no wipers. It barely had gears. The car had passed down to him from Yeager, via Scott Crossfield, who passed it on to Joe Walker, who'd given it to him after his first run in the X-15. It was a wreck. Irony with wheels. Harrison liked a tradition, even a new one, as much as the next man. And the next man, as far as he was concerned, was Bob White. Bob White was reserved, quiet, a thinker; different, somehow, from the rest of them. An engineer as much as a pilot. Hell, Harrison could feel the guy clipping at his heels. Well, that wasn't anything new. He remembered what some of the old heads had said when he first started flying rocket planes. But things change. Not a damn thing you can do about it. A man could spend a decent chunk of his life trying, but it would do no good. Things never stood still. Life was a fucking mess. The rain hammered hard on the roof. He backed out and drove home half-blind.

Harrison arrived home. The nurse's car was still outside. He frowned. Loose stone crunched beneath his heavy boots as he walked toward the front door. He pushed it open, it closed behind him.

Hi, Grace said. She was standing by the staircase.

Nurse still here? he said, surprised.

Grace nodded.

How's Duck? Is she okay?

She's asleep.

What'd the nurse say?

It's Joan; she's coming down now.

Joan stepped into the living room.

Hello, Jim, she said.

Joan, he said. What's goin on?

His words hung in the air.

Florence has got pneumonia, she said.

He looked at his wife; Grace held him up with her eyes.

She's very weak, Joan said, but in good spirits. That's a good sign. She's such a gay little thing.

Harrison didn't say anything.

He looked around the room. Jesus, he said. What a mess.

He began collecting glasses, picking up newspapers and books and dropping things into drawers.

Jim, it's okay, please, Joan said. That really isn't necessary.

Grace looked over to Joan. Harrison disappeared into the kitchen with mugs between his fingers and plates balanced on his hands. He came back.

Jim, Grace said.

It's fine, he said.

Jim, she said.

Hang on, he said, and moved Milo's basket back into the corner by the window.

Jim.

He looked up at his wife. He stopped. He sat down. Grace went to him.

Lapitus said something like this might happen, she said.

Harrison shut his eyes. The room went divergent. The outside of the envelope, he thought. Son of a bitch.

I'll need to run through a few things with you, Joan said.

I want to see her, he said.

Let her sleep, Grace said. She's coughing pretty hard. She'll be awake soon enough.

Is she okay?

Apart from the cough, Joan said, she's breathing very fast, and wheezing, but there's no sickness, at least not yet, and no fever.

I'll make some coffee, Grace said.

They sat around the kitchen table and talked for an hour. The radio broadcast the news in the background. Outside the rain threw itself against the glass windows and thudded on the porch. When there was nothing left to say they just sat and let the radio talk for them.

Saigon, Harrison said after a while. Shit.

You think he knows what he's doing? Grace said.

Sure as hell hope so; he's got plenty enough advisers.

Four hundred combat troops sounds like an awful lot, Joan said.

And thirty-three choppers, Harrison said.

Thing I like about Kennedy, Joan said, he takes advice, but makes up his own mind.

I guess this is it then, Harrison said.

Haven't we already given the Laotian government helicopters? Grace said. What's the difference?

Difference is, Harrison said, those were operated by the Civil Air Transport of Taiwan. These will be flown by Americans.

Direct military support, Joan said.

You mean war, Grace said.

Yeah, Harrison said.

The rain stopped. Joan said she'd be back in the morning. Grace and Harrison were alone.

Florence woke, coughing, gasping, every twenty minutes or so. They took shifts, sleeping on the rug by her bed, sitting up to comfort her until she slept again.

It was late, dark, some time around three.

Daddy? Florence said.

Huh?

Daddy?

I'm here, Duck, he said, sitting up.

Her face was milky-white, pale like the moonlight that fell into the room. He stroked her face, brushing hair from her eyes. She looked confused.

Hey, Duck, he said. It's okay. I'm right here.

She settled slightly, coughed, smiled. He smiled back.

Hey, he said.

Why you call me Duck, Daddy? she said.

He looked at her. He stared at the rug. He bit down hard on his cheeks until they bled.

Well, Duck, he said, when you were born uh, when you were a few days old; this tiny thing; I used to, used to hold you, against my chest, walk about, and sometimes you'd uh, push your face into me and make this strange sound, like a quack, like a duck, so I started callin you a little duck and uh, yeah.

I'm tired, Daddy.

C'mon, he said, let's go back to sleep.

Harrison woke on the floor, the early sun lighting the room. He stood and crept over to the window. There were no clouds; the sky was a beautiful blue. He looked over to where Florence slept and something inside him broke.

Grace was in the kitchen when he came down, her hand on the handle of the fridge. He stood in the doorway and didn't move. She looked at him, and he looked at her, and she knew, and her fingers fell from the handle.

———

The low sun leaked pale light along gaunt tallowy clouds and bleached the bone-cold December ground white.

This is not a eulogy, Irving said. This is a lament. *Whither shall I go from thy spirit? Or whither shall I flee from thy presence? If I ascend up into heaven, thou art there. If I make my bed in the depths, behold, thou art there. If I take the wings of the morning, and dwell in the uttermost parts of the sea; even there shall thy hand lead me, and thy right hand shall hold me.*

All test planes had been grounded. Jim and Grace sat with Joe and Grace Walker. Pancho sat with Chuck and Glennis, together with Jack Ridley and almost every pilot and engineer the Harrisons knew, and plenty they didn't. Annie couldn't make it and it was too far for Hal, Grace's father, to travel.

If I say, surely the darkness shall overwhelm me, and the light about me shall be night; even the darkness hideth not from thee, but the night shineth as the day. For thou didst form my inmost being. Thou didst knit me together in my mother's womb. Let us pray.

They prayed. The silence was as hard as the earth.

Irving spoke some more. A slight breeze picked up and they heard horses bucking and snorting from the ranch close by. The men and women sat very still. The mares whinnied into the cold air. Then the wind changed direction and all that remained was Irving's strong voice and his steady hands and a small wooden coffin sitting on the hillside in the freezing December morning.

Harrison held his wife's hand hard and she gripped it until he thought it would turn blue. He turned around, behind him, and whispered, say, Ridley, got any Beemans? Ridley looked at him, nodded, and reached into his jacket pocket and pulled out a stick. With his free hand Harrison unwrapped the gum and put it in his mouth then heard Irving say his name and Grace released her grip and he stood and walked to the podium. He pulled a typed index card from his pocket and placed it carefully on the stand. He looked up and said,

Oh, I have slipped the surly bonds of Earth
And danced the skies on laughter-silvered wings;
Sunward I've climbed, and joined the tumbling mirth

Of sun-split clouds—and done a hundred things
You have not dreamed of—wheeled and soared and swung
High in the sunlit silence. Hov'ring there,
I've chased the shouting wind along, and flung
My eager craft through footless halls of air.
Up, up the long delirious, burning blue,
I've topped the windswept heights with easy grace
Where never lark, or even eagle flew—
And, while with silent lifting mind I've trod
The high untresspassed sanctity of space,
Put out my hand and touched the face of God.

He sat down. Grace squeezed his hand.

Suffer little children to come unto me, Irving said. *For of such is the kingdom of God.*

She shook and he held her tight.

Pancho stayed with them for the weekend. She cleaned and cooked and fed Milo and answered the telephone and drove home Sunday night and on Monday morning Harrison returned to work. He sat at his desk and studied diagrams for an adaptive control system he'd been developing with engineers from Minneapolis-Honeywell to automatically monitor and change the X-15's gains. Voltage alterations were required to adjust the flight control system, and the stability augmentation system used in previous flights was not an effective solution.

It was impossible to set the gains in the flight control system to a single value that would be optimum for all flight conditions. The speed range was too wide. The MH-96 prototype was designed for high altitude flights outside of the atmosphere. It would automatically combine both aerodynamic and reaction controls, compensating for the reduction in effectiveness of the aerodynamic controls as altitude increased. It consisted of electrical modules and mechanical linkages designed and tested in the simulator, which had analogue computers to replicate the nonlinear aircraft dynamics.

He drank hot black coffee. He stared at a schematic of the inner-loop control architecture.

He was scheduled to make the first X-15 flight with the MH-96 installed that Friday. It was also the first flight test of Reaction Motors' XLR-99 rocket engine, also known as the Big Engine, capable of fifty-seven thousand pounds of thrust.

He studied a memo from Bob Bridshaw at Honeywell.

Bridshaw warned that the MH-96 was a rate-command, attitude-hold system and might not observe usual speed stability characteristics if the thrust did not match the drag. More problems: the system was designed to maintain a limit cycle oscillation at the servoactuator loop's natural frequency. The laws of gain adjustment made Harrison wonder if the gain valve would lag behind the optimum setting. It would still be a better solution than the standard stability augmentation system with pilot-selectable gains, especially during reentry.

He grunted and took another sip of coffee. Ridley walked in.

Jim, he said, surprised. Wasn't, uh, expectin to see you today.

Runnin a program, ain't we?

Ridley thought for a second, considered the situation.

Sure are, he said.

You think the MH-96 might disengage in flight? Harrison said.

It's been designed to run for seventy-five, seventy-six thousand hours between failures, Ridley said.

Uh-huh.

Reset the system, you shouldn't have any problems.

Yeah.

Want a coffee? Ridley said.

Got one here.

How long you been here?

Couldn't sleep. Goddamn coyotes, Harrison said.

Mating season, Ridley said.

If it was up to me, Harrison said, I'd gather a posse and hunt down every last one of em.

Thankfully it ain't up to you.

Where we launching?

Over Silver Lake.

I reckon landing might be a problem, Harrison said.

With the lakebed?

With the stick. I usually have to pull it back, keep increasin the force to keep her on the angle as I slow. I reckon the stick will have to stay dead center.

You might be right, Ridley said.

Only one way to find out, Harrison said.

Ridley sat down opposite him.

We'll climb at seventy-five percent thrust, he said, level out at a hundred thousand feet. Then accelerate to Mach five; hundred second burn; shutdown. Then you can evaluate the system's responses by making a series of yaw, pitch and roll inputs.

Sure the lakes are dry enough now? Harrison said.

Hell, yeah, Ridley said. Driest goddamn winter I ever seen. Joe and Neil tested em on Saturday. Say, here's something I found out from Walker. You know why your flight was delayed til Friday?

Thought Jerry said there was a problem in the coupling?

Nope, Ridley said. The air force was conducting an ejection seat test using a tranquillized bear.

You made that up.

Did not. His name was Little John.

They named him?

On my mother's life.

Little John?

Ejected at forty-five thousand feet.

How'd he pull the cinch ring?

Guess a bear's got claws.

How fast was he goin?

One point four Mach.

He was supersonic?

Fastest damn bear in the world.

They should put him on the cover of *Life*.

Who's been sit-ting in my chair?

That's the funniest goddamn thing I ever heard.

Made one helluva mess.

He bought it? Harrison said.

Chute didn't open, Ridley said. Poor bastard hit the runway like a sack of shit. Bull's-eye, right in front of everyone. Damn thing exploded. Hell of a mess. They had to close the runway. Walker had to take a shower after.

This is the greatest story I ever heard, Jackie, Harrison said. How come you're just tellin it to me now?

Ridley looked at the desk. You were kinda busy over the weekend, Jim, he said.

Oh, Harrison said. Right. Still a goddamned funny story.

Harrison spent the next four days preparing for the flight. Touch-and-go landings in an F-104, forty hours in the simulator. He was hardly home. Friday morning, the Big Engine performed beautifully. After the flight, he typed up his pilot's report on the spare desk in Ridley's office. DATE, PILOT, FLIGHT NUMBER, FLIGHT TIME, LAUNCH LAKE, LANDING LAKE, LAUNCH TIME, LANDING TIME. He pulled on a cigarette as he filled in each. ABORTS: NONE.

He looked up from the typewriter and frowned. He filled out the names of the four chase pilots and the B-52 crew. Under PURPOSE he wrote MH-96 EVALUATION. CONFIG: VENT ON, SL INDICATOR ON INSTR PANEL. BURN TIME: 82.4 SEC. THRUST: 100%. He sighed, looked around for his coffee, then typed RESULTS: MAX L/O RETURN FROM ~ 45 SOUTH OF BASE DUE TO BOUNCE AND OVERSHOOT FOLLOWING REENTRY. He looked at what he'd typed. He hadn't realized how far up the nose had gone after he'd reentered the atmosphere. He'd ballooned out again and couldn't turn. Sailed on by the landing lake at Mach three. Dropped back into the atmosphere over Pasadena with barely any fuel left, turned, made it back, landed safely—just.

Shit, he said, and unspooled the paper.

Walker came in.

I hear Pasadena's nice this time of year, he said, grinning.

Harrison looked up, stubbing out his cigarette in a heavy glass ashtray.

I think you set some kinda cross-country record, Walker said.

All right, all right, Harrison said. I heard about Little John.

Oh, boy; that sure weren't pretty.

Don't doubt that.

I'm headin home. Give Gracie my love.

Thanks, Joe.

Harrison got home at nine. Grace was dozing on the sofa, Milo's head resting on her lap. She stirred as he came in.

What time is it? she said, half asleep.

Did I wake you?

I left you dinner—it's in the stove. I didn't know when you'd be back.

Me either.

How was it?

Harrison didn't answer. He stared out the window.

Jim?

Piece of cake, he said. I feel fine.

He walked into the kitchen. She sat up. Milo yawned. A few minutes later he came back in.

I'm going to bed, he said.

What about dinner? she said.

I'm not hungry.

He went upstairs.

C'mon boy, she said to Milo. Let's get you some water.

Milo followed her into the kitchen. She refilled his bowl. The house was silent. She switched off the kitchen light, locked both doors, said good night to Milo and went upstairs. She could hear her husband moving around the bedroom. She stepped into the bathroom. By the time she got out, he was asleep.

The next morning Grace said, you haven't forgotten we're going up to Harper Farm have you? He said no and left for work.

Harper Farm was her father's ranch. Hal's heart had kicked and squeezed the previous summer, leaving him a sloppy gait and unstable hands. His world contracted. Grace tried to persuade him to sell up and come live with them in the Mojave but he said he couldn't leave her mother. That Grace's mother had died decades ago made no difference. She'd been buried on the ranch and, every night for a week after she'd gone, he'd lain right on top of the soil. Kevin, one of the hands, once told Grace that he'd seen her father testing out the spot for when his time came. The most crucial decision seemed to have been whether left, or right, of the existing plot would work best, with the less conventional top-to-tail also trialed. Grace wanted to talk to her father about it but could never bring herself to raise the topic. Recent events had affected Hal deeply. He'd taken to long and potentially hazardous night walks when the moon was fat enough for him to see. He ate dinner at breakfast and breakfast in the evening. When he slept, he slept on the floor. It was as though his life had been inverted by a powerful force he had no control over. In what was perhaps an attempt to restore some order to his life, Hal had decided to bring the wider family together for a reunion over the holidays.

Grace and Jim arrived at the farm early Christmas eve morning.

Daddy, Grace said, hugging her father on the stoop of the main house.

I'm sorry I wasn't there, he said. His arms, still strong, mollified his willowy child.

Daddy, she whispered into his chest. They parted.

Jim, he said, shaking Harrison's hand. Come on in.

Good to see you, Hal, he said.

We'll bring the gifts up later, Grace said.

Aunt Carolyn hasn't stopped asking me questions about you, sweetheart, Hal said. I'm glad you're here.

Mixie here too? she said.

Sure is, Hal said.

Stevie?

Stuck in Utah. Work.

What's he do?

Could be one of those goddamn astronauts for all I know.

She fixed him a look.

He's a lawyer.

Oh.

Yeah, that's what I said when Mixie told me.

Mind if I use the bathroom? Harrison said.

Go right ahead, Hal said. You know where it is. Let's all go in. Gracie, there's a bunch of folks in here dyin to see you again.

Wish me luck, she said to Harrison.

Hal pushed her through the door to the living room and a cheer went up from inside.

Jesus, Harrison said to himself, and went upstairs to use the john.

By the time Harrison joined his wife downstairs she was on her second glass of Hal's lemon, nutmeg and honey-palm hot toddy, stuck by the sofa with cousin Dave. Harrison smiled and looked around for a drink of his own.

Anyone seen Kevin? Hal said, over the noise.

Yonder, Tom, another of Hal's employees, said from the window. Saw him go into the barn not ten minutes ago.

There was a cry; a rough and throaty noise from outside. The men looked at each other and the women looked at the men and the men turned to Hal, who put down his drink and moved quickly from the room. They followed him outside. The air was cold and the sod was hard and frosted. Kevin came out of the barn and yelled something to them. Harrison couldn't make it out. They picked up their pace. Kevin had blood on his shirt. He came over to them.

What happened? Hal said. Are you all right?

One of the foals is dead, he said. Looks like a coyote done it; don't know how the sumbitch got in though.

Shit, Hal said. Shit. Those fuckers.

This happened before, Hal? one of the other men said.

Never, Kevin said. Not in the barn. Maybe a coupla times, out in the pasture, sure; but sheep, sometimes cattle. Never a foal. Never a foal.

Okay, Hal said. Let's attend to her. We can work out what to do later. Fellas?

The men walked to the barn. Harrison hesitated at the door.

Jim? Hal said. You okay?

Harrison nodded. It started to snow. He waited outside while the men took care of it.

Inside this trim, modest suburban home is Annie Glenn, wife of astro-naut John Glenn, sharing the anxiety and pride of the entire world at this tense moment but in a way that only she can understand.

Grace snorted a worn indignation from the sofa.

One thing has prepared Annie Glenn for this test of her own courage and will sustain her and that one thing is her faith . . .

Nancy Bloom stood on the Glenn front lawn in Arlington. She held the microphone close to her glossy lips. In the background, the living room curtains were closed. Around her, a steel city had been erected, founded by television people.

Jesus, Harrison said, sitting next to his wife. Why are they re-porting from the Glenns' front yard?

. . . faith in the ability of her husband, her faith in the efficiency and dedication of the thousands of engineers and other personnel who provide his guidance system and her faith in Almighty God.

Light the candle already, Harrison said. I bet that slimy Texan sonofabitch is sitting round the corner in a limo waiting to shake her hand in front of those news crews.

CBS turned to Cronkite in the studio. Harrison stood and switched to NBC.

We should have popcorn, he said.

It was late February. Thousands of people crowded the Cape, waiting to see the first American orbit the Earth. Shepard might have been first up, but there was something about *orbiting the Earth* that reached deep inside people; people who were afraid. Everybody stared at the Atlas rocket as it sat, quivering, on the pad. Then came a terrific rumble and the Atlas left the pad and Glenn left the Earth. Harrison drank his beer and thought, Glenn's got his hatch and Glenn's got his window. Hell, some people were even calling him the pilot. Well, good for him. That was the way it should be. The Seven still weren't doing much actual flying, but at least they had a decent view now.

Grace got up and left the room. Harrison pulled his cigarettes from his pocket. He stuck one in his mouth and lit it and waved the match until it went out.

Who knows what's out there, Herb, Al Mann, one of the reporters, said. *This is just the beginning.*

Harrison sat forward and sucked hard on his cigarette.

John Glenn is about to enter the heavens, Herb said. *Since mankind first walked upon the Earth and gazed up at the night sky, he has wondered.*

The rocket rolled. Harrison stared at the screen.

Ahead lies the great tapestry of Creation, Herb said.

The face of God, Harrison thought. He blew smoke at the floor.

Glenn slid into low orbit. The g-forces fell away. Glenn floated.

Oh! That view is tremendous.

Harrison stepped outside. He pulled on the end of his beer. Above him, the sky went on forever. Somewhere up there, Glenn soared.

Harrison dropped the cigarette onto the porch and went back inside and shut the door.

I'm just thankful I live in the same world as John Glenn, a voice said from the television. On the sofa, Harrison reached for another cigarette. The voice continued, *In him we have a fearless protector.* Harrison stopped. He looked up. He stared at the reporter.

This is an NBC special news report brought to you by the Gulf Oil Corporation. . . .

Harrison felt something, but didn't know what. The pack of Lucky Strikes in his hand was empty. There was a fresh pack by his bed. He got up and wondered where Grace was. He went upstairs and stopped dead. Grace sat against the shut door of the empty bedroom, eyes fat with tears. She looked up at him and he felt the air leave his lungs and his heart lurch. He stumbled into the bathroom and shut the door. His face was wet. It tasted like the sea. He wiped his forehead, his temples, his chin; his heart was trying to bust out of his rib cage like an inmate during a prison riot. He gripped the sink and knew fear. Grace was on the other side of the door. Then she was on the stairs. Then she was in the kitchen. Something dropped away, and his hammering heart settled. He sat down on the floor. He was dizzy. His pulse slowed. His breathing grew shallow. He was exhausted. He sat in the bathroom for a long time. Then he washed his hands and went downstairs and saw John Glenn waving from the deck of the *Noa*.

———

Christ, Harrison said, walking into the office one morning in late April. Glenn is everywhere.

Yup, Ridley said, not looking up from the report he was typing.

It's been two months!

He's a Man Destined To Do Great Things.

He's probably got his own room at the White House now, Harrison said. Who's next?

Uh, Carpenter, Ridley said, swigging his coffee.

The diving guy?

The very same.

Where the hell did they get these pilots? Harrison said. Pull names out of a hat?

Ridley looked up. Beats me, he said. Is Deke comin back?

Heard he's gonna run the Astronaut Office.

What happened?

Some heart thing.

Jesus, Ridley said. One minute you're fine, the next—

Only two ways you can walk out a doctor's office, Harrison said. Fine or grounded.

He sat down and flicked through the mail.

Joe around?

Ridley nodded.

Harrison got up and left the room. Between Ridley's office and the staircase that led down to the hangar and locker room was a small lounge area that led to two other offices. The walls were covered with safety posters and maps of the surrounding desert. Old magazines sat in piles on hard blue sofas. The latest issue of *Aviation Week* caught his eye and he stooped to pick it up. He walked to the window and flipped through the pages. At the end of the news section was a small piece headlined NASA WILL ADD NEW ASTRONAUTS. He read the copy. *Between five to ten additional astronauts for NASA's manned space flight program will be selected this fall.* Project Mercury would end soon and NASA had already begun work on Project Gemini. The new two-man spacecraft had been contracted to Mc-Donnell. They were scheduled to deliver the first ship in sixty-three. Harrison skimmed until he got to the selection requirements: *The applicant must be an experienced test pilot ideally engaged in flying high performance aircraft. He must have attained experimental flight status through military service, the aircraft industry or NASA. He must have a college degree in the physical or biological sciences or engineering. He must be a US citizen. He must be under thirty-five years of age at the time of selection. He must be six feet (or less) in height.* The report noted the deadline, the first day of June. He tore out the page and put it in his pocket.

Harrison found Joe in the hangar with Neil. He talked to the two men. Neither of them mentioned the announcement. Had they seen it? It was nearly noon. He stepped outside for a smoke. Shallow clouds roamed slowly through the tin-colored sky. The air felt heavy. A memory of his mother came to him. She was collecting eggs from their chicken coop as rain fell on its corrugated tin roof. He thought about it for a minute then drove home, the folded magazine page pressing against his leg.

He cut the engine outside the house and stepped out of the car and walked to the back door. He stopped and stared at the door for a long time. Then he sat down on the stoop and put his hands over his face. The wind was warm around him. He walked quickly back to the car and drove back to work.

At the end of the day Harrison said to Neil, Pancho's? and the men drove over. They sat in the corner with a beer each and talked about hypersonic lift-to-drag ratios and trans-atmospheric cross-ranges and controlled lifting reentry. Pancho came over and called them a pair of miserable bastards and Neil smiled and sketched out Boeing's mock-up of the delta-winged X-20 Dyna-Soar space-plane on a napkin and Harrison ordered a scotch and felt good.

When he got home, Grace was upstairs in the empty bedroom. Harrison stood outside and watched. There were piles of folded clothes on the little bed. Grace picked up a pile at a time and placed them in large black bags.

What are you doing? he said.

You know what I'm doing.

He went downstairs. He found a mug in the kitchen and poured an inch of rye. He sat down at the table. Grace came down the stairs and the back door banged. He picked up his mug and went to see what she was doing. Grace stood on the stoop. There were several black bags outside the back door.

I didn't want them in the house anymore, she said, walking past him. I'm going to bed.

It's still early, he said.

Turn the lights out when you come up.

He watched her disappear upstairs. He looked at the back door. He went back to the kitchen and topped off his drink. Then he went out to the stoop and knelt down by the bags.

What the hell? he said, looking inside the first one.

Grace! he said. He yelled again. Grace!

He pulled out handfuls of dresses, vests, cardigans and skirts. Some he discarded. Others he collected next to him. What the . . . ? Grace!

What's the matter with you? she said, appearing behind him.

What the hell are you doing? he said.

What?

What the fuck do you think you're doing?!

You know—

I thought you were clearing out a few old things; stuff we didn't want anymore—this, this is everything! Look.

He held up a yellow dress with white lace skirting the hem.

You know what this is? he said.

Her eyes swelled with tears.

Of course I know what it is, she said.

Then why the hell is it out here? Here with the trash? The god-damn *trash*?

It's not the trash, she said.

What?

It's—I'm giving it to Jane Boham—she's just had a little—

The hell you are!

Jim I'm sorry I—

Harrison was frantically searching though the last bag.

Oh you're sorry are you? You're sorry.

Please Jim, don't do this—

Just go away, would you? Leave me the hell alone.

He started stuffing clothes back into one of the empty bags. She stood behind him and cried.

Just—leave me alone, he said.

He heard the door bang behind him. He fell back and wept into the yellow dress.

———

What the hell are you doing here?

Quit being such a hard-ass.

Pancho, I'm serious, it's not like the old days. You need clearance. You need—

I need a drink, is what I need.

Jesus. What do you want?

You know she goes every day. To Rosamond Park Cemetery?

Look, Pancho, I'm flyin in forty minutes.

Did you know that?

No, I did not know that.

You wanna know how I know it? I drive her there every goddamn day. I been spending more time at your place than you have.

Don't come over here, start playing that card, Pancho; that I'm working too hard, that I don't know my own wife.

You don't know your own wife.

Get out.

Shut up.

What's this?

An envelope.

Is she leaving me?

It's from me you dope. It's a thousand dollars.

What?

Take her away someplace, Jim; someplace nice. Just the two of you.

I'm runnin a program here, Pancho, I can't just—

Screw the program.

F'chrissakes.

Speak to the old man, get some time off. Hell, everyone knows you need it.

So now everyone knows what's good for me.

No, just me.

Right.

You were back on the flight line three days after her funeral!

I couldn't protect her, Pancho.

It wasn't your job to, sweetie.

Something ached inside him.

Yes it was, he said.

——

He sat in the middle of Muroc Dry Lake with the canopy up and waited for the ground crew. His pressure suit was tight and uncomfortable. Boy, that was a ride, he thought. The Big Engine had failed to ignite when he was dropped. Hell, he'd fallen fast. There was only time for one relight in the X-15. It lit. Waiting for the truck with the sun on his face he thought about what he'd seen up there, across the top, above the dome. Black space, blue Earth; the globe curling away beneath him. He'd looked down on everything he'd known, for a brief window, a few minutes. He'd flown weightless, on reaction control, hand on the stick squirting hydrogen peroxide from the thrusters. He felt free. Then he dropped back into the atmosphere and the Earth pulled him down.

When the crew arrived they helped him from the cockpit and quizzed him on the malfunction. High speed flights always made him hungry so they'd started bringing him a sandwich to munch on in the truck. Baloney and mustard. He rode back to base.

Phone call, Jim, Ridley yelled when they pulled into the hangar.

Who is it? Harrison called up.

Didn't say.

Harrison climbed the stairs in his pressure suit. In the office, he picked up the receiver.

Hello? he said.

I'm looking for Jim Harrison, a voice said.

This is he, Harrison said.

Jim, it's Deke Slayton.

Harrison looked up. Ridley had gone down to the hangar. He sat down.

Jim, you there?

Yeah, uh, Deke; I'm here.

You still want to come fly for us? Deke said.

Sure, Harrison said.

Good. Great to have you. We need you to come down to Houston for the press announcement, day after tomorrow, but, look, we want to keep things secret til then, so I want you to catch a flight down here tomorrow and get a cab to the Rice Hotel. Have you got that?

Harrison fumbled for a pencil on Ridley's desk and wrote RICE HOTEL on the back of an envelope.

Uh, yeah, Deke, I got that, he said.

When you get there, say you have a reservation in the name of Max Peck.

Right, Harrison said. Ask for Max Peck.

No, Deke said. Tell them *you're* Max Peck.

Oh, right, he said. Deke?

Yeah?

Who's Max Peck?

You'll find out.

The line went dead. He replaced the receiver and looked at the phone. A small smile crept across his face. He picked it up again and dialed two digits, then stopped, put it back, and sat and thought until Ridley came in and said, was that Deke Slayton from NASA? And he said, yeah. Wanted to ask about Walker.

What'd you say? Ridley said.

Told him to speak to Walker, Harrison said.

Walker's thirty-six, Ridley said. He's too old.

Yeah.

He'd be good, though, ol Joe. Yeah. He'd show them a thing or two.

Yeah, Harrison said.

He headed home late afternoon. Milo leapt up when he got in. The dog was slowing down, getting old, enjoying the warmth of the sun through the window more than chasing jackrabbits between the Joshua trees.

Milo, he said, kneeling on the floor, rubbing the dog's head and playing with his ears. Milo yelped with excitement and Grace stepped into the room from the kitchen.

Hi, she said. You're early.

He stood up and kissed her.

Thought I'd slip away while no one was lookin, he said.

How did it go this morning?

It was okay. Listen, hon, I need to be in Seattle again tomorrow—

Again? she said. You spent an entire *week* there just last month—and another before that.

Honey, I'm sorry, you know how important this is. The Dyna-Soar is the next step up from the X-15 and I'm part of the pilot-consultant group. It's not my fault Boeing's shop is in Seattle. Hell, I wish it was round the corner.

Can't Neil go instead?

Neil's going with me.

Grace looked at him. Just so you know, she said, *Dyna-Soar* is a stupid name.

It's just slang, he said. It'll be designated the X-20. Look, hon, I know things have been tough recently. And the program's stepped up and gotten real busy and I haven't been around as much as you'd like. I'm sorry. Things'll be better when I get back, I promise.

Grace sighed. I'm sorry too, she said. Just feel like I'm on my own sometimes, that's all.

You're not, he said, putting his arms around her. Come on, let's head over to Pancho's. It's been an age since we were there together.

You're leaving early tomorrow?

He thought about what time Deke wanted him in Houston.

I'll be fine, he said.

Guess I'd better make the most of you while I can.

That's my girl. C'mon, let's grab a bite there too.

Milo ran around the room then disappeared into the kitchen.

Let me just get changed, she said.

———

Houston was humid. He wanted a cold shower as soon as he arrived. He dropped his bag in front of the reception desk at the Rice Hotel and looked around. Nice place. Can I help you? a girl said.

Sure, he said. I'm Max Peck. I've got a room booked for two nights.

I'm sorry? she said.

I'm—uh—Max Peck, he said. I have a reservation?

I don't think you are, she said.

He didn't know what to do. What should he do? A man appeared behind the desk. His nametag said GEORGE SWARTZ. Ah, George Swartz said, yes; I'll take care of this, Paula, thank you. Mr. Peck?

Paula looked as confused as Harrison.

Uh, yes, Harrison said.

Welcome to the Rice Hotel, George Swartz said. We're very glad you could make it. He reached beneath the counter for a brown envelope. Here's your key. Please let us know if anything isn't to your satisfaction.

Thank you, Harrison said, looking around.

The elevators are right through there, George Swartz said, pointing toward a set of glazed double doors. You're on the fifth floor.

Thanks, Harrison said. He picked up his bag and, envelope in hand, went to find his room. In the elevator he loosened his collar and hit five. There was a sign above the panel that said, WELCOME TO YOUR HOST IN HOUSTON! WE HOPE YOU ENJOY YOUR STAY! MAX PECK, MANAGER.

What the hell? Harrison said.

His room was dark and cool. He sat down on the bed. Was all this really necessary? The phone rang.

Hello? he said. The line was silent. Hello?

Who's this? a voice said.

You phoned me! Harrison said. Who is this?

I'm Max Peck.

Are you the manager of this hotel? Harrison said.

I'm a guest and I think you have my room.

Look, son, Harrison said. I don't know who you are but I can assure you this is *my* room and *my* name is Max Peck and if you've got a problem with that, I suggest you take it up with the manager. I believe his name is Max Peck!

He slammed the receiver back in its cradle.

I need a drink, he said to the empty room. He showered, changed, and headed down to the bar. As soon as he saw Pete Conrad with a tumbler in his hand he knew who he'd been speaking to on the telephone.

Pete Conrad, Harrison said. The Lovelace washout.

Mr. Peck, I presume? Conrad said, turning and smiling. The men shook hands.

I thought I recognized the voice, Harrison said.

Conrad laughed. How the hell are you?

Good.

What'll it be?

Scotch, thanks. So are we all Max Peck today?

Yup, Conrad said.

Well, I can't wait to meet the others, Harrison said. How many are we, anyway?

Nine, Conrad said. And here comes another one now.

John Young, a navy pilot and Pax River alumni, walked over, drink in one hand, fat cigar in the other.

Mr. Peck, Conrad said. We've been waiting for you.

Shit, Young said. You too? What the hell's Deke playing at?

John, Conrad said, this here's Jim Harrison.

Young stuck his cigar between his teeth and shook Harrison's hand.

Real pleasure, Young said.

Likewise, Harrison said. Hell, am I the only air force?

Nope, Conrad said. The same loophole you snuck through let in a couple more.

Well that's a damn shame, Harrison said, smiling.

The bartender approached them.

What'll it be, gentlemen?

Same again for me, Conrad said. Plus a scotch and—John?

Make that two.

Coming up, the bartender said.

And here comes Shaky! Conrad said, spotting Lovell wander into the bar, looking apprehensive.

Damn, Lovell said, seeing the men. It's like the fleet has landed.

Drink? Conrad said.

Well, if you insist, Pete, Lovell said, then, turning to the others, Jim, John; pleasure to see you gentlemen here.

Likewise.

When the bartender returned with their drinks, Harrison said, say, let's take these through to the lobby; see if we can't spot a few more Max Pecks coming in.

Great idea, Conrad said.

They sat and drank and watched five other men experience the same confusion they had at the reception desk. As each man left with his key, the group would holler and cheer and the new arrival would look up, smile, shake his head and walk over. Harrison knew Frank Borman, Tom Stafford and Jim McDivitt; all flight test instructors at Edwards. He shook their hands and introduced them to the others. Ed White came over. He was tall, athletic; a West Pointer with a generous grin. He'd been doing all-weather testing at Wright-Patterson. Harrison only knew him by name.

Eight down, one to go, Lovell said.

The men ordered another round of drinks and then Harrison stood up as a short man with a wry smile approached the group.

Neil, you sly dog, Harrison said, shaking his hand and laughing.

Damn, Neil said. I was a week in San Antonio for those tests and a week here at Ellington for assessment and I didn't see you once!

They must've staggered us, Harrison said.

Two X-15 pilots? Conrad said. We are truly blessed.

I guess this is us, then, huh? Borman said, looking round.

Guess so, Harrison said.

Not bad, Conrad said. Not bad at all.

The next morning they traveled to Ellington Air Force Base, close to where the vast Manned Spacecraft Center was rapidly being constructed on the thousand acres of murky scrubland at the edge of Clear Lake. Deke wanted them to meet the NASA brass. The men made their way to the large hall where the meeting was supposed to take place.

Jim, Deke said as the men entered.

Deke, he said, shaking his hand.

The hall had no windows and the light was poor. There were two suited men standing and talking together on the far side who looked up and began to walk toward them.

Glad you could make it down, Deke said.

Well, it's good to be here, Deke, Harrison said. How's Marge?

She's good thanks, good. Gentlemen, welcome, Deke said to the others. I'll be with you in just a minute. He turned back to Harrison.

Listen, I'm sorry we didn't get the chance to chat more, you know, back in December.

Oh, sure, Deke, Harrison said. Thanks.

Deke slapped his shoulder. Sure good to have you here, he said.

Harrison nodded.

Okay, gentlemen, Deke said, as the two suited men joined him, good morning. We've got a lot to cover today so I'm just gonna get straight on with it. You know me and I sure as hell know more than I'd like to about you after all them tests.

The men laughed.

First I'll introduce you to Walt Williams, head of Flight Operations, who some of you may already know, and Bob Gilruth, director of the Manned Spacecraft Center, who headed up the original Space Task Group for Mercury. They'll be plenty of missions for you all. We got eleven manned Gemini flights on the schedules, followed by at *least* four Block I Apollos, which will lead to a number of Block II Apollo missions—one of which will attempt the first lunar landing. You're no doubt aware, from observing the boys who have already gone up—

And those that haven't, Gilruth chipped in.

Yeah, Deke said, yeah; them too—that you'll receive a great deal more attention than, uh, you've been used to in the flight test business. I know you don't like it, I know you don't want it, but I also know by the fact you're here today that you're willing to put up with it in order to achieve our goals. Now there'll be plenty of pressure and temptation, no doubt about that. Be careful about accepting gifts, freebies, that kinda thing, especially from companies competing for contracts. And with regard to gratuities, if you have any doubt, just follow the old test pilot's creed: anything you can eat, drink or screw within twenty-four hours is perfectly acceptable.

The men laughed and Gilruth shook his head and Williams said, within reason, within reason!

I'm gonna hand you over to Shorty Powers now, our public affairs officer, Deke said. He's gonna brief you on the press conference later. And you'll remember from mine how much I hate press conferences. This time we got the University of Houston's Cullen Auditorium. There'll be reporters, crews from all the television networks, radio, the wire, plus national and international newspapers and magazines. There's eighteen hundred seats in that auditorium and every one of em will be taken. The world is waiting to see who America's new astronauts are. Keep your answers brief, obvious, and impersonal, like good pilots. We already have, he said with a smile, one John Glenn, and God knows that's enough. You'll meet Chris Kraft and George Low later but, for now, here's Shorty.

Deke looked around.

Shorty? he said again.

He's on his way, Williams said.

Okay, Deke said. Any problems, talk to me. I got your backs. And we'll need you down at the Cape October third for Wally's launch, so mark it off in your schedules.

The doors banged and a small balding man appeared in the gloom.

Shorty, Deke said. Jesus Christ. Come on, or we'll never get to the goddamn moon.

Harrison flew back to Edwards that night. He'd hated every minute of the press conference. So had the others. But they answered the questions, posed for photographs. Then they got the hell out.

He landed on the main runway. He felt good. He couldn't remember the last time he felt good. After he got changed, he drove home. Grace was asleep on the sofa when he walked through the door. She stirred when she heard him.

Hey, you're back, she said, half asleep.

He dropped his bag on the floor.

I didn't mean to wake you, he said.

No, it's okay, she said. She stretched. I was waiting up. I must have fallen asleep.

She sat up and yawned.

Where's Milo? he said.

Upstairs, she said. At least, he was. How was it?

He smiled.

What's the matter? she said.

Nothing. How was your day?

Dull, she said. Cleaned the house all morning, then took Milo to Rosamond for groceries. Hey, I ran into Megan Blackman; she was really odd with me.

What'd she do? he said, walking around the sofa to see her.

Nothing really, Grace said. She was just . . . she just made a big fuss over me, and said something like, eight years was plenty enough and to give you her best. And she had this weird smile the whole time. How many times have you spoken to her before? Twice? Maybe three times? And Milo was tugging at the damn leash the whole time, she said.

He sat down next to her. Listen, he said. I got some news.

What? she said.

Pack your bags, he said.

What? Why?

We're moving.

Moving? she said. What? Where to?

Houston, he said.

HOUSTON,
TEXAS
1962

Clear Lake was not a lake. Or clear. It looked murky, but Grace figured Murky Lake didn't have the same appeal. Still. It looked pretty. From a distance. Lots of green. So much green. Trees, too. Trees and green and the murky clear lake. The air was a different kind of hot. It didn't dry out the back of your throat. It had weight behind it. Moisture. The Texan sun was more forgiving; a kind aunt instead of a stern mother. And who could argue with the house? After so many years in their tiny timber ranch house, with its clanky, spurting taps and shit-brown water and splitting wooden walls, and the *dust*, this was like . . . she didn't know what it was like. She'd never seen anything like it.

The house was in Timber Cove, a new development close to Murky Lake and the Manned Spacecraft Center that was emerging in gray cubes from the ground. The Original Seven astronauts, as people were now calling them—the *fellas*—settled here first, picking out lots, their wives choosing their own kitchens. The streets were tidy. Pine and oak trees shaded the sidewalks from the hot sun.

The week following the press conference, members of the New

Nine—as *they* were now being called—flew down to Houston to pick out lots of their own. Grace had known all about the deal that the Original Seven cut with *Life*; she'd read the personal pieces (ghosted, naturally) by the astronauts and their wives. Exclusive rights to their stories; half a million bucks between them. And Leo DeOrsey, the lawyer that NASA had turned to for advice, refused to take a fee, or even be reimbursed for his expenses! It was a new kind of crazy. After she'd settled down and taken in the news that Jim had hit her with, after that, her mind had found itself thinking about such things—compensations—the *goodies*—but she simply couldn't believe that this particularly fat goose, *Life* magazine, would ever lay another egg, even a silver one. She was wrong. An agent was immediately found for them, the Nine, an ad exec from Philly called Harry Batten. Grace liked Harry from their first meeting. He was thin and tall and dressed in a variety of gray suits cut so precisely she could hardly believe he could move. He laughed loud, and he laughed a lot. And he got them their own *Life* deal. Split nine ways this time, sure, but she wasn't about to complain. After years on the pay of an air force captain, it was hard to take in. It hadn't stopped there, either. The Timber Cove developers, so eager to have *astronauts* living in their homes, offered large mortgages with practically no interest and proposed they custom-build the houses to whatever specifications they wanted.

Timber Cove was becoming an astronaut village; the wider area a NASA community. The Harrisons lived next door to the Lovells, around the corner from the Whites and the Glenns. Everyone was a short walk away. She felt safe. The sadness she felt at leaving the high desert (and she wasn't about to pretend to herself or her husband or anyone else for that matter—*Life* deal or no *Life* deal—that she didn't ache with sadness) had just been buried under a mudslide of good fortune, of goodies.

There were times, like that morning, when she felt physically dizzy; a kind of emotional vertigo. On those occasions, she'd walked down to Clear Lake and gaze at the horizon. She felt deep comfort at the space; the absence of everything but the gloomy rippled surface of the water and the blue sky banking overhead. She didn't even take Milo. She wanted to be alone. It was in those moments that she allowed herself to think about Florence. At home, and everywhere else, she could think of nothing *but* her. However, staring across the filthy lake, a silty fug of oil from the refinery across the bay thickening the hot air, there, she was able to consciously, deliberately— tenderly—think about her daughter. Silent tears would fall like carnival ribbons and she'd think, how—*how*—did something that had only been in her life for two years, something that *hadn't even existed* for the first thirty years of her life, how did the loss of this . . . this . . . *thing* destroy so much? She'd carried her, nurtured her, given her life, then brought her into the world, which had then slowly killed her. She hated the world for what it had done. The earth, the soil under her feet, everything. It could all go to hell. She couldn't escape it. It was everywhere. She was part of it. It was her. She would look into the murk and want to drown. She would slide down onto the grass and cry. She'd cry for her daughter, lost, and she'd cry for the thoughts she had in her head. And when the emotion passed, and it always did, she felt exhausted, but, somehow, better. The sun was still warm. The horizon constant. There was so much sky. She'd think about the program. What they were trying to achieve. So many people. So many people. And how she was part of that now.

Back at the house, in the kitchen, she ran her fingers along the cool smooth surface of the countertop. She had an integrated blender, a Thermador double oven, a double sink, a dishwasher. Across a wide breakfast bar was a combined living and family room, with paneled walls, stone hearth and a high cathedral ceiling with beams.

There was a separate dining room with floor-to-ceiling glass that looked out over an abundant garden with a patio area and swimming pool. Upstairs were three bedrooms and a study. She'd argued with the draftsmen about the bedrooms. We only need one bedroom, she'd said, plus a guest room. He told her that it would be foolish *not* to have a third bedroom when it came to reselling. With the layout you've chosen for the ground floor, he said, adding one wouldn't even be a problem. And a lot of folks looking round here will have children. Tired, she'd relented. Now, it was an empty hole howling above her head. She poured a glass of cold Coke and sat outside on the patio. The chairs and table were new. Almost all of their furniture was new. They'd hardly taken anything from the old house. It was all too decrepit, too small, so they'd left it. It was cheaper and easier that way. The air force had yet to lease the house, so they could return for anything if they wanted. They'd left so fast. So little time to say good-bye. That was military life though. Pancho was pretty beat up about it. She never said so; someone like Pancho didn't need to. She was pissed at Jim. She couldn't figure out why he'd want to throw away the Blue Suit to sit in a tin can. She had this phrase, *chimp mode*, whenever she talked about him. *So*, Pancho would say when Grace called her from Houston, *is he in chimp mode today?* Meaning, was Jim testing the new systems. It rankled her, but Grace knew Pancho was hurting. She could barely look Jim in the eye when they'd gone over to say good-bye. The telephone helped, but there was something about not being in the same place. You moved on; that was it. This time Grace felt different though. She felt tethered. She felt sick when she thought of her little girl all alone in that cemetery. She felt *black*.

Oh, God.

She stood up quickly and walked around the garden. She was barefoot and the grass felt cool where it had been shaded from the morning sun. The garden was planted up and alive. Deep greens, yellow, indigo-blue. Enclosing it was a wooden fence that ran the length of the house's rear perimeter. The wood was stained light brown. At the back of the garden, parts of the fence were still exposed where the plants hadn't yet thickened out. The fence was six feet high. She stood looking at it for a long time. She reached out her hand and touched it. Then she went back inside.

Grace sat on the sofa and read for an hour. She grew restless. Milo was asleep in the sun upstairs. She collared him, found her sunglasses and headed out again. She thought about calling on Marilyn Lovell next door. She liked Marilyn, and their husbands got along well. Not that either of them were ever around. Deke had been working them hard from the get-go. Wally—Jo Schirra's husband—and the rest of the Mercury boys were concentrating on the next flight, scheduled to launch in a few weeks time, and the New Nine (she already hated the name) were learning as much as they could about Project Gemini. Jim would leave the house early and arrive home, exhausted, late. They were working out of rented offices in the Farnsworth-Chambers Building downtown, since the Manned Spacecraft Center was still being built. There was something about the speed that everything was happening at. It unsettled her.

Milo pulled on the leash. Grace felt sorry for him. He'd never had to wear one before. He wasn't used to the cars, or the intricacies of a suburban neighborhood. He pulled her on. Maybe, she thought, she might bump into one of the other wives. Annie had been so sweet to her, and Pat kind. The others she wasn't so sure about. She'd picked up on a strange hostility from the Original wives. Did they think she didn't deserve to be in Timber Cove? That they weren't entitled to their slice of the *Life* pie? Marge Slayton had organized a lunch for them not long after the Nine had arrived in Houston. It had been oddly tense. As though the

Mercury wives resented these nine rookies and rankled at their attitude, like an older sister punishing her younger sibling for simply arriving and benefiting from her hard-earned privileges. Grace understood the pecking order. God knows she'd been a military wife for long enough. Unofficially, the wives rose in rank with their husbands. Living somewhere as remote and godforsaken as Muroc in the early days, it wasn't something she'd really encountered. Hell, if you were living on some desert outpost to God knows what, who really gave a damn? But then, she knew she wasn't like the others, and Jim was more than a cut above the pilots who'd been selected for the first monkey shots. The boys at Edwards were an elite few. And the other wives knew it. Marge was trying, with Susan Borman, to formulate the equivalent of the Officer's Wives Club for them in Timber Cove.

Coffee, every month, Marge said. We'll rotate homes. And we'll call it the AWC.

None of the other wives needed to ask what the *A* stood for; like their husbands, nobody uttered the word itself. Grace had picked up on the code early on. It was always *the men*, or *the boys*, or *the fellas*. Grace had neither the time nor the patience for the kind of organized horseshit that came with the service. All the other wives wanted to talk about was *Jackie's wardrobe*, or how Jackie *wore her hair* at such-and-such occasion. Grace didn't give a damn. And over that first coffee, when she dropped cigarette ash on Marge's new shag-pile rug and said, goddamn it, the others looked at her like she was trash. Jeez Louise, she'd thought. Was this really her world now? Jan was different though. Neil was a civilian and had been flying for NASA so they didn't follow the same rules. She liked Jan. But Grace was used to being alone and that's the way she wanted to keep it. She wasn't planning on attending many of the AWC meetings.

At the corner of Shorewood and Whispering Oaks she paused

and lit a cigarette. Then she walked back down to the edge of Clear Lake.

Grace sat opposite Marilyn at the Lovell kitchen counter drinking coffee. She hadn't spent long at Clear Lake.

I promise, she said.

Marilyn was slender and tall with black hair that erupted from her head in dark curls twisted into a beehive. She tapped her cigarette into a glass ashtray on the countertop and leaned forward.

I'm pregnant, she said.

Pregnant? Grace said, putting down her mug. I—wow—that's, uh—goodness, congratulations. Sorry. You just caught me by surprise.

You're not the only one caught by surprise, Marilyn said.

That's wonderful news, Grace said, it really is.

Yes, it is, she said, but with three monsters already—well, two; my eldest is practically—honey? Marilyn said, breaking off.

I'm sorry, Grace said.

It's okay, Marilyn said, moving her coffee out of the way and reaching for Grace's hands. What is it?

Oh, God, Grace said.

Come on, you can tell me, Marilyn said. Friends *and* neighbors.

It's not right for me to come into your home and hear your wonderful news and—

It's fine, Marilyn said, really—I'm the wife of a test pilot. I've had to deal with *much* worse, *believe* me.

Grace laughed through her tears.

Have another cigarette, Marilyn said, offering her the pack. Grace took one and lit it and told her everything and when she was done Marilyn hugged her and told her she couldn't imagine going through what she'd been through and Grace felt a little better.

What's Jim been like? Marilyn said from the other side of the kitchen, putting another pot of coffee on.

Grace didn't say anything.

Figured as much, Marilyn said.

Grace lit another cigarette.

You know, Marilyn said, returning to the bar with fresh coffee, I remember this bad string we had a few years back at Pax River. Probably the worst I've known. I mean, it was *grim*. We lost twenty-two pilots over an eleven-week stretch. That's two a week! About halfway through my Jim comes home—on time, thank God—and I say to him, how was your day? Like a good wife. And he says, super, super. So I ask him, you know, did you fly? And he says, yup, lotta fun. And that was it. He started asking me about dinner or something. I found out later that he'd been practicing low lift-over-drag landings in a F-104 with John Murphy in the backseat. The idea was—and I only half understand these things—to land the thing at about two hundred knots using the afterburner for speed and stability, flaring the flaps . . . well, that was the idea. But the afterburner malfunctioned. They lost thrust, and dropped like a rock. Murphy told Jim he was gonna punch out if they couldn't regain power. He's in the backseat and the tail woulda hit first, right? So the tail hits the runway. Murphy ejects. Jim decides to stay with the plane, which hits the ground and screeches down the runway at God knows what speed before smashing into the mesquite.

She stopped and gave a small laugh at the memory and stubbed out her cigarette.

Jim was fine. Behind him, where Murphy had been sitting a few seconds earlier, was the engine. Murphy was fine. And if Jim had punched out as well?

What? Grace said.

His ejection mechanism broke on impact, Marilyn said. He would have been killed either by partial ejection or the nitroglycerine explosion. *Super, super; lotta fun.* So, your Jim? It doesn't surprise me. It's what they're like.

I know but—

I know.

Grace stared into her coffee. Marilyn lit another cigarette.

You have a beautiful home, Grace said.

Why, thank you. Let's go outside.

The women left their drinks and sat out by the pool on green chaise lounges.

It all feels so . . . normal, doesn't it? Marilyn said.

Grace thought for a second, then said, yeah.

So normal it's weird! Marilyn said.

I know what you mean, Grace said.

You know, Marilyn said, I was so thrilled when Jim told me about this astronaut business—no, thrilled isn't the right word, it was more than that. Relief. That's what it was: *relief.* It was only a matter of time—and that's all it is, time—before some officer or base chaplain was going to walk up my path and knock on my door. Now, Jim will tell you that every time you go up, the clock gets reset—you know, that the odds aren't cumulative? That's bullshit. Only a matter of time before he got killed testing airplanes for the navy. But he's out, thank the Lord, and with NASA now. And this astronaut business? I know where he is pretty much all day! And when they put him on top of that rocket? I'll be able to watch the whole thing on television right from the living room! I won't have to wait and wonder and watch the clock as it pushes itself toward five and he still isn't home. I won't have to phone the wives of other guys in the group to find out if anything's happened. I won't have to call the base and demand to speak to my husband.

Yeah, when Jim told me he was going to be spending the next few weeks in class—

Ha!

I almost cried!

And, Marilyn said, NASA says they're even going to give us these little *squawk boxes*—at least, that's what Chris Kraft called them—like an intercom, only one way—so we can listen in on the communications between the spacecraft and the ground. How about that?

Sounds pretty neat, Grace said.

This is *the life*, Marilyn said. The classroom, the office, the simulator . . .

And the only thing you have to worry about, really, is the launch, Grace said. Which, frankly, seems a hell of a lot safer than testing every crazy plane the air force dreams up.

Well, all I can say is that it's about time, Marilyn said. So, *enjoy* it.

Yeah, Grace said, looking at the still pool. God. I feel so *angry*. At God. At Jim.

There aren't many people who can go through what you've gone through and come out the other side, Marilyn said. But I believe you are one of those people, Grace. I really do. And we both know that God doesn't cause cancers.

Why didn't He cure it then? She was a *child*, for chrissake! How could He allow it? Miracles have happened before, you know—the blind man, the leper—why not my little girl?

She started to cry. Marilyn held her hand.

I don't know, honey, she said. I don't know.

I miss her so much, Grace said.

Is there anyone back west that you'd like to come visit? Or maybe you and Jim should take a few days, head back, see a few people; maybe spend some time at her grave? I know it sounds strange, but it's helped me before at times like this.

Grace shook her head. No, she said. Jim won't go back. He won't do it. I don't think he can. And I couldn't go back by myself. I'm so sorry—you're about to have a baby and I'm—

It's fine! Marilyn said. Did I tell you how Jim found out?

Tell me, she said.

I was terrified. Terrified of telling him. I didn't know what NASA would say. I thought they'd stop him from going up. I mean, talk about a distraction, right?

He hadn't noticed?

He's never around long enough to notice anything, she said. Unless I get my hair fixed in a way he doesn't like. And I was terrified our doctor would tell him.

Can he do that?

I don't know, but he's always getting me confused with Jane Conrad, so I think I'm safe.

Grace laughed.

I can see the resemblance, she said.

Early on, Marilyn said, he had to give me this examination and—you'll never believe this—while he was *down there*, he says, *you remind me so much of Mrs. Conrad.*

No!

To which I replied, inside or out?

Grace laughed harder.

Oh, boy, Marilyn said.

That's priceless, Grace said.

Isn't it? So, anyway, my dress is getting tighter and tighter and every time we went out in the car, I had to make Jim stop all the time so I could use the bathroom. I told him I had a bladder infection. I'd gotten into the habit of hiding crackers under my pillow at night; they really helped with the morning sickness. I used to nibble on them in the dark when he was asleep. So, a few weeks ago, I was lying in bed, eating these things like crazy, and he wakes up and says, why are you eating crackers? So I had to tell him.

What'd he say?

He said pinch me tomorrow and tell me I had a nightmare. Then he went back to sleep.

Grace laughed.

He told me he didn't mean it in the morning.

So what *are* you going to do?

Keep it to ourselves for as long as possible. Jim thinks they'll realize he's indispensable soon enough.

Grace looked at the pool again. A slight breeze formed ridges where the blue grew dark toward the far end and she wondered how deep it was.

———

The sky set thickly gray and Grace lit a candle in the living room and carried it through to the dining room. Harrison walked in and looked at her.

It's your birthday, Jim, she said. We're having a candle.

He didn't say anything. She walked past him, back to the kitchen, and said, they'll be here soon; would you go and get ready?

What's wrong with what I got on? he said.

You look like a mechanic, she said.

The hell does that mean?

I'm not doing this now, she said.

What? Grace.

She turned and faced him.

It means, she said, that it looks like you don't give a damn.

I don't, he said.

I know that, Jim; you've said it enough times today, but do you want them to think that?

Frank and Shaky won't care and the women can think what they want, he said.

Jim, I'm the one who has to live with these women while you're at work, she said.

He sighed and looked at the floor.

All I'm sayin, he said, is that you didn't have to do this.

Go change, she said.

Grace set the pot down in the middle of the table.

Rabbit stew, she said, removing her oven mits. Old recipe from back home.

Rabbit stew! Rene Carpenter said. Grace, you're so *talented*!

Grace held together a smile.

Grace, honey, it smells wonderful, Marilyn Lovell said from where she was seated next to her husband.

The barbecue Grace originally planned had turned into a more intimate dinner when only the Lovells, the Bormans, Louise Shepard, and Rene could make it. The others were busy or couldn't get sitters at such short notice (how was two weeks short notice?) and the other fellas were either at the Cape, or McDonnell, or the office, or wherever the hell else they were when not at home. She wished the Glenns had been able to come but they had taken a trip back east to visit John's folks. It was fine. Easier this way. And she had a surprise for Jim too. It would be a good night.

Susan Borman filled her wineglass and Frank smiled at the smell from the pot.

Beer, Frank? Harrison said. Shaky?

Hey, you can only get away with calling me that if you're navy! Lovell said.

Harrison laughed.

Beer'd be good, Borman said.

Make that two, Lovell said.

Comin up.

Harrison walked into the kitchen. The doorbell rang.

I'll get it, Harrison said.

This our mystery guest? Lovell said.

Hope so, Grace said, and stared at the candle.

Harrison walked across the living room to the front door. The doorbell rang again.

All right already, he said. Jeez.

He opened the door.

Happy birthday, you miserable son-of-a-bitch, Pancho said.

What the hell are you doin here? he said.

I'm your birthday stripper, she said. Jesus, don't look so goddamn terrified. Grace invited me. Surprise. Let me in, would you, the bottom just fell out of the damn sky.

She pushed past him into the dry. He shut the door.

Oh, she said, looking around, nice; fancy. What in god's sweet name is *that*?

She was pointing at a portrait on the wall above the fireplace.

It's a portrait, he said.

Of what?

Of me.

Pancho snorted.

Take my hat, she said. Make sure you hang it up; don't just toss it down someplace. Cost me two hundred bucks.

For a hat? he said, looking it over in his hands before hanging it on a peg by the front door.

Hey, I didn't drive all this way for a lecture on my financials. I brought you something.

She handed him a wrapped paper package.

It's sure good to see you, he said.

Knock it off, would you. My ass is killin me, sat in that car so long.

You drove straight here?

Hell no, dummy; I got friends all along the border.

Harrison pulled open the paper. Inside was a framed photo of her, him, and Ridley, leaning against the bar of the Happy Bottom Riding Club.

Pancho, he said. I love it.

Don't go gettin all mushy on me, she said, it's just a goddamn photo. Where's Grace?

Pancho started toward the kitchen, muttering about the decor. He followed her across the living room, through the empty kitchen and into the dining room.

Well if it ain't the prettiest bunch of people I've ever seen in one place, she said.

Grace jumped up and hugged her hard.

Good to see you too, kiddo, Pancho said.

Let me introduce you to everyone, Grace said. Harrison caught his wife's eye and smiled.

I gotta take a piss first, Pancho said. I been squeezin so hard since San Antonio I think I pulled a goddamn muscle.

Gracious, Louise said.

Rene's eyebrows arched; Borman laughed.

I'll show you where the bathroom is, Harrison said.

Why? You gonna watch? Pancho said.

Come on, he said, moving her toward the door.

Jeez Louise, he said as soon as they were alone. Tone it down a bit, would you?

What's the big deal? Pancho said. Those tight-asses could do with loosening up.

You don't even know them, he said.

I'm right though, right?

Harrison didn't say anything.

Ha!

This is gonna be a hell of a night, he said. What was Grace thinkin?

She wanted to have a real woman at your birthday party, Pancho said.

It's not a party, he said.

It is now, she said. Now, where's the john?

Pancho told stories all evening. The men laughed and the women frowned at the men; Harrison couldn't remember the last time he'd seen his wife so happy.

How's business anyway? Harrison said to Pancho as Grace cleared the table.

Goddamn FBI launched an investigation after some weenie lieutenant wrote General Holtner a letter sayin he'd paid one of my girls for sex—accused me of runnin a whorehouse! I'm filin suit against the U.S. government. Never run away from a fight in my life, Pancho said, and I sure as shit ain't about to now.

Uh, Pancho, Harrison said, trying to avoid looking at Rene and Louise.

I told the FBI, Pancho continued, if I was really runnin a whorehouse, they would've found out about it in a couple of days, not the fourteen weeks it's taken them to find out not one goddamn thing!

That's terrible, Marilyn said.

Sure is, honey, Pancho said. The fellas are gonna have to find someplace else for sex now.

Who wants coffee? Grace said, appearing in the doorway. There was a show of hands.

These stories are so fascinating, Louise said, but perhaps we could tone them down a little, or maybe talk about something else? This is a dinner party after all!

The atmosphere around the table stiffened.

I'm sure glad you said that, Pancho said. Tell you the truth, I'm havin a helluva time cleaning these fucking stories up.

Louise blushed and Grace said, do you all know who her grandfather was? Thaddeus Lowe, father of the damn air force—invented aerial reconnaissance; scouting Confederate positions in a balloon for Lincoln himself!

Okay, honey, Harrison said.

He built the Mount Lowe Railroad—that's why it's called the Mount Lowe Railroad!

Yeah, Pancho said, but all he had left when he died were his Civil War medals, a couple of gold-headed canes, a sword, a pistol and a watch—and one lousy share of stock in the Pasadena Land and Water Company. He was a smart man; genius even, hell of an entrepreneur; goddamn terrible with money. After the funeral, all in all, we owed seven hundred bucks.

Nobody knew what to say, even Harrison, but Pancho lit one of her ten-cent cigars and told them about the time she yelled at John Wayne for interrupting her lunch.

That night, in bed, Harrison said, boy, that was a lot of fun.

Grace pulled off her dress and smiled at him in the low light.

Happy birthday, she said.

Come to bed, he said.

She kicked her underwear onto the floor and slid in next to him.

I'm cold, she said.

He pulled her onto his chest.

I thought Louise was gonna have a stroke when Pancho started on about the whorehouse, he said.

Grace laughed. I can't believe she'd rather stay above some bar downtown than here, she said.

Well, her and this Blackie Rowan go way back, apparently.

Don't doubt that.

Yeah.

Was it okay? she said. Dinner? I don't want you getting in any trouble because—

It's fine, he said.

Really? she said.

Yeah, he said. Talk about a cat among the pigeons. I miss the old days.

Grace was quiet.

Hon? he said.

Me too, she said.

What's the matter? he said.

Nothing. Grace rolled away. Can we turn out the light now?

Thought we were talkin?

I'm tired.

Grace—

Don't, Jim, she said.

Don't what?

Can we just go to sleep?

What's the matter? he said.

Nothing is the matter, she said.

They stared into the hard silence until they slept.

———

Deke called a late pilots' meeting to discuss launch preparations for Wally's flight the next day.

Take the T-33s, Deke said. Get down there tonight. Each of you has a room at the Holiday Inn, Cocoa Beach. The manager, Henri Landwirth, is expecting you. I'll see you down there.

The Astronaut Office kept a fleet of aircraft—T-33 Shooting Stars, mainly; a few F-102s—for when they were needed on short notice halfway across the country. The pilots also used the airplanes to keep up their proficiency and would take them into the sky as often as they could. Plus, there was extra pay. The men complained that the 102s, on loan from the air force, were barely capable of going supersonic, topping out on a good day at about Mach one point two five, like some beaten-up old hatchback. Deke reassured them he was working on procuring a few Delta Darts, the kind of airplane you could really fly balls-out.

Around the table, the men started to collect their things.

Hey, Jim, Conrad said as they stood. You spoke to Rathmann yet?

Sure have, Harrison said. When we were at the Cape for the prelaunch training. Fixed me up real good.

What color you go for?

Powder blue.

Nice.

You want to see it? It's out back.

You can do that?

Do what?

Park there?

Yeah.

Aw, hell. I've been parking over at the—never mind. Listen, I can't; I gotta run, but let's take em out when we get back, go for a little rat-run, yeah?

Sounds good.

See you at the Cape, Conrad said, slipping out the door.

Jim, Deke said. You got a minute?

They were the only two men left in the room.

Listen, Deke said. Marge ran into Grace the other day, down by the lake. Why don't you two come over for dinner one night after we get back?

Sure, Deke, that'd be swell, he said. I'll tell her.

How's she doing?

Fine. Good. Enjoying the house after all those years being fried like an egg out at Edwards.

Yeah, Deke said.

I don't think she can get her head around how many rooms we got now, Harrison said.

I'm not sure any of us can.

Yeah.

You know, you're one of the best pilots in this group, Jim, Deke said.

Sure appreciate that, Deke, he said.

Deke grunted.

Guess I better go home and pack, Harrison said.

Just take care of yourself. I'll see you down there.

Thanks, Deke.

Harrison turned the key and gunned the Corvette's big block V8 engine. Not bad for a buck a year, he thought. Conrad had put him on to a guy named James Rathmann, a General Motors auto dealer twenty miles south of Cocoa Beach. Grissom and Shepard had met him at a party, become friends. Ever since, any of the fellas could lease any Chevy they wanted from him at a dollar a year. Rathmann, an Indy 500 winner, was good pals with Ed Cole, who ran Chevrolet. They liked to cut loose and race the boys along A1A, tearing up the asphalt then shooting the breeze with the astronauts after. It made them feel pretty good.

The early fall rain fell hard as clouds murmured throaty rumbles above Houston's low buildings. The tall ones were lost, slunk into the murky wet gray. Harrison drove home on dark roads slick with water that sprayed from his tires. He pulled up outside and silenced the engine. It shuddered and stopped. He looked at his watch. Almost four. He sighed. He'd be in the air soon, above all this. He sometimes wished he could stay up there. He got out of the car. It was gloomy outside. The house looked dark. He hoped Grace wasn't caught out in the rain. He slid his key into the front door and stepped into the hall.

You look wet, Grace said.

Harrison frowned, and looked around.

Why are all the curtains shut? he said.

Guess I didn't get round to opening them, she said. Not much point now, I suppose.

Busy day? he said.

She shrugged and sat back down on the sofa.

Looks like you didn't get round to dressing either, he said.

Grace looked down at her pink gown.

Milo doesn't mind, she said.

Jesus, he said. What if someone comes to the door?

No one comes to the door, she said.

What's gotten into you?

Nothing.

You haven't been out today?

It's hardly dog-walking weather.

He looked at Milo, who looked miserable.

What's going on? he said.

Nothing's going on, she said. What's the difference anyway? You only ever see me in bed these days.

The program—

Yeah, I know about the goddamn program, she said.

The program, he said, is just getting started. Honey, we've all just got here. There's a hell of a lot to learn. It means I might not be around as much as I was before.

Because you were around a lot then, right?

I have a job to do.

No, you have a job you want to do.

You enjoying the house? The food?

I enjoyed it when we had nothing.

You enjoyed living out in the middle of the goddamn desert with only the Joshua trees for company? You enjoyed the sandstorms and the porch steps you had to stretch over in case they snapped?

I miss our home.

This is our home.

This is not our home. I want to go back.

You want to go back? You can't go back. You want me to tell Deke, sorry Deke, I've changed my mind? You want me to tell the president? Sorry, Jack, my wife misses the goddamn Joshua trees! You want me to be the astronaut that never flew? And what do you suppose the guys back at Edwards would say about that? Oh, they'd have some fun with that, let me tell you. No. My career would be *finished*. And I'd be a national joke. This is our life now.

This is our life? she said. No, Jim, this is *your* life. Your choice. You didn't even talk to me about—

Because you would have said no!

You're goddamned right I would have said no! But I would have gone with you. I would have come. But you lied. Didn't you? You lied to me about where you were when they interviewed you, when they did their tests. You said you were in Seattle. You lied. To me.

Honey, I—

Did you even say good-bye to her?

What?

Did you even go and see her?

Harrison stared at Grace.

Did you? she said.

She's not there, Grace, all right? When are you gonna realize that? She's *not there*!

Jim—

Grace started to cry.

She's gone, okay, Grace? She's *gone*!

Can you not even say her name? Grace said through her tears.

Just get the hell away from me, he said, backing up.

Jim—

I need to pack a bag.

Where you going?

It's Wally's flight tomorrow, he said. I'm going to the Cape.

He went upstairs and she fell into the sofa and sobbed. When he came down, she was sitting up at the breakfast bar with a glass of milk.

Jim, she said.

He looked at her from the hallway. Then he turned and left.

———

The men met in Henri's, in the basement of the Holiday Inn. It was dark and cool. Small lights lit bottles of brown, deep red and yellow on the shelves behind the bar. Harrison sat down and ordered a whiskey sour and pulled his cigarettes from his shirt pocket.

Got a match? he said to Cooper, who sat next to him.

I got a lighter? Gordo said.

That'll do.

Gordo flipped the lid and struck a flame that spat and flickered in the low light.

Thanks.

The two men heard a boisterous laugh somewhere behind them. It was Wally, maintaining an even strain.

At this rate, Gordo said, they might as well wheel him straight out to the tower and strap him in.

Harrison laughed.

He'd still do a better job than Carpenter did on the last flight.

Jesus, that was like the Bay of Pigs in space, Harrison said.

Tell me about it, Gordo said. What the hell happened to the holy notion of *operational*?

Beats me, Harrison said. Guess that's what happens when you put up a deep-sea diver.

You shoulda heard Kraft in the Control Center. He was *in-candescent*. Actually stood up and yelled, *that sonofabitch will never fly for me again!* I thought his goddamn eyeballs were gonna pop.

Well, there you go, Harrison said.

Yeah.

Jeez.

The bartender brought over his whiskey sour and Harrison thanked him and took a mouthful.

Say, Gordo said. Fancy comin water-skiing after the launch tomorrow?

Sure.

Great, Gordo said. We can do a little trout fishin after. Cocoa Beach is the goddamn saltwater trout capital of the world.

Sounds good.

Harrison pulled at the end of his cigarette then pushed it into a nearby ashtray.

I gotta split, Gordo said. Got me a little date later.

Later? Harrison said. It's almost midnight.

It sure is, Jimmy, he said, smiling. It sure is.

Gordo slid off his stool and went up to his room to shower. Harrison ordered another whiskey sour and walked over to where Deke and Gus were talking under a painting of a Polaris missile surrounded by green palms. Before he reached them, he heard a voice call out behind him.

Well, shit. If it ain't Jim Harrison, former pilot.

I know that voice, Harrison said, turning around. Joseph Walker, cowboy of the west. What brings you out here to the future?

Ho ho, Walker said as the men shook hands. Hell, I just wanted to be in the same room as an astronaut.

Harrison smiled.

Naw, Walker said, NASA just gave me a coupla days off to see the launch. Gonna be quite a show, by all accounts.

You wanna drink?

Still workin my way through this one, Walker said, holding up a bottle of beer.

You call that a drink? Harrison said. Come with me. He walked back to the bar.

Two old-fashioneds, he said to the bartender,

Nice, Walker said.

Seemed appropriate, Harrison said. It's good to see you, Joe.

Place ain't the same without you, Walker said.

That so.

Damn sight safer, for one.

Thought I'd give some of the other fellas a chance to do some proper test work.

Real generous of you, Jim.

Well I'm a generous guy.

How's Grace? Walker said.

She's good. How's Pancho?

Still pissed at you.

Well, I'm not gonna change that anytime soon. Maybe they'll let me name a crater after her or something.

This really happening, ain't it?

Yeah.

First lunar landing, Walker said. That's the ultimate flight test. Y'know, if I was younger, I might have applied myself.

A girl approached them from a tight circle of friends who watched from the end of the bar.

Walker looked at Harrison, then laughed.

Howdy fellas, she said.

Howdy, Harrison said.

My name's Lucy, she said.

Pleasure, Harrison said.

Nice to meet you, Walker said.

Are you an astronaut too? Lucy said.

Joe's the best test pilot you'll ever meet, Harrison said.

When you going up? Lucy said to Harrison. He glanced at Walker.

Soon, he said.

Yeah? she said.

You live round here? he said.

For now, she said. Wanna come to a party?

Maybe later.

Well, all right then.

Okay.

Okay.

She smiled and slipped back to her friends who looked over at him and bowed their heads and giggled and he sighed and turned back to his drink.

Holy moly, Walker said. Maybe I should've signed up after all.

Let's go get some air, Harrison said.

The next morning, the nine rookies were up before dawn. Henri always made sure his kitchen was well stocked with steak and eggs and coffee—a pilot's breakfast. Wally had left at midnight for the crew quarters up at Hangar S. Deke had gone with him. The tradition, formed after only four flights, saw Deke wake the slumbering astronaut on the morning of the flight and take him to breakfast with Walt Williams, Bob Gilruth and Marvin Hoffman, the flight surgeon. Then the astronaut would get suited up, taken out to the pad and inserted into the spacecraft.

Jolly Wally had been laughing and joking and lollygagging it up all morning. He gave off the aura of a man about to go on a fishing trip, not into space. Even after they sealed him into the capsule, he was still Wallying around. Then they lit the fuse and blasted him into space.

Schirra stayed in beercall buddy mode all the way up. He'd named his spacecraft *Sigma 7* and would make six orbits to Carpenter's three; the objective to use half as much fuel and land on target. Carpenter, distracted by experiments, had gotten behind on his checklist, wasted fuel, almost fried on reentry and landed two hundred and fifty miles off-target. It was a near-fatal fuckup; some were even saying he'd *panicked*. Schirra was determined to show the world that a real pilot could still hang his hide on the line the old-fashioned way and coolly bring it home; a real operational flight test. And he did exactly that. Everyone from the flight director down celebrated that night in downtown Cocoa Beach, then poolside at the Holiday Inn. There were so many of them, with contractors, support staff, the contractors' support staff and NASA personnel, it felt like they were an occupying force celebrating a victorious invasion. Even Von Braun's German rocket team were out, knocking back pilsner and *Glühwein* and singing *Oh du lieber Augustin* long into the hot night.

When Harrison woke the next morning he swung his legs out of bed, lit a cigarette and called Grace.

Are you okay? he said.

Yeah, she said. You?

Yeah, he said. Sorry about before.

It's okay, she said. Me too.

He said he wouldn't be home for a few more days, perhaps even a couple of weeks.

A couple of weeks? she said.

Uh yeah, he said. Deke wants us to get familiar with operations while we're down here; Von Braun came down for the launch too, so we gotta go meet him as well.

Jim, a couple of weeks though . . .

Probably be more like a week, no more. Don't worry about it.

That's easy for you to say. Guess I'll see you, then.

Don't be like that, he said.

I need you here, she said.

Kennedy—

I know what John Kennedy said, she said.

We've only got seven years, he said.

Sure sounds like a long time, she said.

Not if you want to travel a quarter million miles into space, it isn't, he said.

Guess I should be thankful you're only in Florida.

I miss you, he said.

I miss you too, she said.

I'll be home before you know it, he said. Enjoy the peace and quiet. Enjoy having the place to yourself.

Sure, Grace said.

Invite the girls over, he said. Maybe do a dinner.

Good idea.

Okay then.

What about clothes?

I'll pick up some new stuff down here.

Okay.

I'd better go, he said. I'll call you tomorrow.

Okay then. Bye, she said.

Bye, he said.

In Houston, she put down the telephone and sat thinking for a minute, then got up and walked into the garden. She walked around and around, circling the perimeter, then sat down on the grass and cried.

———

Harrison was in Wolfie's, in downtown Cocoa Beach, when he heard the news. It had been a good morning. Deke had called an unscheduled pilots' meeting first thing. The conversation was lively as the men took their seats around the table and waited for him. Consensus was, he was going to announce the crew selections.

Gentlemen, good morning, Deke said, walking into the room. Let's get to it. First thing. If I have a guy, and I keep him around, he's eligible to fly. That's it. Second, there are no *copilots* here. We have commanders, and we have pilots.

Harrison smiled.

All astronauts are created equal, Deke said. But some are more equal than others. And I gotta plan long-term. Fellas, we're going all-up now. We don't have time for Von Braun's baby steps, so we're getting rid of any dead-end equipment and tests. Coupla things before we go on. Glenn's out of the running.

He retire already? Gordo said.

A few laughs.

Kennedy's not gonna let him go up again, Deke continued, so he won't be flying Gemini. Neither will Carpenter.

A few more laughs.

So that's you nine, plus you Gordo, plus Wally and Gus.

What about Shepard? Borman said.

Grounded, Deke said.

The men exchanged glances.

You serious? Conrad said.

Serious as hell. Doctor says he can't fly. He's been having some problems with dizziness since May. Turns out he's got something called Ménière's disease. It's an inner ear problem. He's out, at least for now. But who knows.

Shit, Borman said.

We gotta do something, for Al, Conrad said.

Already did, Deke said. I've given him my old job. He's now in charge of the Astronaut Office. I've resigned my commission from the air force and I'm now a civilian employee of NASA. Assistant director for Flight Crew Operations.

Deke? Harrison said.

General LeMay grounded me permanently because of this god-damn heart thing, so I quit. If I wanna go up someday, I gotta keep flyin. And as a civilian, I can fly NASA aircraft, as long as I've got a qualified copilot with me. And as long as that copilot isn't Al.

More laughter.

That's as good as I'm gonna get for now, he said. I'll be keeping up my astronaut training with you fellas; see what the next few years bring. So. The first manned Gemini missions: Grissom-Young. We need to find out if a manned spacecraft can maneuver in space. Backup crew: Schirra and Stafford. That's Gemini III. The first two will be unmanned tests. Next up, Gemini IV: McDivitt-White. We're thinking, first EVA. Ed, you fancy taking a walk in space?

Guess I could give it a try, White said, folding his arms behind his head and sitting back.

You'll have Borman and Lovell backing you up, Deke said. Gemini V, first week-long flight. Cooper and Conrad. A hundred and twenty orbits. Guidance and navigation. Backup: Harrison and Armstrong. Gemini VI, first rendezvous in space—we can't land on the moon without it. We'll be using an unmanned Agena that we'll send up in advance. Give us something to rendezvous with. Schirra and Stafford; backup Grissom and Young. Gemini VII, long duration. Fourteen days in space. Borman and Lovell. That's gonna be tough. Two weeks in a tin can with Frank.

Hey! Borman said.

All that, Deke said, is subject to change. We're in the middle of selecting a third group of astronauts—fourteen more pilots—so we'll come back to crew selections for the remaining missions after that. Bobby Kennedy wants a black astronaut, but we can't find a black pilot that's good enough. It's not racist, just the way things are. A pilot either has it or he doesn't. Nothing else matters. If anyone asks you about it, or mentions the name Ed Dwight to you, tell em to speak to me. Now. What else? Gemini is a manned system, start to finish. Laid out the way a pilot likes things. Gus did that, working with McDonnell. You can buy him a beer. That's it, gentlemen, except for this: the program doesn't need a scandal. I don't give a damn what a pilot does in his spare time; if he plays around or not is his business. It's not my concern unless it affects his work. Which is what a messy divorce would do. Land yourselves one of them and it's a one-way ticket back to wherever you came from. It's not a moral thing, it's not a PR thing, it's a practical thing. I don't want anything distracting you from your job. Now, that all said, what say we head down to Wolfie's and grab a bite?

It was Lovell who first noticed that something was wrong. The men sat at a long table drinking beer and eating sandwiches. Wolfie's had a radio, usually tuned to WXBR. But the music had stopped.

Listen, he said to Harrison, holding up a finger. That's Kennedy, isn't it?

Harrison stopped eating and listened.

Yeah, John Young said. Hang on.

He called over to Stan, the owner, standing behind the counter.

What's goin on? Young said.

You haven't heard? Stan said.

Heard what?

Stan came over. Cuba, he said. Last night.

What about Cuba? Harrison said.

Come out back, Stan said. I got a television. You'd better see for yourselves.

The men left their lunch and followed Stan through a set of doors near the back, through a minuscule kitchen into a small office with no window where a woman sat hunched over thick scarlet accounting books, smoking and sighing to herself. He turned on the set and changed it to NBC.

Hold on, he said. They've been playing it all morning.

They just had it, the woman said. I turned it off. Try ABC.

Stan turned the dial round and the president appeared on the screen.

. . . *policy of this nation to regard any nuclear missile launched from Cuba against any nation in the Western Hemisphere as an attempt by the Soviet Union on the United States, requiring a full retaliatory response upon the Soviet Union.*

Jesus Christ, Harrison said. What happened?

Soviets installed nuclear missiles in Cuba, the woman said. In secret. Weren't you listening? A U-2 spy plane snapped pictures of the damn things.

Cuba's only ninety miles away, Harrison said.

Oh, that's where Cuba is? the woman said. I'd been wondering.

Holy shit, Borman said.

You see? Stan said.

How the hell did no one call us, Deke said. Gilruth must have known. We must be at DEFCON 3, at least.

To halt this offensive buildup, a strict quarantine—

What the hell's a quarantine? Borman said.

—on all offensive military equipment—

Fancy way of saying blockade, Conrad said.

Legal way of saying blockade, Lovell said.

—under shipment to Cuba is being initiated.

When did this go out? Harrison said.

Seven last night, Stan said.

All ships bound for Cuba will, if found to contain cargoes of offensive weapons, be turned back.

Something tells me these ships ain't gonna stop for some blockade line, Conrad said.

Damn right, Young said.

Why the hell aren't we launching a strike against them? Borman said. Christ, did that kid not learn anything from his father?

Jack Kennedy's got a cool head on him, Harrison said. And his brother's a smart guy. I need to make a phone call.

Yeah, me too, Conrad said. The others nodded.

Thanks, Stan, Young said.

Don't mention it, fellas.

They shuffled out.

Finally, said the woman as Stan pulled the door shut behind him.

Back at the Holiday Inn, Harrison tried calling Grace, but she wasn't in. It was hot. He stunk. He sat for a moment, then stood and changed his shirt. Then he went down to the bar. He called again early evening.

Hello? Grace said.

Hey, he said. It's me.

Jim, she said.

I called earlier but you weren't in.

Where the hell have you been?

Where have *I* been? Where have you been?

I've been trying to get ahold of you since last night!

What? I've been right here. Who did you speak to?

I don't know—some woman.

Well that makes things easier.

She didn't say and why would I ask? She told me you weren't staying there.

Harrison sighed.

Henri's given us our own rooms; we're off the guest booking sheets. What time did you call?

Right after the broadcast, she said. About seven-thirty.

We were downstairs, he said. I'm sorry. I'll sort this. We only just found out. I called as soon as I got back.

I'm scared half to death, Jim, she said.

I'm coming home, he said.

Really? she said. When?

We all are. First thing.

Thank God. Jim, she said. I haven't been doing too good.

Are you sick?

I don't know.

Well, you're either sick or you're not.

Jim—I—can we not do this now?

Grace—

Please. Just come home.

I already said I'm coming home.

Please, Jim.

What?

Nothing. I miss you.

I miss you too. Sorry it's been a couple of days.

Are you okay? she said.

Yeah, we've just been so busy. And we just got our crew assignments.

That's good, she said. Do you want to tell me now?

I'll tell you when I get home, he said.

Okay.

I'd better get packed, he said. I'll see you tomorrow, okay?

Jim? she said.

Yeah?

I love you.

I love you too, he said. Everything is going to be okay.

Okay, she said.

Stay in the house. Don't go out unless you have to. Keep the radio on. I'll be home real soon.

The following night they sat together on the sofa and watched news reports of the blockade and of the ships turning around and of the *Marucla*, which didn't, and were frightened. They went to bed and didn't talk. When he was sure she was asleep he turned onto his back and stared at the ceiling which was white from where the curtain cracked in the middle and let pale moonlight in. He lay awake for a long time. It felt to him as though the world had paused. The only sound was that of his wife sleeping alongside him. He realized with acute clarity that the past was nothing, it did not exist; it could not be *lost*, and the future was merely an abstract concept. He lay very still. Then he turned over and slept till morning and in the morning he rose early and dressed quietly and went for a run in the rain. When he got home she had fixed a pot of coffee, and eggs, and they sat together and listened to the radio in silence. Then he left for work.

In the evening he took her out to the pool and said sorry for how things had been and they held each other. Then they went inside and Harrison called a few friends he had higher in the air force who told him the country was now at DEFCON 2. He told her what it meant and she sat down at the table with her head in her hands.

I'm going for a walk, she said. I need to get some air.

Don't go far, okay? he said.

I won't.

Want me to come?

No.

Do you want to take Milo?

No.

When she got back he said, where did you go, and she didn't answer so he asked again and she said Clear Lake. They sat up and watched the news on CBS and Grace asked him what DEFCON 1 was and he said *nuclear war imminent* and she said I wish I hadn't asked.

What can we do? she said. We must be able to do something.

Nothing. There's nothing we can do. Except wait it out.

And pray. We can pray.

He thought for a second then said, yes, we could pray. So they sat closer together and shut their eyes and Grace said a prayer which lasted no longer than a minute.

Let's go to bed, he said, afterward. No sense staying up waiting for something to happen.

They went to bed and lay together in silence and he found himself thinking on his daughter's grave and he didn't know why. He thought of something else, of McNamara, of Sorensen, of Bobby; men like him, no different, all breathing the same air as him, dressing in the mornings as he did, all lying in dark rooms wondering what tomorrow would bring. He felt uneasy and hot and he couldn't get comfortable. He shut his eyes. He saw the cemetery, the grass, the stone angel on the tomb near the gate. He felt short of breath. He tried to think of something else, but he couldn't get the image out of his mind. He sat up and turned the light on. His back and legs were wet from where he was sweating. He smoked a cigarette and tapped the ash into a tray he balanced on his chest. When he'd finished, he moved the tray back to his bedside table, turned out the light and pulled Grace closer to him. She slid her feet between his and he fell asleep.

First light was cool and gray.

Do you want some coffee? Grace said, getting out of bed.

That'd be good, he said. Guess the world's still here.

She let out a little laugh.

Maybe it's just us? he said.

If it is, she said, I'm taking you to Hawaii.

How would we get there?

You could fly us.

They went downstairs and read the morning paper together over breakfast.

Anything new? Grace said.

Yeah, he said. Emergency meeting of the Security Council last night. I always thought Stevenson was a sorry sonofabitch but it turns out he's got some balls after all. Asked Zorin about the missiles straight out. Zorin refused to answer. Then Stevenson said he was prepared to wait til hell froze over for an answer! Told Zorin he'd present the evidence himself if he continued to ignore the question.

What happened? Grace said.

They set up an easel at the back of the room and showed everyone the photographs—look.

He showed her the picture in the paper.

Three photos, he said. One twenty-four-hour period.

The Cubans built all that in a day? she said.

Well, they had plenty of help from their Red friends, he said.

Jesus.

There's more, Harrison said. Lots more. Read the rest of it, right there. Those goddamn lying Soviet bastards.

And this was yesterday? she said, reading.

Yeah, he said, pouring himself another coffee.

She folded the paper and sighed.

Listen, Jim, she said. I need to talk to you.

Can it wait? he said, glancing up at the clock.

You're not going in again are you?

Damn right I'm going in.

Jim, please; I need you here. Who the hell knows what'll happen?

I have to, he said.

I'm your wife and I'm asking you to stay.

I have to go in.

The program's more important than me?

Jesus, Grace.

Is the program more important than me?

Come on.

Answer the goddamn question!

Yes, he said. The program's more important than you.

You son of a bitch, she said.

Grace—

No. Screw you.

Listen a minute, would you. This isn't about you or flyin anymore. This is about *them* and *us*. Look at this, he said, picking up the newspaper and tossing it down. *Look* at it. We can't afford to lose.

This—all this—we're at *war*. And we have to beat the Soviets. We have to dominate. We have to win. And I have to work.

———

Harrison sat at his desk and read through his memos. Rain hammered against the mottled glass window behind him. Deke had assigned each of the Nine an area of specialization. Harrison got Guidance and Navigation, which was better than Boosters or Recovery. McDonnell was falling behind building the Gemini spacecraft. Grissom had been directed to oversee the work full-time up at the McDonnell plant in St. Louis. The first unmanned flight was just thirteen months away, in December, sixty-three. Harrison doubted they could deliver on time. He sighed, lit a cigarette, sat back. He was tired. He'd slept badly. He thought back to the craziness of the previous day and then an unrelated thought, generated by some foreign part of his mind, appeared, and the thought was of Florence's frail body in the ground.

Jesus! He sat up, coughing on the smoke in his lungs. His forehead pimpled with sweat. He shook his head, as if to physically dislodge the thought from his consciousness, but it wouldn't shift. How could he think that? Jesus Christ. What the hell kind of person was he? He tried to think of something else, but couldn't; it snapped back. It moved from thought to image; vague to detailed. Christ! He rubbed his face and cried out in horror. He stood up and walked around the room. His hands trembled. He sweated harder. There was a knock on his door.

Shit.

It was Lovell.

Yeah, Harrison said.

Hey, Jim, Lovell said. Do you—are you all right?

Huh?

You look awful.

Oh, yeah, thanks, I'm fine; just tired.

Listen, can I show you something? Lovell said.

Yeah, Jim, sure, Harrison said. Just—could you give me a minute?

Sure thing. Come find me.

Lovell left. Harrison wiped his brow. His gut felt liquid. He walked fast to the men's room, locked himself in a cubicle, tried to focus on what Lovell might want with him.

When he got home that night he went straight upstairs and sat on the bed and loosened his tie. The rest of his day had passed without incident. Lovell's interruption had been enough to knock him back to reality. His mind kept drifting back to what had happened, but he sensed danger in dwelling on the specifics, so he hauled it in and focused on the present. He went down to the kitchen.

Honey? he said.

Outside, she said from the patio.

What you doing out here? he said, joining her. It's miserable.

Thinking, she said.

He took off his tie and sat down.

How you been? he said. Good day?

I went over to Sue Borman's for coffee.

All the wives?

She nodded.

What's the matter?

Ugh, it's terrible, Jim, just . . . awful.

Awful?

It's all so . . . phony. I hate it. I guess the relief of leaving flight test has worn off for everyone and been replaced with the holy terror of the *launch*. And the subsequent thought of three dead husbands circling the moon forever. No one will talk about it though. Not even with each other. I want to shake them and say, my God, who *else* are you gonna talk to? They do this stupid skit—Rene came up with it—she calls it the *Squarely Stable* routine. I guess it was meant to be funny, keep everyone's spirits up from dealing with the press—and maybe it was the first time—but they do it *every* time and it's driving me crazy.

Grace stood up and held her fist to her mouth, as though holding a microphone, and started acting out Rene Carpenter impersonating a television correspondent they called Nancy Whoever.

We're here in front of the trim, modest suburban home of Squarely Stable, the famous astronaut, who has just completed his historic mission, and we have here with us his attractive wife, Primly Stable. Primly Stable, you must be happy and proud, and thankful at this moment.

Grace's tone shifted slightly.

Yes, Nancy, that's true. I'm happy, proud, and thankful at this moment.

Grace continued.

Tell us, Primly Stable—may I call you Primly?

Why, certainly, Nancy.

Tell us, Primly, tell us what you felt during the blastoff, at the very moment when your husband's rocket began to rise from the Earth and take him on this historic journey.

Honey, Harrison said.

To tell you the truth, Nancy, I missed that part of it. I sort of dozed off, because I got up so early this morning and I've been rushing around taping the shades shut so the TV people wouldn't come in the windows.

Okay, Harrison said. I get it.

Well, would you say you had a lump in your throat as big as a tennis ball?

That's about the size of it, Nancy, I had a lump in my throat as big as a tennis ball.

And finally, Primly, I know that the most important prayer of your life has already been answered: Squarely has returned safely from outer space. But if you could have one other wish at this moment and have it come true, what would it be?

Well, Nancy, I'd wish for an Electrolux vacuum cleaner with all the at-tachments.

Grace lowered her fist.

And then they roll about laughing for the next ten minutes, she said.

Harrison grunted. Grace sat down and said, all I want to say to the press when they ask me how I feel is, nobody cared before, so why the hell bother now? I wish Pancho was here. I wish she was at Sue Borman's goddamn coffee mornings.

She'd sure put them in their place, he said.

Grace sighed. Her heart sunk low in her chest.

I miss her, she said.

They shot down a U-2 over Cuba today, he said.

I don't care, she said.

He noticed the envelope on the table for the first time.

What's that? he said.

It came this morning, she said.

Can we go in? It's freezing out here, he said.

Sure.

They went inside.

What is it? he said.

She handed him the envelope. He opened it.

I don't get it? he said.

It's a thousand-dollar gift certificate to Neiman-Marcus, she said. It's a fashion store downtown.

Who sent you this?

She gave a little laugh that was sad and ironic and bitter all at the same time.

It's a gift from an anonymous priest, she said. We all got one. The nine of us.

Why the hell would a priest—

So we can afford the right clothes, she said. The right clothes for the society parties, the drinks receptions, the press conferences, the launches.

You're kidding me? he said.

Wish I was, she said.

Jesus, he said. That's a little odd.

A little odd? she said. A little odd? A so-called priest giving me a thousand bucks to go shopping? Yeah, Jim, I'd say that was a little goddamn odd. On the upside, I can now buy dresses I don't like for parties I despise. A black backless number, maybe? Some feathers and sequins? Some daytime attire from Yves Saint Laurent? Because that's what's missing from my life? I'm sick of it, Jim—I hate it; I hate this. I miss the desert; the wilderness. I want to ride a horse if I want, or take a walk with earth not concrete under my feet. And this, this is the worst kind of suburbia. This has been *created*. There's nothing authentic about any of it, apart from the goddamn lake, and that's one giant goddamn oil slick. I'm sorry, Jim; I want to go back.

You just want to go back so you can visit the Rosamond Park Cemetery every day, he said.

Jesus, she said. You still can't say her name, can you? It's *Florence. Florence!*

He didn't say anything.

And she's dead because the cobalt killed her, Grace said.

It was the only option left! There wasn't anything else we—

Yes there was! she said. Nothing. We could have done nothing. And if we had, she could have gone on, she could still—

Nothing? How could we have done *nothing*?

That's the thing with you, Jim, she said. You've always got to be doing *something*. Even if it means—

She broke off.

What? he said.

What the hell does it matter.

We had *no choice*! Harrison said.

There is *always* a choice! Grace said.

So it's my fault, is it? My fault she's—

He hesitated.

It was a decision we made *together*, he said.

You sure about that? she said. Duck would be three and a half now.

Don't, he said.

Don't what? Talk about it? You want me to be like you? Do you have any idea what it was like—what it *is* like—being married to you? You left me on my own to deal with it! You never *ever* talked to me. You *never* talked about it.

Doesn't mean I didn't—

I know that, she said. I know it devastated you. It broke you. I could see it. I could tell. I knew how much you loved her. I know.

His face was wet.

You shut yourself off, she said. You went straight back to work. That hurt me so much. I needed you . . . desperately. I was so angry. You knew that. You just kept as far away from it as you could. You kept away from me.

Tears fell silently down his face.

I can't stay here, she said. I want to go back. I want to go home.

I can't go back, he said.

But I can't stay here, she said. I know the program needs the perfect marriage. So I'm just gonna go. You can tell Deke whatever you want. Tell him I'm sick. I owe you that much.

Harrison didn't say anything.

I'm going to stay in a hotel downtown tonight, she said. I booked it after I got back from Sue's. Tomorrow I'm flying to LA. Grace

Walker is picking me up from the airport. Air force hasn't leased the house to anyone yet, so I'm going back. They'll be happy to get it off their hands again. I miss our home. I miss my friends. And I miss my little girl. I feel close to her there. I like being surrounded by her life. I'll call you in a few weeks.

He didn't say anything.

I've got a bag, she said. It's in the guest room.

She went to get it. Then she left.

———

The next day, a deal was reached; Khrushchev and Kennedy talked under the table. Grace had taken Milo, and he was alone. He spent the morning rearranging his office. There was too much clutter. He tidied stationery into drawers, filed away paperwork. The filing system was inconsistent and it made him uneasy. He instructed his secretary to deal with it when he was gone. He was due in Baltimore that afternoon for a tour of the Martin Company, who were assembling the Titan II rockets for Gemini. He unpinned the photograph of Grace from the corkboard on the wall and put it in the middle drawer of his desk underneath a technical report on the feasibility of landing the Gemini spacecraft on a dry lake using a paraglider. Who wanted to be churning around on the swells waiting for a bunch of goddamn swabbos to come unbuckle you? Plus keeping most of the US Navy on active standby for the length of the mission was incredibly expensive. It would be a hell of a thing to set foot on the moon only to drown in the stinking sea of the Atlantic as soon as you made it back to Mother Earth. Imagine that. He didn't like to. He pulled everything else from the corkboard and put it in his drawer with the picture. Then he cleared off his desk. It was hot. He buzzed his secretary.

Maggie, he said. Is the goddamn air on?

Maggie poked her head in.

Sorry, Jim, what was that?

What's the point of having an intercom if you're just going to come in anyway? Is the AC on?

I believe so, she said.

Okay then, he said.

Are you all right?

I'm fine. I'm going to Baltimore.

Poor you.

Yeah, he said. I need to speak to Deke when I get back. Could you get me the first five minutes he has?

Of course, Maggie said.

No—wait, Harrison said. Scratch that. I'll catch up with him in Sacramento.

Any advance on that? she said.

No, he said, I—

A thought hit him hard.

What? she said.

Shit.

Jim?

Wait! he said. Sorry. Could you, uh, just give me a minute? Sorry.

She pulled the door shut. He fell back on his desk, leaning against it, sweating, through his face, his hands, the back of his legs. *What if Grace was right?* What if it *was* his fault? No, they had come to the decision together. *You sure about that?* He remembered them sitting by Duck's hospital bed as she slept. He remembered Lapitus leaving them to talk. He'd been so tired; so tired he could barely function. What had they said to each other? How had they decided? He couldn't remember. *Shit shit shit.* He shut his eyes tight. Something about reaching the end of the line—or had he imagined that?

Duck being strong. What had they said? He couldn't remember. *C'mon, c'mon.* He felt something. Then it was gone. What the hell was it? He rubbed his face with his hands. *Decisiveness.* Why had he felt suddenly decisive, f'chrissakes? He tried to experience the feeling again. His recall triggered a memory: Duck's bedside, Lapitus gone, talking to Grace, feeling *decisive.* Lapitus, his voice; that hospital, its empty hallways. He suddenly saw the janitor; his slow gait, that steel bucket, loping along the hallway as Lapitus talked about cobalt for the first time.

Fear held Harrison hard.

That was it—right there!—watching the janitor walk away. He'd thought, *if it comes down to it.* He *had* decided. Alone! Right there in the goddamn hallway! Jesus Christ. *A measure of last resort!* He'd decided, he'd talked to Grace, he'd given Lapitus the go-ahead, despite Lapitus saying she wouldn't be able to take it. *He'd decided.* Without discussion, without deliberation—because, because—*why?* Why had he done that? He pushed further into himself. Because he liked being in control; because—*yes, go on, say it you sonofabitch*—because *being in control makes you feel good*—no, worse—*because it makes you feel important.* Jesus Christ. He had killed her. He had killed his own daughter. Because of his ego. His heart wailed. A new thought invaded his mind—his hands around his daughter's neck, crushing her windpipe, squeezing the life out of her. In the office, he cried out, pushing his fingers to his forehead, trying to rid himself of the intrusion, the thought, but it came back, again and again and again, each time with more power. And now she was looking up at him, in pain, in horror, at what he was doing. No, he cried. No!

His heart tried to bust out of his rib cage and his body was a hundred and sixty pounds of panic.

Maggie buzzed him. He looked up at the door.

Not now! he yelled. Blood beat in his ears. Had she heard? Would she come in? His legs were numb. He held onto his desk, walking around it, then sat in his chair, feeling dizzy. His mouth was dry.

The door opened.

Jim?

Maggie, he said. Uh, sorry. Come in.

It's okay, she said. It can wait. God, you still look peaky. Let me get you some water. You never drink enough water. Hold on.

She disappeared and he pulled at his clothes where they were stuck to his skin. He wiped his face and ran his fingers through his hair. Maggie returned with a tall glass of water.

Here you go, she said.

He took the glass and drank it in one long gulp.

Better? she said.

He nodded.

See? she said.

And he did feel better. His pulse slowed to a steady thump. His head felt clear, but his mind tugged at the thoughts he'd had. Maggie cut them off.

Look, if you feel well enough, go to Baltimore, she said. If not, go home. We're not going to the moon this afternoon.

I'm fine, he said. I'm going to Baltimore.

He gathered his things and left.

They had rooms at the Lord Baltimore, a twenty-three-story hotel housed in a French Renaissance building that once hid a speakeasy in the basement. The tour of Martin had been productive. The Titan II was on track. The engineers were doing solid work. Good job too; it would be his ass on the line soon enough.

Harrison dropped his bag off in his room and went down to the bar. The soft Art Deco golds and browns and reds soothed his eyes. He ordered a scotch, which soothed him further. The others were still upstairs, in their rooms, taking showers. He hadn't bothered. Deke appeared from an elevator and Harrison waved him over.

What are you doing here? Harrison said.

Last-minute meeting with Larry about the booster. I'll have one of them, Deke said to the bartender, pointing at Harrison's glass. The bartender nodded, and walked away.

So what do you think?

Of the scotch? Harrison said.

Of Martin.

They're on schedule. What else is there?

You okay?

Fine, Harrison said. But, look, Deke, I got something I need to tell you.

No good conversation ever started out like that, Deke said.

I was gonna tell you in Houston, but, shit, Deke, he said. Grace has gone back to California.

On vacation?

Permanently.

Right.

Look, I respect you more than anyone around here, so I wanted to be straight with you. I know the program doesn't need a divorce and, hell, it might not even come to that, but, well, it's been a long time comin, I guess. I mean, Christ, I wish it wasn't happening but . . . It's been a tough few years.

Deke didn't say anything. The bartender returned with Deke's scotch.

All we're doing is living apart, Harrison said. Grace told me we could say what we want. Say she's sick; that she's gone back to rest, away from all this. She doesn't care. She was dyin here, Deke.

Look, Deke said, picking up his drink. We're not the morality cops. I just need you focused on the right thing.

And I am, Harrison said.

Good, Deke said. Then that's all there is. That's me talking as your boss. As your friend, I sure am sorry to hear it.

Yeah, Harrison said. She took Milo.

She took the dog?

Yeah. And the goddamn coffee machine too.

The coffee machine?

It was a good one.

I'd like to see someone put that in a blues song.

Glad I'm here to keep you entertained, Harrison said.

Deke looked over at the elevator.

I gotta go, Deke said. Here's Gus.

Harrison looked around and saw Grissom approach them.

Now, Gus here, Deke said. He's a gruff little fella, but he sure knows how to cut loose when called for.

Where you headin? Harrison said.

Gonna find us some fun, Gus said.

You wanna come? Deke said.

I'm gonna sit here, finish this drink, then grab some food with a few of the boys.

Well, okay then, Deke said. Guess I'll see you at the Cape on Tuesday.

Sure thing.

Take it easy, son.

The two men left. Harrison sighed, lit a cigarette, finished his drink. Then he went up to his room, ordered a hamburger, ate half, fell asleep. He had strange dreams. When he woke his legs were half off the bed and someone was knocking at his door. Where the hell was he? What day was it? He sat up, groggy, rubbed his face. There was no one at the door. Maybe he'd dreamt it. He lit a cigarette and walked to the window and looked out. Baltimore fell below. Jeez, he was up high. He hadn't realized. His room was pretty nice too. Was he in one of the penthouse suites? He looked around.

He was. This astronaut business sure had unexpected perks. He drew on his smoke and felt pretty good about himself. *Ego.* It hit him hard. Inside his belly, his gut moaned. *He'd decided. His ego had sentenced her to death.* His guilt crippled him. He felt sick. *Grace was right. She was right about him.* What if *others* found out? The *press?* His face, the headline, MURDERER. Ruin. No way out. One way out. How would he do it? He could jump off the twenty-third floor of a building. Maybe he should do it now? Jesus, no! He wasn't suicidal! Why had he thought those thoughts? Maybe there was something to it? Maybe he *did* want to kill himself? His daughter was dead. His wife had left him. Maybe he'd see Duck again? *He was suicidal!* Panting, sweating, gut heaving, he fell back from the window and locked himself in the bathroom. Stop. Just because he'd had a thought about killing himself didn't mean he'd thought about killing himself. It was just a thought. It just popped into his mind. It wasn't his fault! Jesus Christ. He was going crazy. Maybe he would kill himself? Jesus Christ!

Okay, stop. He held his head in his hands. He replayed the entire sequence of thoughts in his head. He felt worse doing it, but he had to do it, he had to know! If he could hang his hide on the line, day in day out, he could do this. He did it. He was not suicidal. He was sure of that now. He was hot, shaking, exhausted, but felt better.

What time was it? How long had he been in the bathroom? He'd woken at six. He remembered glancing at the time before getting up to see who was at the door. He remembered thinking, *kinda early?* Harrison looked around for his watch. It was in his bag. It was nearly nine. Three hours! That was impossible. His watch must be wrong. There was a small alarm clock by his bed. It said nine. How had three hours passed just thinking about—

The thought of strangling Florence violated his mind. He cried out, but it was too late. He sat on the bed, pushing fingers into his forehead. He would never do that. He sat up, thinking hard. He would *never* do that. He hadn't ever done that, had he? No, Christ, of course not. Don't be ridiculous. He'd decided to start the cobalt treatment though. He'd laid it down, to Lapitus, to Grace. She'd submitted. He remembered now. He went over it again, and again, and again, until his body shook. He'd decided. He'd made Grace agree. *Her body was too weak. She suffered.* It was his fault; it was all his fault.

He showered at eleven and was two hours washing. He ate nothing for lunch. *It was his fault.* Whenever the thought occurred, he would sit on the bed and go over the conversations with Grace, with Lapitus, unable to get up, unable to move on, until he'd reassured himself that the decision to use cobalt was considered, justified, shared. Those moments, that reassurance, he wanted to save, store, for the next time. Often, his concentration would be interrupted by a noise in another room—a flushing toilet, a slamming door—and he'd scream in frustration, having lost his place in the process, and have to start over, often hearing distant knocks or water creaking pipes or another door slam, which would send him back to the beginning again, as though he were climbing an impossibly slippery slide.

It was almost six. He called down, ordered a hamburger. It came at seven, he ate it at eight-thirty, cold. It tasted good. He tried to leave, for the bar, several times. Parts of the suite were now acutely familiar to him, having sat staring at them as he tried to rationalize the distressing thoughts that erupted in his mind with increasing severity. Now, those areas of the room waited, like booby traps, to trigger the original thoughts themselves. At several points he was surprised again by how much time had passed and he'd go over exactly where the time had gone, which meant recalling the original thoughts, which caused him great distress. Sometimes, if this process took time, at the end, he would be surprised by just how much of it had passed, and would go over exactly where *that* time had gone too. He was trapped, by his mind, by the room, by his desperate attempts to feel in control. At times, he would be lost to frustration, then despair, then dealing with thoughts of suicide, and, always, intruding into his conscience, was Florence, and he would hate himself for desecrating her memory.

It was Saturday. He had the room until nine the next morning. He set his alarm and tried to sleep. He was exhausted. He wanted the nightmare to end. He craved unconsciousness. He was now in such a state that images automatically appeared every time he shut his eyes and ridges in the bedsheet reminded him of the weak limbs of a dying child and he cried into his pillow until, at last, he fell asleep, and ten minutes later, at half past seven, he was awoken by his alarm.

———

He flew commercial back to Houston. His body was a wreck, but he felt a little better. Something about sleep—even ten minutes of it—had erased the loop he'd got stuck in. He didn't think about it. That much he was able to do now. He focused on the program. On his work. He slept in the cab from the airport to the house. Later that night, he picked up the telephone and dialed the Happy Bottom Riding Club. He had no cigarettes so girded his fingers around the green cord of the telephone.

What? Pancho said.

It's me, he said.

Figured.

Guess you know.

Yeah.

She okay?

Are *you* okay?

Christ.

Come home, Jim.

Yeah, he said, maybe.

They talked some more, then hung up. The house was silent. He couldn't go back. He packed a large bag, threw the bag in the Corvette, fired the engine and drove out of Timber Cove, out of Houston, and to the Cape.

———

CAPE CANAVERAL
COCOA BEACH,
FLORIDA, 1962

He was three days reaching the Cape. The roads were long and hot and empty. He drove through the southwest prairies of Louisiana, skirted the lowlands of Mississippi and Alabama and crossed into Florida at Pensacola. He stayed in hot motels and ate late in all-night diners with hard-bitten loners, wastrels and drunks sitting alone drinking cold coffee and smoking around him. He'd sit up at the counter, order meatballs and french fries and feel like he belonged. On occasion, a couple of cops on night patrol would roll up and eat with him, radios crackling quietly beneath the table. He felt a strange peace. During the long drives, he'd developed a system to help him cope with his troubled mind. He applied engineering principles to the problem, which was, he established, terrifying thoughts. Rather than spending time thinking through these thoughts, reviewing their content, seeking to reassure himself of their falsity, he came up with a system, a short-cut; bullet points. There were five in total. The points could be applied to any troubling thought he had. The real genius lay in their automation. He realized he didn't actually have to *consciously recite* each of the points. He could simply count them out on his fingers. Or tap them out with his foot. He would be reassured, the thought would go, and he could move on. It was simple.

From a pay phone out the back of Joe Mac's he called Pancho. The line connected, but he hung up after the third ring. It was his last stop before hitting Florida.

He arrived at the Cape, drove down to Cocoa Beach and parked up at the Holiday Inn. Henri was pleased to see him. He gave Harrison a room for as long as he needed it. He unpacked, then went down to the bar. Later that night, he called Grace Walker from his room.

Jesus, Jim, she said. What happened?

I don't know, he said.

How are you?

I'm okay.

Look, I'm not taking sides on this—nobody needs that—but I feel very protective toward Grace; you understand that, right?

I do, he said.

She's been through so much.

We both have.

Yes, but she's been dealing with it.

And I haven't?

Honestly, Jim? No, I don't think you have. Look, so much has happened, and so fast . . . You both need some time. All I'm saying is, don't be too hard on yourself. I know you're under a lot of pressure at work, but maybe you could take a week or so off? Or even just a few days? I really think it would do you good. I could make up Robbie's old room; you could stay with us.

How's Pancho?

She's the same. Where are you?

The Cape. Need to be here most of the time anyway.

What about the house?

Figured we'd sell it . . . Grace can keep whatever we get.

Why don't you come back, Jim? It would be good to see you. Joe would get a kick out of having you stay.

Harrison didn't say anything.

He told me he ran into you at the Cape, she said.

It was real good to see him, Harrison said.

Joe said the same, she said.

There was a pause.

Is she okay? he said.

Yes, she said.

It's good to hear your voice.

And yours, Jim. You call me anytime you want, okay?

Say hi to Joe for me.

I will. Take care of yourself.

Bye, Grace.

Bye, Jim.

The next day was Monday. That meant pilots' meeting, first thing. They convened in the small room next to Deke's office up at the complex. The light was a white strip with a rectangular table sat beneath it. Deke stood at its head like a father at dinner. Behind him, on the wall, was a blackboard. Blinds were lowered across a wide window that overlooked the parking lot outside.

Gentlemen, he said when they were all seated and silent. Nineteen sixty-two is almost over. The years are gonna pass fast from now on. If you think you've been busy so far . . . We have a deadline, and we're gonna make it, with time to spare. We've got some stuff to figure out, but we will figure it out and move on. You all look pretty relaxed there in your Ban-Lon shirts. That's gonna change.

He pointed at the blackboard behind him. *Environmental Training*—exposure to acceleration, vibration, noise, weightlessness; simulated lunar gravity, wearing a bulkier pressure suit. Some of you will have more experience at this stuff than others. Doesn't matter. *Contingency Training*. We're gonna run survival schools in the desert and the jungle. In an emergency, who knows where you'll come down. Also, ejection seats—in case there's any of you who haven't punched out of an airplane—and parachutes. *Indoctrination Program*, where we'll practice moving and working in zero-g. And we'll all ride parabolic trajectories in the zero-g airplane; a modified KC-35. What else? We'll have engineering briefings and reviews, make sure you're all up to speed on vehicle design and development. Some of you navy boys will find the next part old hat: *Water Safety and Survival* at the navy's preflight school in Pensacola. And you'll ride the wheel at Johnsonville, you lucky sons-of-bitches. Anyone who stays conscious at twenty-g's will have a free steak dinner on Max Faget. Glenn did sixteen. So that's the one to beat. It will be a special kind of torture. We're gonna build our own centrifuge at MSC too. And we'll be doing a lot of simulator work, of course.

What about flyin, Deke? Conrad said.

Yes. After the hell the Mercury fellas raised, we've decided to formalize it. You'll all go through an *Aircraft Flight Training* program. So. Sixty-three through sixty-four will be dominated by training and developing your areas of specialization as Gemini progresses. We got a lot of ground to cover and not much time.

John Young, sitting on Harrison's right, leaned back and sucked on his pipe. Harrison pulled out his cigarettes and gestured for a light.

I'll have one of them if they're going round, Borman said.

Harrison slid the pack across the table to him.

And you might want to cut back on those too, Deke said. None of you are gonna be smoking in a hundred percent oxygen environment so you better get used to it. All right. There's gonna be a lot of memos floatin around. Make sure you read them. Being on a flight crew means your time will be dominated by your upcoming mission but you'll need to stay on top of your paperwork. Now. Get the hell out of here.

They thanked Deke and picked up their pads and pens and got up.

Jim, you got a sec? Deke said, as the others filed out.

Sure, Harrison said.

Deke waited until they were alone and shut the door.

We've had a few calls, he said.

Press?

Yeah, Deke said. You okay with me sayin she's sick?

Yeah, Harrison said.

Okay, Deke said, listen. If you get asked about it, either ignore it or confirm it; don't deny it, even if it's your first instinct. We need to be tellin the same story.

Harrison nodded. Sure thing, he said.

Right, Deke said. Let's get back to work.

Out in the lot, Harrison slipped into his Corvette. The leather seats were hot. He should have parked in the shade. He put the key in the ignition switch and checked his mirror. He felt too far forward, so adjusted his seat back, then forward, then back again. He adjusted his mirror. Was the door shut properly? He wasn't sure. He opened the door and shut it again. He readjusted the mirror. The seat was too far back. He moved it forward and wiped the sweat from his forehead. Christ, it was hot. He reached over to turn the key but stopped and retracted his hand. No. He wasn't ready. He reached for it again, held it between his finger and his thumb, then withdrew again. Shit. *Shit shit shit.* He hit the wheel with his fist. He wound the window down. He moved about in his seat. He touched the mirror. He tapped the brake pedal with his foot five times. He reached for the key, started the engine, and drove off.

He spent Christmas at the Cape studying. His flight manual was already two inches thick. Orbital mechanics, principles of rocket flight, reentry mechanics, rendezvous mechanics. It was a hell of a holiday. He spoke to Grace once, on Christmas eve, in the early evening. It was only the second time they'd spoken since she left.

How you doing? she said.

Okay, he said.

How's work? she said.

Same old, he said. I miss you.

Are you eating? she said.

He told her that he was.

He wanted to ask her about selling the house but couldn't bring himself to churn up the conversation.

Some of the stuff I said before I left . . . she said. I'm sorry. I was in a pretty bad place.

I'm sorry too, he said, trying not to think about it.

I've been going along to church, she said, in Rosamond. It's helping.

I'm glad.

Merry Christmas, Jim, she said.

Merry Christmas, he said.

The line was silent, then it was dead. He tapped on his leg once, twice, three, four, five times, then went down to the bar and felt sorry for himself.

Sixty-three started in the centrifuge at Johnsonville, riding the wheel, using all his strength to keep conscious as it spun. He managed sixteen g's. He came off, felt like hell, walked slowly toward the men's room.

How was it? Conrad said, passing him, up next.

Easy, he said. Nothin to it.

Then he went into the john and vomited.

———

It was the end of January. Harrison waited in the lobby of the Holiday Inn for Lovell. The two men were due to meet George Smathers, ex-Marine officer, former assistant attorney and now senator for Florida, at a cocktail reception at six. Smathers was close to John Kennedy and Harrison admired him. The man had fought hard with LBJ on his decision to site the Manned Spacecraft Center in Texas instead of at the Cape. Harrison brushed dust from his suit and looked around.

You're early, Lovell said, walking in from the stairwell.

You know how I love time in the barrel, Harrison said.

Best advice—and this is from Gordo—arrive late, leave early.

That's some good advice.

All they want is a handshake, photograph with an astronaut, and a smile. That's all. Then we get the hell out.

Getting the hell out sounds good, Harrison said.

We should go someplace tonight, eat something half-decent for a change, Lovell said.

Harrison agreed.

You ready? Lovell said.

Sure.

Let's walk, Lovell said. It'll take longer.

The Cape Canaveral Hilton was on North Atlantic Avenue, right on the beach. It looked like a white brick, an icebox coated in lumpy stucco render. Outside, the men finished their cigarettes in the cool air.

I heard Connie Hilton's coming tonight, Lovell said as they walked inside.

No shit, Harrison said.

The receptionist directed them toward the lobby.

Jesus, Harrison said, as they stepped through the door. Gilruth's here.

So's Webb, Lovell said.

Well, he ain't exactly one to miss an opportunity, Harrison said.

Come on, Lovell said. Let's get ourselves some liquid propellant.

Harrison and Lovell found a waitress carrying champagne and helped themselves to a glass each.

There's Deke, Harrison said.

They walked over to him. The lobby, with its fake Baccarat crystal chandeliers and replica Versailles paneling, was crowded. Women laughed and swung glasses around themselves while serious-looking men stood close by and smiled. The carpet was deep crimson, snagged and fraying in parts, cigarette burns scattered like black seeds.

Jeez, Lovell said. Even the Hilton looks low-rent here.

Cocoa's finest, Harrison said.

Fellas, Deke said when they reached him.

Looks like a busy night for you, Harrison said.

Up to my ears in bullshit already, Deke said. I'm gonna need a shovel to get out of here.

Harrison sipped his drink and tapped his leg five times, the sharp edge of a shovel triggering a thought that immediately arrested his mind. Stay calm, he thought.

Is Hilton still here? Lovell said.

Connie?

Yeah.

No. Left half an hour ago, Deke said.

Smart guy, Harrison said.

Do I detect resentment at barrel-duties, Harrison? Deke said.

You're goddamn right you do, Harrison said.

Well suck it up, Captain, Deke said. Everyone's gotta do their time, unless they're on the next flight, and even then, I guarantee you, some sonofabitch who needs reelecting will want to come on the loop to shoot the goddamn breeze while you're up there. Hell, I hear the president himself wants to speak to whoever makes the first landing by telephone.

From the carrier? Lovell said.

From the surface, Deke said.

The *surface*? Harrison said. Because they've got nothing better to do after traveling a quarter of a million—

I know, Deke said, I know.

For the love of God.

We were thinking, *For All Mankind*, actually, Deke said. Got a nice ring to it, hasn't it?

Sums it all up, Lovell said.

I thought so, Deke said.

All right, all right, Harrison said.

Who's been bitin your ass? Deke said.

Just can't stand these sorta things, Harrison said, flexing his fingers five at a time.

Well try to enjoy your drink at least, Deke said.

Harrison felt his back prickle with sweat.

You know fellas, Harrison said, I'm just gonna step outside, get some air—be back in a—

Heads up, Lovell said. Here comes Smathers.

Senator! Deke said. Well it's good to see you too. I've got a coupla people I know you're gonna want to meet. Jim, Jim—this is George Smathers; George, this is Jim Harrison and Jim Lovell, two of our finest astronauts.

It's a pleasure, sir, Lovell said, extending his hand.

The pleasure is all mine, I assure you! Smathers said.

Senator, Harrison said, shaking his hand after Lovell.

The two Jims! Smathers said. Thank you for all your hard work and dedication.

It's a pleasure to serve, sir, Lovell said.

This here's my good friend, Herb White, Smathers said.

Pleasure, Harrison said, shaking White's hand.

Very, very pleased to meet you both, White said, gripping Lovell's hand and grinning.

We were just talking about the possibility of getting Kennedy down for a tour sometime, Smathers said. You know, the launch facilities, see the rockets up close, show him firsthand the nuts and bolts of his vision, that kind of thing.

Give him a warm Florida welcome, Herb said.

Sounds good, Deke said.

Indeed, Smathers said. I'm going to bring it up when I'm back in Washington.

How long are you here for, Senator? Deke said.

Just a few days, sadly. I'd like it to be longer, but there's a lot going on right now.

Have you talked to Gilruth or Webb yet?

I'm meeting with them later, Smathers said. Let's just enjoy ourselves for now, shall we? I don't get out much these days.

The men laughed.

Say, Smathers said. Do you gentlemen like my new suit? I was in London last month and had it cut at Savile Row.

He held it open at the waist.

What do you think? Cobalt blue.

Harrison's heart exploded; his gut turned liquid, his face gushed sweat. He felt unreal. Blood pumped hard behind his eyes.

Oh, Jim, Smathers said. Are you feeling all right? You look a little, ah, off-color.

Uh, yes, sir, I feel fine, he said, tapping and tapping his leg. A number of violent thoughts filled his mind. He began to blink in sets of five, hiding his actions by pretending to scratch his forehead. When that didn't work, he rubbed his eyebrows, shielding his face, trying to go over his thoughts manually, but it was impossible, standing there, in front of them. He needed to be alone. He needed time. His anxiety grew. His heart rate bordered on apoplectic. He needed time. He needed to be alone. He rubbed his forehead.

Uh, he said. Uh.

Jim? Deke said.

I'm fine, he said.

So, I was saying, Smathers said, picking up the conversation. Do—

Hang on a minute, Harrison said.

Jim, Deke said.

Hang on, he said.

For what, exactly, Captain? Smathers said.

Just, uh—

Thoughts begat thoughts. They stacked up on top of him. The more his stress rose, the more they came, too powerful to ignore.

Jesus, Jim, Deke said. What the hell?

Senator, I don't think Jim is feeling too well, Lovell said.

Harrison grimaced as his gut cramped. Jesus. He couldn't hold it in. He needed the men's room, right away. It lurched and gurgled inside him. The force was unbearable! He fought hard against it. Then his mind connected cause and effect together like a powerful magnet and presented the newspaper headline: ASTRONAUT SOILS SELF AT HILTON COCKTAIL PARTY. It was too late. He felt something run down the back of his left leg. *Christ*, he thought. Keep it in!

Uh, I don't feel too good, he said.

Maybe you should get some air? Lovell said.

Sorry, Senator, Deke said.

Not at all! Smathers said. I just hope you're all right?

We need you in tip-top shape to beat the Russians! Herb said.

Harrison turned to leave. Think I ate something bad, he said to Deke.

Take my room, Deke said, pushing a key into his hand. Gilruth gave it to me for tonight. I'll head back with Lovell.

Harrison turned quickly and left.

Poor man, he heard Smathers lament behind him.

The lobby was crowded. He walked carefully, as fast as he could without making the situation worse. He didn't know where the john was so headed for the elevator ahead. *Please, God, help me*, he said, over and over in his head. The porter saw him approach and opened the elevator doors. Harrison stumbled in, the porter smiled, Harrison nodded, and the box swallowed him up. He fell into the room, locked the door and stumbled to the can. He tapped and tapped his leg and said I'm sorry, I'm sorry, over and over. Afterward, he stripped off his clothes and lay down, exhausted, humiliated, ashamed, in the bath, and cried out for his wife.

———

They sold the house the following summer. It went for a decent sum. Timber Cove was a desirable area. *Astroville*, the real estate agent called it. Grace insisted he keep half the money. You need to get a place of your own, she said. You can't live in a motel forever.

He had no time to think about it. He was on the backup crew for Conrad and Gordo's Gemini V and training hard. It was a complex, challenging mission. Harrison found the extreme focus of training helped him live with, what he now termed, to himself, his *affliction*. He could live with it. His coping techniques had evolved. Over time, their effectiveness would diminish, but a new one would always present itself. After the incident at the Hilton, he considered going to Deke, telling him everything, but how could he? He was unable to tolerate the thoughts himself, let alone tell another. What would Deke think of him? No. And Deke would make him leave the program; that much he was sure of. And he had nothing else now. More than that, though, he wanted to go up; he had to go up. He yearned for it.

———

It was late, quarter gone eleven, Harrison stood alone outside Walt's. The air was cool. He could smell the sea; the salt and the sky. Across the street, a man and a woman stood sharing a cigarette, their thin shadows falling across the sidewalk, the warm sun long sunk beneath the sea. He imagined them eating together across the tight vinyl check of a restaurant tablecloth; how each reflected back the best of the other. Harrison fingered the box of matches in his pocket. His arms glowed neon indigo from the sign above the door. Cars drove downtown, taillights casting red trails inside his eyes. The man parted from the woman and crossed the street toward him.

You got a light? Harrison said as he approached.

The man looked up, said, sure pal.

Harrison pushed a Lucky Strike between his lips. The man pulled a lighter from his pocket, struck it, Harrison leaned in.

Thanks, he said.

Pleasure.

Busy here, huh.

I guess.

You got something to do with this damn program they're runnin? Harrison said.

Hell, no, the man said. Take it easy, pal.

He walked away, leaving Harrison smoking alone in the neon glow. He drew himself together, dropped the cigarette on the sidewalk, pushed open the door.

Evening, Jim, the bartender said. Usual?

He nodded.

Coming up.

In the corner, a television set showed the news at low volume. Harrison sat down at the bar.

Here you go, Walt said, setting the glass down on a paper napkin.

Thanks, Walt.

Jesus, have you seen this? a voice said.

There were two men, older, at the bar next to him. They were watching the news.

They've gone at them with tear gas and goddamn billy clubs.

Harrison looked up at the television set.

Six hundred blacks, marching in Alabama? I can believe it.

This ain't America.

This the news?

They interrupted *Judgment at Nuremberg*. Walt, turn it off, would you, I don't want to watch any more.

Can I get another? Harrison said.

Sure thing, Jim, Walt said, clicking the set off.

You're Jim Harrison, right? the first man said.

He nodded.

Bill. This here is Eb.

Pleasure, Harrison said.

Mind if I ask you a question?

Depends on the question.

Well, Eb and me, we been wonderin. Why we spendin American dollars puttin men up to do a monkey's job?

Harrison glanced at his glass, turned it with his hand, looked up at him.

Well, he said, those early flights, yeah, they were designed to be automated, sure. It was quick and dirty, but Eisenhower was in a fix; the press were goin nuts, remember?

Sure we do, Eb said.

All the engineers wanted the occupant to do was flick a few damn switches, Harrison said. But you know what? The Mercury boys, they said, no, we want to fly the thing, like a pilot, case we need to. Good job, too, or ol Gordo would have fried.

Gordo Cooper? Bill said.

Yeah, Harrison said. His flight, the last one; designed to be the longest of em all. Twenty-two orbits.

How many'd Glenn do?

Three.

Jesus.

Harrison continued. Gordo's first eighteen orbits, everything goes swell, then, on the nineteenth, the electrical system shorts. Next orbit, he loses all attitude reading. Then the whole automatic control system goes off. Temperature in the capsule hits a hundred and, because of the electrical problem, carbon dioxide starts building up in his suit. Mission Control, well, they're getting themselves in quite a twist. Gordo figures he's in a tight spot, so takes over. He's gotta line up the angle of reentry manually, with his eyeballs, holding the capsule steady with the stick. On his final orbit, he approaches daylight over the Pacific, checks his orientation with some lines he's drawn on the window with a pencil. Then, using his wristwatch for time, manually fires the retro-rockets at exactly the right moment, and splashes down alongside the carrier. Hell, they were so close, you could toss a ball between them. Ol Gordo, yeah; that's how you do it.

Hey, Walt, three more, Bill said.

Coming up.

Have to say, Eb said, glad we ran into you.

Harrison nodded.

These Gemini flights, he said, they take real piloting. Besides, you can't put a monkey on the moon. What's the poor sonofabitch gonna say?

Reds'll blow us all to hell before we get to the moon, Eb said.

Could be worse, Bill said.

Eb looked at him. How could it be worse?

In your guts, you know he's nuts!

The men laughed. Harrison smiled, his face creasing along old lines, eyes narrowing into half-moons.

Oh, boy, Eb said, Goldwater; that crazy sonofabitch. Christ, though, what about Johnson's daisy girl?

The way her eye filled the screen during the countdown? Bill said. Then, *kaboom!* Honest to God, I wet my goddamn pants first time it ran.

Say what you want about Johnson, Harrison said, but that broadcast was genius.

Love each other or die, Eb said. What an asshole.

Was a hell of a slogan, Harrison said.

Vote for me or the other guy will kill you?

Whatever works, I guess.

Thank God it did.

The Reds ain't stupid, Bill said. It's a suicide button; they know that, everyone does. Something's changed. Don't know what, all I know is we now got men on top of missiles, not bombs.

Still plenty of bombs, Eb said.

All I want to do is fly, Harrison said.

An hour later it was half past midnight and the bar was quiet.

Jim? Walt said. You okay?

He looked at the light, it hurt his eyes.

What happened?

Fellas left a while ago.

Harrison's mouth was dry.

Sorry, Walt.

You're always welcome here, Jim.

He stood, his legs were weak.

You okay?

Sure.

You don't look too good.

I'm okay.

He dropped some bills on the bar.

No need, Walt said. Bill took care of it.

But after they left—

That too.

Guess I'll have another, then.

He ordered a scotch and stared at the bar and sat there for a long time.

When he left, it was very dark. He stood on the sidewalk. The alcohol was messing with his processes; his reasoning. He couldn't think straight. He didn't feel good. C'mon, he thought, *c'mon.* He pushed his hand hard against the wall. He lived by one rule: *don't fuck up.* If someone saw him struggling, if it got back to Deke, he'd be out. It was the only thing that mattered. He'd gotten good at hiding it, but all it took was one *fuckup.* He walked back to the Holiday Inn.

Gemini V splashed down at twelve fifty-five on August twenty-ninth, nineteen sixty-five. *Eight days in a garbage can,* Conrad said. *Wish I'd taken a book.*

Three weeks after Harrison's backup duties on Gemini V ended, Deke assigned him and Neil to the prime crew of Gemini VIII. Fifty-five orbits, the world's second rendezvous, followed by the first docking of two spacecraft in space. Rendezvous in Earth orbit was a dark art, requiring the pilot to *slow down,* rather than accelerate toward his target, in order to drop into a lower orbit, increase his centrifugal force, and *speed up.* Orbits in different planes, of varying shapes, complicated matters. The whole enterprise took exceptional piloting skills. In addition, there was an ambitious EVA in the flight plan; much longer and more complex than Ed White's spacewalk on Gemini IV. It was set to be a hell of a mission. As commander, Harrison relished the challenge, immersing himself in the details. Gemini VIII would launch in March. He and Neil worked long and hard; eight, nine, ten hours in the simulator, straight, almost daily. The technical detail kept his mind calm, his attention focused. *Don't fuck up.*

He tried to be careful.

Then in late February one of the new fellas from the third group was flying from Houston to the McDonnell plant in St. Louis in heavy rain and came in too low and too slow—bad news in a T-38 that often stalled below two hundred and seventy knots—so gunned the afterburner for another pass and turned and crunched into the McDonnell hangar and was decapitated in the parking lot.

That evening, after the news broke, Harrison sat on his bed, smoking, reviewing his black notebook. It was divided into six sections: SCHEDULE, SYSTEMS BRIEFINGS, EXPERIMENTS, FLIGHT PLAN, MISCELLANEOUS, OPEN ITEMS. He sighed, rubbed his face. There were a hundred and eighty-four open items, each numbered in his tight black hand. He stopped reading, dropped the book on the bed. It was late, almost eleven, the telephone rang.

Jim Harrison, he said into the receiver.

Jim, it's Deke. We need to see you here urgently.

Where are you?

MSC.

I'm at the Cape.

I know.

What's it about, Deke?

Tomorrow, eleven-thirty, my office. We'll talk then.

The line went dead. He didn't have time for a round-trip to Houston. Four weeks before the flight? What did Deke want to see him about? Jesus—had he been found out? No, he'd been careful, discreet, trained harder than anyone; no one could deny that. Maybe Deke wanted to talk Apollo crew selection? That was more likely. Or the new fella's funeral. He went to bed, rose early, flew down to Houston in a T-38. He landed, taxied, popped the canopy. It was a sunny day.

Thanks for coming on such short notice, Jim, Deke said, from behind his desk. Have a seat.

Uh, no problem, Deke, Harrison said, and sat down.

There was a knock at the door.

Yup, Deke said, and Marvin Hoffman, the flight surgeon, came in and sat down. As soon as Harrison saw him, he knew.

Jim, it's come to my attention, Deke said, that you're not doing too good.

I'm fine, Deke.

Come on, Jim, Hoffman said.

Does Marvin have to be here?

Yes, Deke said. Look, I know the last few years have been pretty tough on you—

Deke—

And you've been through shit that—God forbid—none of us will ever have to experience—

I don't want to talk about that, Harrison said.

I know you don't, Jim, but I do, Deke said. And if this goes on much longer the whole world will be talking about it, and I'm pretty sure neither you, or Grace, want that.

Harrison didn't say anything. He began to feel *not good*. He'd stopped using stupid techniques a while ago. He'd realized that he was a *test pilot* and, if he treated every instance as *a test pilot in a tight spot*, he could easily maneuver out of trouble. He didn't realize that this was simply another technique.

Harrison stood.

I got a flight to prepare for, he said.

Jim, you're mentally unwell, Hoffman said, rising.

Marv, Deke said.

Are you grounding me? Harrison said to Deke.

Deke got to his feet.

Yeah, he said.

This is flight surgeon *horseshit*, Deke! Harrison said, pointing at Hoffman.

You need to look after yourself, Jim, Deke said. You need to get some help. Marvin can help you with that. We've got people you can talk to now. Hell, you've been doing a pretty damn good job of keepin on; you've done good work, you should be proud of that. But now's the time to stop, before you do something stupid and auger in. We sure as hell don't need another astronaut clobbered before he's even been into space. Or, worse, what if we send you up, and something happens, and NASA's got two dead men orbiting the Earth? There'd be no damn program *left*.

He's right, Jim, Hoffman said.

A month before the flight, Harrison said. You're taking me off a month before the flight.

That's why we have backup crews, Deke said.

Look, Harrison said, Dave Scott's a fine pilot but—

Dave will do just fine, Deke said. And no one came to me. It's important you know that. It was just, a little thing here, a little thing there; Marv and I spoke.

Deke—

I'm sorry Jim, Deke said.

I'm sorry too, Harrison said.

Conrad's downstairs, Deke said. He'll fly you back to the Cape, if that's where you want to go.

He stared at Deke, then nodded.

Marv will make you an appointment to see one of our people right away.

Where can I reach you? Hoffman said.

Holiday Inn, Harrison said.

I'll need a permanent address.

That is my address.

Deke waved his hand at Hoffman.

Right, Hoffman said. Deke, I gotta run.

Sure. Thanks, Marv.

Jim, Hoffman said. I'll be in touch.

Harrison nodded and Hoffman left, leaving the two men in the room together.

No reason why you can't get back in the rotation for Apollo if things go well, Deke said.

Guess I'd better find Conrad, Harrison said.

The heat hit him hard outside. He felt sick. He was sick.

You'd better not do that in the cockpit, Conrad said, stepping out of his Corvette.

Pete, Harrison said.

Or my car. Tough break?

Something like that.

C'mon, Conrad said. Let's get back, sit by the pool, have a beer.

Harrison said, a beer sounds good, and Conrad drove them to Ellington and they flew back to the Cape.

———

He didn't go to the launch. The night before, he drove up to pad nineteen, parked the Corvette and looked across at the vast Titan II rocket. The small Gemini capsule sat on top of the fat booster, black and silver and white. He looked at it for a long time. Then he drove back to the motel. That old pilot's saying: *only two ways out of a doctor's office.* He went down to the bar and drank and smoked. He thought about all the work Neil and Dave were now having to do before the launch. He looked at his watch. Ten-thirty. They were probably still in the simulator. He felt bad. He was falling into a funk. It started as soon as he and Conrad landed at the Cape and had gotten progressively worse. He wasn't going up. Something else was slipping away too, but he didn't know what. He took a bottle back to his room.

The next morning, he got one of the engineers to install a squawk box by his bed. He might not be attending the launch, but he sure as hell wanted to listen in.

Sure appreciate this, Lou, he said to the engineer as he finished up.

No sweat, Jim, Lou said.

Harrison headed downtown and bought cigarettes, bags of potato chips, Budweiser.

The Agena target vehicle—that Neil and Dave would rendez-vous with—launched on an Atlas booster at three seconds past three. When he heard the rocket boom and roar, he stepped onto the walkway outside his room and looked up, shielding his eyes from the sun. It shrieked into the sky and the Agena popped it-self into a one hundred and eighty five-mile circular orbit with-out blowing up. Gemini VIII was scheduled for an hour and thirty-four minutes later. He went back inside and lit a cigarette and sat down and smoked it. Twenty minutes later he turned on the squawk box.

This is Gemini launch control coming up on T minus seventy-four min-utes and counting; mark; T minus seventy-four minutes and counting on the Gemini VIII mission.

The technicians, under Gemini Pad Leader Guenter Wendt,

were busy in the white room during the final phases leading up to hatch closure. Finally, at four forty-one and two seconds, Gemini VIII left the pad for orbit. Harrison's heart stuck in his throat and he opened a Budweiser that foamed onto the floor.

Over the squawk box he heard Dave Scott say, *Guenter Wendt? I vonder vere Guenter Vendt?*

Harrison finished his beer and opened another.

You're looking good, VIII.

How about that view?

Coming up on five minutes.

Boy! Here we go!

Harrison got up to find the potato chips. He took another beer from the fridge and added more. He sat back down and felt a deep misery. The mission proceeded right on the book. He knew every stage, every task, every burn. They rendezvoused with the Agena.

Outstanding job, coach!

Way to go, partner!

Boy, that was really slick.

The two spacecraft, a hundred and fifty feet apart, flew around the Earth at seventeen and a half thousand miles an hour, passing in and out of contact with NASA's global tracking stations that relayed communication and data between the spacecraft and Houston. Harrison listened as Armstrong flew the spacecraft around the Agena, inspecting the vehicle for launch damage.

Man, it flies easy.

Really?

Nothing to it.

Harrison lit a cigarette and cracked open another can. The crew were given the go-ahead to dock with the Agena before they passed into the darkness of the next night. Harrison sat forward, ear cocked toward the squawk box, sweating the taxing maneuver. The spacecraft eased closer to the Agena. Jim Lovell, the CAPCOM for the mission, gave the final go to dock.

Flight, we are docked. It really is a smoothie.

Roger. Congratulations. That is real good.

The spacecraft, now coupled with the Agena, moved out of range of the Tananarive tracking station and into another communications dead zone. Harrison found half a bottle of scotch on the side table. He held the neck to his lips and drank. The squawk box spat static and Harrison fell asleep.

Scott's urgent voice jarred him awake.

We have serious problems here. We're { . . . } we're tumbling end over end.

Holy shit.

He sat up, groggy.

We're { . . . } disengaged from the Agena.

Harrison grabbed the box and listened. What the hell was—

We're rolling up and we can't turn anything off.

The spacecraft was spinning wildly out of control.

Continuously increasing in a left roll.

Armstrong's voice, clipped, calm.

Shut down the main thrusters! Harrison said.

We have a violent left roll and { . . . } can't { . . . }

{ . . . } can't fire { . . . } we have a roll { . . . } stuck hand control.

Shut them down! Harrison said.

The spacecraft spun faster until the motions began to couple. Holy shit, Harrison thought: pitch and yaw and roll! It's inertia coupling; inertia coupling carried into space. *I gotta cage my eyeballs*, he heard Armstrong say, as Gemini VIII tumbled like a gyro at three hundred and sixty degrees a second, and he wrestled with the stick.

Stand by.

C'mon! Harrison said. If it went on much longer, they'd lose consciousness and the ship would break apart. In the spacecraft, Armstrong and Scott were beginning to gray-out. Their vision blurred and distorted. Armstrong reached above his head, trying to focus on the switch that shut down the thrusters. The panel stretched and contorted as the blood pressure in his brain fell rapidly. Holding his head at a certain angle, he managed to get a clear visual fix. He hit the switch. The thrusters shut down.

Harrison was on his feet. He had to get to the Cape Control Center. No one knew the ship or mission like he did. One of the Gemini's OAMS thrusters must have stuck open; there must have been a short. Only one thing could bring the ship under control now: the Reentry Control System—small thrusters on the nose, reserved for reentry. But Armstrong would have to leave enough propellant in the tanks for reentry, otherwise they'd be stuck in orbit; quickly dead. He had to get up to the Control Center. Harrison's blood turned fast. He began to sweat, from his face, from his back, from his legs. He looked around the room. He turned off the box, found his car keys and grabbed at the door. Wait. Had he turned the bathroom light off? He didn't know. He had to check. In case it caused a fire. He went back to the bathroom, lit in yellow, and flipped the switch. He turned the AC off too. Then he unplugged the fridge. He went back to the door. The pants press! He went back and unplugged it. He looked around the room. The squawk box was plugged in. He got down on his knees and looked under the bedside table. A thin black wire trailed out of the back of the box, curled in a bundle on the floor and disappeared behind the bed. He looked under the bed. It had been hardwired into the socket. Shit! He yanked it out of the wall. Sweat fell from his face. Then he realized his mistake: what if there were residual electrical discharge in the wire? He couldn't just leave it on the floor, under the bed, with all the dust. It could spark and ignite. He began to pull it out, quickly, but the wire was tangled under the bed with the telephone cord. He lay on his front and tried to untangle them. His arms were wet, his pulse rate high. It took him half an hour. He wound the wire around the squawk box and stood it on the bedside table, making sure the exposed end didn't touch anything. He looked around. Everything was fine. He switched off the main light and held the door handle but froze. He removed his hand. He looked around in the gloom. He reached out for the handle again but stopped before he got to it. He looked round again. He turned the light on. He turned the light off. He went for the handle. He stopped midway. He tried again; his hand barely left his side. He tried again and held the handle and gripped it tight and pushed it down then stopped and let go. He cried out in frustration. He tried again and again. Blood throbbed in his ears. He stopped, stumbled back into the room, fell on the bed and wept. It was too late. He was too slow. The crew were dead and it was his fault. His head felt heavy, lilting with guilt and scotch. He staggered into the dark bathroom, pissed on the floor, then found a bottle of gin in the cupboard and began to drink.

He came round several hours later. He was on his side, on the floor. His keys lay by his face. He looked at them for a long time. Then he picked them up, stood, and walked out of the room.

He drove fast up the stretch, slipping behind other cars before pulling hard past them; past the Starlite, the Satellite, the Polaris. Past Wolfie's, past Walt's. The steely blue eyes watched him speed toward the hard beach. His tires squealed on the oily road as he swerved onto the flat sand. A solitary runner pounded the coast. Harrison roared past him. The low sun sprang off powerful breakers as he gunned forward pushing the needle high and waves hit the shore and he turned and spun and tumbled, flipping violently across the iron sand, the car landing silently on its hood.

———

Jesus. Okay. Thanks. Do you have any cigarettes? Where can I then? Fine. Thanks. No, let me handle that. I'll handle that too. That won't be necessary. And he's stable? We can move him? Now, if possible. Okay when? Tonight? Okay. I'll sign them. No. No immediate family. Separated. California. Yeah. I'll take care of that. Uh-huh. No. We'd appreciate that. I'm sorry this is more complicated than—I'm sure you do. I appreciate that. The program. Yeah. Leave that with me. Yes, please. That won't be necessary. No, that won't be necessary. Okay. And who do I speak to there? Right. We'll do that. Okay. Fine. Thanks.

Deke? Harrison said. It was dark. He didn't know if he was asleep or awake. The voice had come from someplace else. He slipped into his own black place and thought no more.

———

The sound of fluttering curtains drew him back to the world. He felt cool. And peaceful. There was a purity, a simplicity, in his consciousness. He lay still. There was some pain, but it was distant, like old heartache. He sensed the room around him. It was small. He was alone. It was very dark.

———

Voices woke him. He felt vexed. The voices were loud. Not shouts, but not whispers either. Normal talk. People were talking normally around him. Two people. They woke him. He moved around in his bed. The breeze had gone. There were other sounds now. Mechanical sounds. One of the voices spoke to him. He was a doctor. Asking how he felt.

Terrible, he said. He opened his eyes. His throat was dry and his head hurt like hell. He groaned.

You're pretty lucky, the other voice, another doctor, said.

Memories returned to him the way memories did. *Neil and Dave.* He shut his eyes again. The doctors sat him up, gave him water, he drank it through a straw.

A fella jogging on the beach saw the whole thing, one of them said. Good job too.

What hospital . . . ? Harrison said.

They took you to the 6550th USAF Hospital down at Patrick Air Force Base. The runner's a captain down there. Deke Slayton got you transferred up here. You're in NASA's medical facility here at Cape Canaveral.

Deke . . . Harrison said.

The second doctor left.

You came in pretty beat up, the first doctor said. Amazingly, you only have two broken ribs and a severe concussion. No damage to your brain, your head, or your spine. Can't say the same for your Corvette.

When can I leave? Harrison said.

Not anytime soon, the doctor said. I want to monitor you for possible intracranial hemorrhaging and both NASA and the air force want to conduct a full psychiatric assessment, which, of course, will have to go on your record. To the outside world, you're being treated for a neck injury as well as the aforementioned ailments, following a little overexuberant rat-racing to blow off steam. Perfectly understandable for an astronaut putting his hide on the line for his country. There's water, if you're thirsty—he motioned to the bedside table—and sleeping pills if you need them.

What's your name? Harrison said.

I'm Doctor Merry.

You don't look so thrilled.

And you look like a fool, Captain.

I just want to get out of here, Harrison said.

I'm afraid that's impossible, Merry said. And my staff will make sure that's the way things stay. Don't forget that you're still a captain in this air force. Orders are orders. And no amount of so-called *astropower* is going to help you here.

I don't need a goddamn shrink, Harrison said.

We'll let the goddamn shrinks be the judge of that, Merry said.

Harrison tried to move. His whole body ached. His ribs were sore. He felt drowsy.

Deke, he said. I need to talk to Deke.

You need to rest. Colonel John Winterbourne, chief of Psychiatry, will see you tomorrow. A nurse will be in at four. Enjoy the food.

Merry left. Harrison shut his eyes. Armstrong was dead and it was his fault. The air was very still. He opened his eyes and stared out the window. He turned his head. The bottle of sleeping pills stood on the bedside table. It was a large bottle. He stared at it for a long time.

Deke, he said, turning away. He had to speak to Deke.

At ten to four, the nurse came in. You got a phone call, she said. I'll bring it in.

A telephone was wheeled to his bed on a small trolley. The receiver sat on its side. He picked it up.

How you feeling, kid?

Deke.

Sorry I can't get up there.

It's my fault, Deke. The crew. They're dead because of me.

Dead? What the hell are they givin you up there? Armstrong activated the RCS, brought the ship under control; kept enough in the tank for reentry. But, as you know, mission rules state an immediate abort once the RCS is activated. So we brought em down right away, in the middle of the damn Pacific, five hundred miles east of Okinawa. Poor bastards had to wait two hours in heavy seas before the *Leonard Mason* could get to them. Gemini VIII; one for the books. I won't lie; it was close. Hell of a job. Hell of a pilot. Glad you're all in one piece. Hope the view is good. Oh, and Merry is an asshole.

The line went dead. He sunk back into his pillows and exhaled slowly. Jesus. Outside, the light was fading. He just wanted to go home. He reached his hand across to the sleeping pills. The pain in his chest was dull. He swallowed one with water and shut his eyes and waited for the darkness to come.

———

The wind flicked the curtain and banged the window. It was the middle of the night. He stirred. Another bang, louder. Maybe there was another tropical storm about to hit the Cape? There hadn't been any concerns for the launch, but those things could move pretty fast. He sat up. His head felt groggy. He tried to get out of bed. His feet fumbled in the gloom for the cold floor. He looked up. There was a figure standing in the window.

Jesus, Harrison said.

What's a pudknocker like you doing in a place like this?

Pancho?

The shadow dropped into the room.

Guess you can drive about as well as you can fly, huh?

What the hell are you doing here? Visiting hours ended at six.

Well I didn't fly two and a half thousand goddamn miles in ten hours to bring a weenie like you grapes. So grab your stuff and let's get the hell out of here.

She stepped forward to see him.

Christ, she said. You look awful.

He tried to get up and cried out in pain. Pancho steadied him.

You're gonna have to quit screaming like a girl if this is gonna work, she said. Leave the light off. We gotta move quick. It's not gonna be long before some goddamn junior crewman on six hundred a year takes a nighttime walk and spots the scarlet marvel on his ground.

Harrison looked at her.

You got the plane *here?* he said.

You bet your sweet ass I do, Pancho said. It's a goddamn air force base, ain't it?

How did you even know I *was* here?

Got a call from an old friend, she said, pulling his arm over her shoulder. Was told to come pick you up. Jeez, you got any pants? Forget it, we ain't got time.

Harrison hadn't realized he was only dressed in a hospital gown.

Steady! he said as Pancho dragged him across the room. Jesus! I broke my goddamn ribs.

Quit your whining, she said. We don't have long. Deke said he'd only be able to give us ten, fifteen minutes tops.

Deke?

Stand here, Pancho said. Don't move.

She pulled his bedside table across the floor and shoved it under the window.

Think you can manage that? she said.

Maybe, he said. My side hurts pretty bad though.

C'mere, she said. Look.

She made a stirrup with her hands and hoisted him onto the table. He looked out the window.

Pancho, we're two floors up.

There's a ladder on your left, she said. You'd better be able to manage that.

He swung himself around, out, onto the ladder. He held his left side and lowered himself down. Pancho followed, giggling. At the bottom, she pulled the ladder down and laid it flat on the grass.

Where's the Mystery Ship? he said.

C'mon! she said.

Pancho led him along the side of the hospital, over the road, between two buildings and against the wall of a hangar.

Damn, he said when he saw it. I'd forgotten what a beauty she is.

The Travel Air Type R Mystery Ship was a low-wing racing airplane, one of only five. Pancho had broken Earhart's airspeed record in it, years before. The wings were thin, braced with wires, the fuselage sleek and streamlined.

Took me three years to fix it up after I won it back, she said. Felt good to get her up again. Now get in.

He got in.

Pancho looked at him and laughed hard.

What? he said from the front cockpit.

If it ain't the funniest goddamn thing I ever seen! One of NASA's world-famous *astronauts* sitting in his underwear in the back of a monoplane. I sure wish the boys could see this.

Hurry up, would you, before we get busted, he said. Plus I'm cold.

Pancho climbed in.

Fastest damn airplane in the world when I bought it, she said. Cost me a goddamn fortune.

Can we go?

All right, all right, keep your peckerwood on; we're goin.

She started the engine. It stuttered and stalled.

Would it help if I got out and pushed? he said.

Quit bitchin, she said.

She fired the engine again and it rumbled and roared and she taxied toward the runway and took off.

Attagirl! she said, as it howled into the air.

The wind whipped through the thin wires and through his hair. He felt the pressure on his face as they rushed into it. He smiled. The engine hacked and spat and Pancho yelled, we got a problem, and Harrison yelled, what?

Outta gas, Pancho said.

Sweet Jesus, Harrison said. Some rescue.

The Mystery Ship dipped and bucked.

Didn't figure on not being able to refuel at the base like normal, she said. Hang on, I know a few places round here.

They made it to a corn farm near Ocala and landed. Pancho said she and Telly, the farmer, went way back.

Far enough to have you bangin on his door in the middle of the night askin for gas? Harrison said.

Least the sonofabitch can do, Pancho said.

Telly appeared in the doorway in his underwear.

Telly, Jim; Jim, Telly, Pancho said. Jesus, am I the only one not standing around in my goddamn underwear tonight?

Telly kept his fuel by his barn. He had an old Stearman 17 he'd converted for crop-dusting.

You need food, water? Telly said as he refueled the Mystery Ship.

We're good, Pancho said. Thanks.

Real pleasure, Telly said.

Come out to the desert sometime, Pancho said. Do some proper flyin.

Hell, I might just do that, he said. He laughed and waved them off.

They hopscotched cross-country, back to California. Pancho flew by dead reckoning, using a compass and Rand McNally road maps, stopping only to refuel at private airfields; nothing more than dirt strips with tin hangars. She gave Harrison a gallon of water and a bag of beef jerky and told him to be grateful. After the third stop, Harrison fell asleep. After the fourth stop the fuselage caught fire and Pancho brought the Mystery Ship down into the mesquite and jumped out to throw sand on the flames and took off again. Harrison stirred and said, what happened? and Pancho said, don't worry your head about it, sleeping beauty.

They got back to Pancho's in the middle of the afternoon, landing on her strip by the back barn.

Upstairs, Pancho said to Harrison.

Exhausted, with a blanket he'd found on the cockpit floor wrapped around him, he traipsed into the house and climbed the stairs. Pancho followed.

That's your room, she said, pointing to a green door at the end of the landing. It's all made up for you. Go to sleep. And no funny business. I don't want you banging on my door in the middle of the night looking for hot sex. Tomorrow we're making a goddamn plan.

You done being pissed at me?

I'm never gonna be done being pissed at you. But I just flew a solid day to bring your sorry ass home.

How'd you stay awake?

Who said I did?

Tuck me in?

Get the hell out of my sight.

MOJAVE DESERT
MUROC, CALIFORNIA
MARCH 1966

———

The next morning Pancho banged on his door early and fixed eggs and coffee for breakfast. After they'd eaten, she took out a pack of Pall Malls and lit one. She offered the pack to Harrison who took one and lit it with Pancho's lighter and sat back and sipped his coffee. Pancho leaned forward and looked at him.

Good coffee, he said.

Here's how this is gonna work, she said. As you know, Deke an I been talkin. You're welcome to stay here for as long as you want. It's your room. But there's three conditions. First off, you help me out with the planes. Maintenance, repairs, refueling anyone who ties up; that kinda thing. Second, you see a NASA shrink. It won't go on your record. Deke's seen to that. Third, you give Deke a call when you feel right. Said he'll give you a seat on the next available mission.

Harrison thought for a moment and said, okay.

Good, Pancho said, because the other option was to drive you out into the mountains and kick you out in your underwear. Speakin of which, there's some clothes upstairs Billy Horner left behind, probably fit you. Landwirth is gonna get your stuff sent down from the

Cape; out of his own pocket too, dumb bastard, so make sure you call him.

I will, he said.

I just thought of another rule, Pancho said.

Are you just gonna make them up as we go?

Rule number four: I don't want to hear any of that crappy NASA jargon round here. I can't stand it. You want to speak like a goddamn robot, you can do that in your room, on your own.

Should I be writin these down?

Rule number five.

Jesus!

Rule number five! Rule number five is no backtalk!

All right! All right!

Harrison got to work on the Mystery Ship, fixing her up after their long flight. He worked outside, hot wind blowing in his face, like it had always done. He'd forgotten how quiet the desert was. He worked alone, and would often have to sit for long periods in the hangar. Afterward, he'd go out and look at the sand and the sky then get back to work. His mind calmed a little. The ache in his side eased as his ribs healed. He wanted to ask Pancho about Grace. He'd not spoken to her for a long time. And Pancho had not mentioned her once.

He'd been back a couple of weeks when he had a phone call from the secretary of a Doctor Baum. Baum was a private psychiatrist NASA had employed while selecting the original Mercury astronauts. He worked a day a week at the Antelope Valley in Lancaster. Harrison would be seen then. They would review progress every two months. The first time they met, Harrison knew they weren't going to get on. Baum looked like a tall glass of tonic with no gin, thin and serious and slightly bitter.

Harrison did not want to be at the Antelope either. It made him uncomfortable. Pancho drove him over every week, partly because rule number six was *no driving* and partly to make sure he actually got there on time. During their third session, Baum said, most of my patients *want* to be here, and Harrison said, really, he didn't see the point. In the fourth session they talked about his mother and flying and Baum prescribed thioridazine, which the hospital's pharmacy dispensed for him. He took them home in a brown paper bag and sat in the hangar and read the advisory notes on the bottle and he read each line over and over and he felt scared and sweated heavily. Then he swallowed one of the capsules and went outside and set the advisory notes on fire with a match. When it fell to the ground he stood on the burning paper and scooped up the black ashes and threw them into a water trough. Then he lit a cigarette and went back to work.

Apart from Pancho, the only people he spent any time with were the Walkers. He'd play with the kids, have a few beers with Joe, stay for dinner. Most nights, he turned in early. He stayed away from the Happy Bottom Riding Club and its regulars. There weren't many he knew at the base now anyway; most had moved on or augered in. Ridley was in France, working for NATO's Advisory Group for Aeronautical Research and Development. Yeager had returned to Edwards and was now commandant of the air force's new Aerospace Research Pilot School, or ARPS, as it was known, designed to produce air force astronauts for both NASA selection and the air force's own space aspirations. When word reached Yeager that Harrison was back, he stopped by the ranch and the two men sat outside the hangar with a beer and talked about the old days. As it happened, one of Yeager's first students, an air force pilot named Dave Scott, had just taken his first spaceflight aboard Gemini VIII. I'll be damned, Harrison said when he found out. He did one hell of a job.

Yeager chuckled and said, feel like a proud father. They sat and talked for a long time.

One night, over dinner in Pancho's kitchen, Harrison said, I hate goin up to the Antelope, and Baum's an asshole. Pancho looked up from her plate and said, you forgotten our deal?

No, he said. But there must be someone else?

Pancho chewed her food.

I'll look into it, she said. Eat your pie.

He ate his pie.

A week later Pancho said, I spoke to Deke; got you someone else.

You spoke to Deke?

Yeah, I spoke to Deke. And I got you someone else.

Who is he?

He's a she, and she's agreed to come out here every week, although God knows why anyone would want to talk to a miserable bastard like you.

A woman?

Thought you might like it. If you ask me she's nuts herself but no one's askin me.

Harrison stood up and hugged her and she recoiled and cursed him loudly.

He met with Doctor Louise Brubaker twice a week, in an old workshop Pancho had behind the barn. Doctor Brubaker's husband, Ed Brubaker, had flown in Korea, chasing down MiGs up the Yalu River. She knew pilots. *I'm familiar with the breed*, is how she put it. It was a good start. As the weeks went on, their talks began to help.

* * *

Pancho gave him Saturdays off. He usually slept late, ran errands, read in his room. His window looked out over the front of the house. The room was small, with barely enough room for a single bed, which he'd wedged horizontally against the window to give him more space. Next to it was a small bedside table with a lamp, pack of Lucky Strikes, matches, two paperbacks and a stick of Beemans. On the far side of the room, behind the door, was a thin wardrobe and an old chair.

He'd spent the morning with Pancho in Lancaster, meeting an accountant he'd finally persuaded her to hire. Harrison didn't like town much. It was busier than it used to be, and he was afraid he'd run into Grace.

They got back to Pancho's at noon. He found some bread, a little cheese, some potatoes and beans in the kitchen and took them up to his room with a glass of water. He sat on his bed and ate. When he was done, he drank a little water and put the glass down on the bedside table and the empty plate on the floor. Then he lit a cigarette and looked out the window. The bed creaked beneath him. He finished the cigarette and picked up the paperback he was reading, *The Deep Blue Good-By.* A few minutes later, Pancho rapped on his door.

Visitor, she said.

He sat up. Reverend Irving poked his head in.

Hello, Jim, he said. Hope I'm not disturbing?

Not at all! Harrison said, laying the book pages-down on his bed. Please, come in, have a seat. Excuse the mess.

Oh, said Irving, pulling up the chair, looks fine to me.

It's good to see you, Reverend, Harrison said. Can I get you anything? Coffee? Water?

I'm fine, I'm fine, thank you, though. I just wanted to see how you were doing.

Appreciate that, Reverend.

Call me John.

Appreciate that, John.

So how are you?

I'm okay, he said, I'm okay.

Pancho told me everything. You've been through a lot.

Would you like a smoke, John? Harrison said.

Ah, thanks.

Harrison offered him the pack, and some matches.

Thank you, Irving said.

Harrison lit one too. The men sat in silence for a moment.

Anytime you want to talk, about anything, Irving said, just give me a call, or swing by the church.

That's very kind of you, John, thank you. I'm doin okay, though, really. Getting there.

Oh, and our service on Sundays is at eight. Come along, anytime; we could use a man like you.

Not sure I'm good for much anymore, Harrison said.

I think God would disagree, Irving said.

That so, Harrison said. Must have missed the memo.

You know, Irving said, looking at his hands. I've been seeing a fair bit of Grace this last year or so.

You mind if I have another? Harrison said, glancing at the Lucky Strikes.

Not at all, Irving said.

Harrison picked up the pack and tapped it on the bedside table and jerked his hand so a cigarette poked out of the torn corner. He raised the pack and put the cigarette between his teeth. Then he picked up the matches and struck one and held the flame against the tip of the cigarette and took the first few drags and looked at Irving and said, how is she?

She's doing well, Jim; she's good. She's been part of church life

now for a couple of years. It's such a blessing. She's been doing amazing work with the children.

She's joined your church?

She gave her life to Christ and He's been doing wonderful things.

Is she happy? he said.

She is.

I'm glad to hear that.

Yes.

You together?

Oh, no, Jim; that's not what I meant. I'm not involved with her
in that way.

Okay, he said. Does she—forget it.

Go on.

Nah. Don't worry about it.

Sure?

Yeah. Thanks for stopping by.

It's good to see you doing so well, Jim, Irving said, rising from
the chair. No need to get up; I'll see myself out.

Harrison nodded. His throat was dry.

Take care, John, he said, reaching for a stick of Beemans. He
wasn't looking, and his hand knocked over the glass which fell to the
floor and smashed.

Shit! Harrison said. Sorry—

It's fine! Irving said, brushing glass from his shoes. Honestly. No
harm done.

He looked up at Harrison and said, it wasn't your fault.

Harrison's conscience reverberated. He was momentarily
stunned.

What did you just say? Harrison said.

Irving moved his chair back beside the wardrobe and said, no
harm done, really; it's fine.

No, Harrison said, after that.

Oh, Irving said, thinking. It's not your fault.

Harrison stared at him, then began to cry.

A few months later, Walker augered in doing a public relations stunt for General Electric. His F-104 Starfighter collided midair with an XB-70 Valkyrie bomber; an evil, delta-winged beast with a horrendous wake vortex off its wingtips. Not long after the funeral, Grace ran into Jim at the hardware store. They shared an awkward hello and embraced briefly.

Nails, she said. I need nails.

Well, you've come to the right place, he said.

Neither of them said anything for a moment.

How have you been? she said. You look healthy.

Good, he said. Thanks. Apart from—

Yeah, she said. Me too. I'm seeing Grace and the kids tomorrow, actually. I still—I can't—I mean, when something hangs over you for so long . . .

Yeah, he said. Yeah.

Thought I might've seen you at the funeral.

I was there.

Oh.

Harrison didn't say anything. He looked away.

Did you go to the other one? she said.

He shook his head. Been to enough of those over the years, he said.

Too many, she said.

Goddamn corporate bullshit . . . he should've never been up there. He's NASA's chief test pilot, f'chrissakes! All for some goddamn *photograph*.

You've got every right to be angry, she said.

Harrison didn't say anything. He was now staring at the floor.

When I found out you were back, Grace said, I wanted to stop by—Pancho . . . She didn't think it'd be a good idea.

Oh, he said. I didn't know that.

Yeah, she said. She was pretty insistent.

She can be that way.

Yeah, she said. Grace and Joe filled me in from time to time.

Same, he said.

She gave a little smile and pulled a finger across the edge of each eye, now wet.

Shit, she said. Sorry.

It's okay, he said.

I promised myself I wouldn't get upset if I ran into you.

I'm sorry, he said.

No, it's okay, she said. It's not you, I'm just getting emotional.

It's okay, he said.

He touched her arm. Between them was a terrible ache.

Goddamn it, she said, trying to stem the flow with her fingers. Then she fell into him and he put his arms around her and he held her tight. They stayed like that for a minute, maybe more; he wasn't sure.

I'm sorry, he said.

I'm sorry too, she said.

They parted. She dried her eyes with her palms. A bell rang as someone entered the shop.

Have you seen Chuck? she said. Air Force brought him back to Edwards.

Yeah, seen him a coupla times. Been huntin once or twice too.

She nodded.

Glennis and I have stayed pretty close, she said.

I'm glad, he said. You should come over sometime. Really. I'll talk to Pancho.

Good luck with *that*, she said, giving a little laugh. But thanks, I'd like that.

Okay, he said.

God, it feels like years, she said.

It is, he said. Or was.

Yeah, she said.

Yeah, he said.

Okay, she said. Well. I'm gonna get my nails, which I think are over there somewhere, but it was good to see you, Jim. I'm glad we ran into each other.

Me too, he said. Say hi to Glennis for me.

I will, she said. See you.

See you, he said.

Grace rose early the next morning, fixed herself eggs and coffee and drove to Rosamond. Her arms ached from shoving the heavy transmission around. It was an old Chevy pickup, three-speed, Mexican-red; thirty bucks from Mac, month before he died. It was a wreck. He'd worked it hard. She'd learned how to fix it up herself. Working outside, with her hands, felt good.

It was almost ten. Rosamond was busy. It had changed so much since the early days, when she and Jim had first moved to Muroc. She could remember driving down Main Street at noon and not seeing a single person. She pulled up outside Howard's General Store. She was due at Grace Walker's for coffee and wanted to pick up some candy for the kids. She cut the engine and the truck shuddered into silence. She stared up at the empty sky. Joe was gone. She'd never seen Jim angry before. She found herself wondering what his room at Pancho's was like. It had been good to see him. She wanted a cigarette. She stepped out into the fresh air, bought candy and a bottle of Coke, which she drank on the sidewalk in the sun. Then she returned the bottle and drove to the Walkers'.

She stayed for lunch. The children played upstairs. The women sat in the kitchen and talked.

Do you want another coffee? I could sure use one.

How are you sleeping?

Not great. But the kids are, which is something. I've got something for you, if I can still find it in all this mess.

She walked over to the counter and began sifting through a pile of papers.

Got it, she said, and sat back down. Here. She slid a photograph across the table. I want you to have this.

Grace picked up the photograph. It was Joe and Jim, standing on the lakebed in their pressure suits, grinning; sky arcing away behind them.

A few weeks later Harrison picked Grace up from church on Sunday and drove them out to the mountains to fish.

Look at you, she said, winding down her window.

Yeah, he said. Finally. Pancho made me do a bunch of tests.

Bet that was fun.

He chuckled.

Think you'll fly again soon?

I dunno, he said. I feel better, but I still get distracted sometimes.

Do you want to get back into flight test? she said.

That's a young man's game, he said. Should have got out years ago. You want one?

He offered her a cigarette.

I quit.

You did, huh?

Yeah.

Really?

John helped me.

Irving?

Uh-huh.

You should come sometime, she said.

To John and Gracie's no-smoking club?

To church. Do you good.

She laughed.

What? he said.

Nothing, she said.

Was sorry to hear about Milo, he said.

Ah, he was an old boy.

A good old boy, he said.

The best, she said. Her arm rested on the blunt lip of the open window and the hot wind blew her hair in all directions. The road turned to track and the car churned yellow dust around them.

Can I ask you something? he said, looking over at her.

Sure, she said.

He pulled the car over and idled the engine.

Hey, she said. Why are we stopping?

It's important, he said.

I'm all ears.

It's serious.

I'm serious.

You don't sound it.

I promise, she said. Look.

She lay back in her seat and shut her eyes.

See? she said. You have my undivided attention. My mind is empty. Like an empty box. My mind is an empty box.

I could have told you that, he said.

She snapped open her eyes.

Who's messing around now? she said.

He looked at her.

All right, come on, she said, or we'll never make it up there by nightfall.

Okay, he said. Irving—John—came to see me. Not long after I got back.

Okay, she said. Sounds like the kinda thing he'd do.

We talked, he said. It was good. When he got up to leave, I accidentally knocked over a glass; smashed it all over the floor, so I apologized and he said, he told me, *it wasn't your fault.*

Okay, she said.

When he said it, when he said that to me—I don't know; something *happened*, I don't know what. He looked up at me, said *It wasn't your fault* and it felt like I'd been hit round the head with a brick. It was like my whole being shook. It was the strangest damn thing. I felt odd for the rest of the day. And a while later, with Doctor Brubaker . . . I don't know. I started to feel better. Do you—do you think it was God?

Talking to you?

Yeah.

She thought for a moment, then said, yeah.

He looked at her, then thought for a minute.

All right, he said. Let's go.

The trout in the mountain lakes were golden; succulent and firm and robust. It was work to reach them, but worth the effort. They liked the cold water high up in the Sierras. Fried up fresh with a little butter, they were the best thing Harrison had ever tasted.

They fished, and camped, then moved higher and fished the next day, eating what they caught. What they couldn't eat, they stashed in a cold icebox. When they got home, they shared the haul with Pancho, who put half in her freezer and half on the menu.

Soon after their trip, Harrison started turning up at Rosamond First Baptist Church on a Sunday, just after the service had started. Soon after that, he started turning up on time.

It was early fall, the end of September; Harrison had started to fly again. He was fixing a sandwich in Pancho's kitchen when the telephone rang. He wiped his hands, walked through to the bar and picked up the receiver.

Yeah? he said.

Heard you got your wings back.

The gruff voice took him by surprise.

Well, he said, someone's got to show this new breed how it's done.

Heh, Deke said.

Pancho stuck some cardboard wings on my chest, Harrison said. Inscription said *ass-tronaut*.

That was my idea, Deke said. How you feelin?

Good, Harrison said.

You wanna come fly for us again? Deke said. Gemini's just wrapped up. Lovell and Aldrin; three EVAs, over five hours outside the spacecraft. Plus we grew some frog's eggs in zero-g.

Yeah, Harrison said, I heard about Aldrin's record.

I'm not gonna say we can't do it without you, because we can. But we got a hell of a lot of work to do in the next three years if we're gonna get to the moon by nineteen seventy and we need all the good men we can get.

I sure appreciate that, Deke, he said. And everything else, I really do.

Deke grunted.

I don't know, though, Harrison said. Tell you the truth, I've been thinkin about quitting; retiring from the air force too. Maybe set up a little trout farm in the mountains, lead a peaceful life.

Sounds like a damn fine idea, Deke said. Might even join you when Apollo slips into the early eighties. Get the hell out, and don't tell anyone.

I'll send Pancho over in the Mystery Ship.

Heh. I'm still owed a flight, so I guess I'll be stickin around for a while longer. There might be something else for you, though, if it takes your fancy. Based at Edwards. Pancho got a teleprinter?

Yeah, he said.

Got the number?

He read out the number pinned on the wall above the telephone.

All right, Deke said. I'll send you something to look over. Call me if you're interested.

He hung up. Harrison replaced the receiver and walked through to the cramped office behind the bar. He sat by the teleprinter and waited. After a couple of minutes, he returned to the kitchen to finish making his sandwich. He heard the bell ring and walked back to the office, eating his lunch. The Fernschreiber 100 spooled paper. He tore it off, sat down, and read.

Pancho was in the stables looking over six new quarter-horse stallions she'd just bought in Oklahoma. Harrison walked in and handed her the teletype.

What's this? she said.

Take a look.

She read it and handed it back to him and turned her attention to the horses.

Well? he said.

She fixed him a look.

You so much as think about turning this down I swear to God and Jesus Christ his son I will hang you upside down by your peckerwood and invite the entire goddamn state of California to throw shit-clods at your balls.

Take it I got your blessing then?

She ignored him and talked to her horses.

A few weeks later Glennis invited him to dinner and he went and Grace was there and it was good. After dinner he followed her onto the veranda for a smoke and they looked into the darkness together and he said I miss her and she turned to him and saw his wet eyes and he said I miss her so much.

She picked him up the next day and they drove to Rosamond and parked in the small lot at the entrance to the cemetery. The day was unusually humid. They walked together down to where their daughter lay and stood in front of the simple stone that marked her grave. The inscription read, FLORENCE MAYTON HARRISON. Underneath her name, it said "DUCK". Then, below that, it said, MAY 7, 1959—DECEMBER 12, 1961. Grace slid her hand into his and they stood for a while. Then they walked back to the car.

EPILOGUE
VICTORVILLE, CALIFORNIA
CHRISTMAS EVE, 1968

The television glowed in the low light of the living room. It was dark outside. The new house was so drafty they'd had to roll up newspaper to block cracks between the wall and the floor and poke balls of it into the holes in the window frames. They'd moved to Victorville that fall. The living room was a small nook, the kitchen larger, and there were two good-size bedrooms upstairs, as well as an old outhouse and a barn outside that they wanted to turn into a stable. An oil-filled heater stood next to the sofa where they sat, warming the room. As commandant of ARPS, Harrison had given himself Christmas off.

The broadcast was live, a ghostly hue traveling a quarter of a million miles to Earth from where Frank Borman, Jim Lovell and Bill Anders were in lunar orbit. Cronkite, erudite, steady, mustache groomed and hair slicked, was anchoring the CBS News Special Report, *Apollo 8: Historic First Flight to the Moon.*

Bet ol Shaky never thought that one Christmas Eve he'd be flyin round the moon, Harrison said.

I just feel sorry for Marilyn, Grace said.

She'll be sweating the Trans-Earth Injection, he said. That's the burn that'll bring them home.

And if it goes wrong? she said.

They'll be spending plenty more Christmases around the moon, he said.

Well aren't you Captain cheerful. What's their odds?

Of making it home?

Yeah.

Honestly?

Yeah.

Fifty-fifty, he said.

Jesus, she said.

This is Apollo 8, coming to you live from the moon, Borman said.

Harrison turned his attention to the television. In the kitchen, the telephone rang.

I'll go, Grace said.

We've been flying over the moon at an altitude of sixty miles for the last sixteen hours.

He heard Grace pick up. It was Pancho. Yeah, Grace said, we're watching.

We are now approaching lunar sunrise, Anders said. *And for all the people back on Earth, the crew of Apollo 8 has a message we would like to send to you.*

Harrison sunk back into the sofa.

IN THE BEGINNING, GOD CREATED THE HEAVEN
AND THE EARTH; AND THE EARTH WAS WITHOUT
FORM AND VOID, AND DARKNESS WAS UPON THE
FACE OF THE DEEP; AND THE SPIRIT OF GOD MOVED
UPON THE FACE OF THE WATERS. AND GOD SAID,
"LET THERE BE LIGHT"; AND THERE WAS LIGHT.
AND GOD SAW THE LIGHT, THAT IT WAS GOOD. AND
GOD DIVIDED THE LIGHT FROM THE DARKNESS.

You got it, Frank, Lovell said.

No, it's your { . . . }

> AND GOD CALLED THE LIGHT DAY, Lovell said,
> AND THE DARKNESS HE CALLED NIGHT. AND THE
> EVENING AND MORNING WERE THE FIRST DAY.
> AND GOD SAID, "LET THERE BE A FIRMAMENT IN
> THE MIDST OF THE WATERS, AND LET IT DIVIDE THE
> WATERS FROM THE WATERS"; AND GOD MADE THE
> FIRMAMENT AND DIVIDED THE WATERS WHICH
> WERE UNDER THE FIRMAMENT AND THE WATERS
> WHICH WERE ABOVE THE FIRMAMENT, AND IT
> WAS SO. AND GOD CALLED THE FIRMAMENT HEAVEN.
> AND THE EVENING AND THE MORNING WERE THE
> SECOND DAY.

Can you hold the camera? Borman said.

You want to pass it over here, Jim? Anders said.

> AND GOD SAID, "LET THE WATERS UNDER THE
> HEAVENS BE GATHERED TOGETHER INTO ONE
> PLACE," Borman said, "AND LET THE DRY LAND
> APPEAR" AND IT WAS SO. AND GOD CALLED THE
> DRY LAND EARTH, AND THE GATHERING TOGETHER
> OF THE WATERS HE CALLED THE SEAS. AND GOD
> SAW THAT IT WAS GOOD.

Harrison sat very still. On the screen was the surface of the moon.

And from the crew of Apollo 8, Borman said, *we close with good night, good luck, a merry Christmas, and God bless all of you, all of you on the good Earth.*

The camera swung up, showing the Earth, hanging in the darkness, burning, blue.

AUTHOR'S NOTE

This work of fiction would not have been possible without the labor of many others. I am deeply indebted to the many writers, biographers, historians and filmmakers who have come before me and documented this extraordinary period in history. In particular, I would like to cite the following works that provided information, detail and dialogue crucial to the writing of *The Last Pilot*:

Across the High Frontier by Charles E. Yeager and William R. Lundgren

First Man: The Life of Neil A. Armstrong by James R. Hansen

The Right Stuff by Tom Wolfe

Yeager by Chuck Yeager and Leo Janos

The Happy Bottom Riding Club: The Life and Times of Pancho Barnes by Lauren Kessler

A Man on the Moon: The Voyages of the Apollo Astronauts by Andrew Chaikin

Moondust: In Search of the Men Who Fell to Earth by Andrew Smith

Lost Moon: The Perilous Voyage of Apollo 13 by Jim Lovell and Jeffrey Kluger

Deke! by Donald K. Slayton with Michael Cassutt

Carrying the Fire: An Astronaut's Journeys by Michael Collins

Return to Earth by Edwin E. "Buzz" Aldrin, Jr. with Wayne Warga

Rocketman: Astronaut Pete Conrad's Incredible Ride to the Moon and Beyond by Nancy Conrad and Howard A. Klausner

Red Moon Rising: Sputnik and the Rivalries That Ignited the Space Age by Matthew Brzezinski

Countdown by Frank Borman with Robert J. Sterling

We Seven by the Mercury astronauts

The Astronaut Wives Club by Lily Koppel

Live from Cape Canaveral by Jay Barbree

Of a Fire on the Moon by Norman Mailer

And the following motion pictures:

The Legend of Pancho Barnes and the Happy Bottom Riding Club (2009; dir. Amanda Pope)

For All Mankind (1989; dir. Al Reinert)

Apollo 13 (1995; dir. Ron Howard)

Thirteen Days (2000; dir. Roger Donaldson)

The Right Stuff (1983; dir. Philip Kaufman)

In the Shadow of the Moon (2007; dir. David Sington)

When We Left the Earth (miniseries, 2008; dir. Nick Green et al.)

From the Earth to the Moon (miniseries, 1998; dir. Tom Hanks et al.)

Rocket Science—The History of Space Exploration (2004; prod. Casablanca Media Television)

* * *

In addition, I would like to credit two poems that appear in the story: *High Flight* by John Gillespie Magee, Jr., written in 1941, and *Oh Little Sputnik* by G. Mennen Williams, first published in *The New York Times* in 1957.

I would like to thank Col Jeff Hosken, USAF (ret.) for graciously fielding my many queries and Charlie Duke for talking to me about his experiences and answering my questions.

Finally, I was fortunate enough to meet Jim Irwin in 1990, and will always be grateful for his generosity and advice.

ACKNOWLEDGMENTS

To Juliet Pickering, my agent; thank you.

To Elizabeth Bruce, my editor; thank you.

Thank you to everyone at Blake Friedmann and Picador USA.

I'm grateful to Arts Council England for their generous grant and to everyone who wrote letters of support.

Thanks also to Kirsty Mclachlan, Anna Watkins, Scott Pack, Jon McGregor, Sarah Savitt, Francesca Main, Annabel Wright, Elena Lappin, Gillian Stern, Kat Brown, Melanie Welsh, Chris Gribble, Sam Ruddock, Laura Owensby, Ian Ellard, Rachael Beale, Rowan Whiteside, Clare Stevens, Amy Farrant, Philip Loveday, Adam Modley, Alireza Afshari, Vicky Howells, Keith and Halcyon Meldrum, Jacqui and Esa Kalliopuska, James and Rachel Webster, Helen and Mike Bansback.

Thank you, Elizabeth Jenner.

Thank you, Susan and Brian Webster.

Thank you, Robert and Delores Johncock; Dad, especially, for introducing me to the astronauts.

Finally, thank you, for everything, Jude, Elsa, Jesse.

ABOUT THE AUTHOR

———

BENJAMIN JOHNCOCK was born in England in 1978. His short stories have been published by *The Fiction Desk* and *The Junket*. He is the recipient of an Arts Council England grant and the American Literary Merit Award, and is a winner of Comma Press's National Short Story Day competition. He also writes for *The Guardian*. He lives in Norwich, England, with his wife, his daughter, and his son. *The Last Pilot* is his first novel.